THE VEIL OF TIME

The Ladies of the Labyrinth
Book 2

Hope Carolle

ARE YOU SIGNED UP FOR DRAGONBLADE'S BLOG?

You'll get the latest news and information on exclusive giveaways, exclusive excerpts, coming releases, sales, free books, cover reveals and more.

Check out our complete list of authors, too!

No spam, no junk. That's a promise!

Sign Up Here

www.dragonbladepublishing.com

Dearest Reader;

Thank you for your support of a small press. At Dragonblade Publishing, we strive to bring you the highest quality Historical Romance from some of the best authors in the business. Without your support, there is no 'us', so we sincerely hope you adore these stories and find some new favorite authors along the way.

Happy Reading!

CEO, Dragonblade Publishing

Additional Dragonblade books by Author Hope Carolle

The Ladies of the Labyrinth Series
The Veil Between Worlds (Book 1)
The Veil of Time (Book 2)
The Season of the Veil (Book 3)

CHAPTER ONE

"TRY TO GO just a day Gabriella, without your mobile. You're constantly checking it. I'd love to see you with your sketchbook instead, using your astute powers of observation we all know and love." Mummy gestured to the wider world over her shoulder. "You might see something wonderful you otherwise might miss."

She tasked me with a rather tall order. Go without my mobile? Wretched idea. What if one of my friends texted and I didn't send a return for 24 hours? They'd immediately ring the police. What if a piece of breaking news happened, and I was the last to know?

And more importantly, what if Albert called, texted, or tagged me on a post? Yes, it'd been two—no, *three* years—but you never know, he might pop up out of the blue. You hear stories like that all the time, don't you? Love rekindled, reconciled after both parties realize what an absolute absurd reason had been used to break up. So, I ran over the man's toe once. It was an *accident*. He said I did it on purpose, but he knows I would never hurt him, even in a heated moment.

"Really, I insist upon it. I'll turn it off," Mummy said, gently reaching across the table, taking up my mobile in her elegantly manicured hand, and then placing it discreetly in her handbag. "There now, that wasn't too terribly difficult?"

"Mum, honestly. This is beyond the pale." I stood up to my full height, reaching across the table, to protest, perhaps even to intimidate. No, not really, but for a woman I'm unappetizingly tall. Model height, if I had a model's body, but no; I like my food, thank you very much. Can't sustain me on a celery smoothie and a kale salad with a one-ounce portion of grilled salmon on the side. I'd murder someone out of pure hanger.

"Do sit down, Gabriella. You'll make a scene."

Mummy and I were treating ourselves to afternoon tea at Fortnum and Mason's. The cost these days was exorbitant, but Mum, otherwise known as Georgianna, the Countess of Swiffingford, every once in a while, and as a thanks for her patronage, would have her bills waived. It was a huge privilege of which we didn't often take advantage.

Though only 59th in line to the throne, making me 60th, the countess was welcome even as a distant member of the royal family and patron. Known for her extraordinary sense of style—today, for instance, she was dressed in a Hermes scarf mixed with Gucci sneakers, a quilted vest, a layered necklace, a smart jumper, and a pair of dark jeans. She was slim but not too slim, hair in a silver bob, her blue eyes intense, and her dark eyelashes a long fringe. She looked wealthy but everything designer she'd found at thrift stores, online or bricks and mortar, or handed down to her through friends.

I sank back into my chair. No, of course I would never make a scene at Fortnum & Mason's. I was brought up properly. My mother always seemed to know what to do with herself, and how to look, so brilliantly, at all times. I completely idolized her. Mummy had raised me alone when she became a widow at an early age, taking sole responsibility for me: earning a living, fulfilling her duties as a member of the royal family, and keeping us out of the spotlight as much as possible. How she'd done it, I don't know. But I do know she missed Daddy terribly, and would not allow another man even a look in. She had the one love of her life, and it was over, and so she focused on me.

I adored and respected her, even to the extent of not protesting too loudly when she put me on phone detox. Me, a grown woman.

A phone addiction wasn't the only thing we didn't share. Style, for example, certainly didn't come easily to me as it did to her, because honestly, my mind is too busy whirring all the time to make much of an effort on my appearance, except when around Mummy or some of my stylish cousins.

What did come easily to me? Academics, specifically, the study of Middle English romances, like *Troilus and Cressida*. Star-crossed lovers. And the art they inspired. For this, you can look at some tapestries, a few pieces of art, for as much as medieval people loved the stories of romance, they *thought* that their art should be from the Bible. But I didn't study the religious art of the time, I studied the secular. The portraits, the political, the scenes of everyday life. What did people wear? What did the villages look like? How did they want to be portrayed? For nearly all the twenty-seven years of my life, I had been obsessed with the dusty visions of the past.

But I digress. Mummy was taking away my phone because I was having a tiny nervous breakdown. I told her, "I truly thought my audition was a smash. Absolute smash. My outfit was on point—thanks to you. My narration I thought sounded nice—a hint of poshness, but not so much as to be annoying. I stood straight and tall and looked into the camera. And oh yes…"

I had forgotten about the hiccups. In the middle of my audition to host the next BBC series of documentaries on legacy of the artwork of Her Majesty (Rest in Peace, you are forever our Queen), I hiccupped. Nothing big, but it gave me the giggles, and I really couldn't keep a straight face after that. The director kept giving me more tries—a second, a third… a seventh, an eighth. I finally got it right on the tenth. But by then, everyone on the set was absolutely fuming, the way I am when I haven't eaten in more than four hours. Jaw fixed, teeth clenched, the director said, "Thank you for your time, Ms. Palmer."

The casting agent texted me not more than ninety seconds later. A new record, I'm sure. I hadn't even left the building. "We're going to go in another direction. Thank you for your time."

I put down the pot of tea I'd been pouring. "Now that I remember it better, Mum, it was a disaster. I had to do ten takes. I'm not cut out for this, and I'm not cut out for that job at the museum, and there's no way I'm working at a bank. Ever. *Ever.*"

Mummy sighed. "I know how you feel about those soul-sucking jobs in the city. People do seem to enjoy them, though. Must be the money—all those smart suits, the private jets, the wheeling, and the dealing."

"And let's not forget about the corruption," I reminded her, "the long history of racial injustices, the sexism. Besides, they want numbers people. I see a spreadsheet and I want to put a fork in my eye."

Mummy screwed up her face. "Please, don't use that type of imagery around me. My imagination is much too vivid. What you need is to just keep pushing on with that PhD of yours, and you'll find a path. You've simply jumped the gun, that's all. Settle back into your thesis, and the work will come." She pushed her chair back, stood, and leaned in to kiss the top of my head. "Must go, Poppet. Be good. I'll hand you that phone back tomorrow, how about, at your flat around noon. Righty ho?"

I shrugged. It was clear I couldn't talk her out of her lunacy.

"Oh, and don't leave your veneers again in that serviette. They're so expensive to replace, darling."

The heat rose to my face. I was *this* close to walking out of the restaurant without my snap-on veneers, only to later realize I was exposing my two broken front teeth. I didn't often take off the veneers in public places, but sometimes hard bits from biscuits got stuck, and we'd been given a corner table. So I'd popped them out, and then forgotten about them.

I discreetly slipped the veneer out of the serviette, and with one swift, practiced movement, popped them back onto my upper row of teeth.

"Thanks, Mummy." I gave her a kiss on both cheeks, and we were off in two different directions.

Noon was just twenty hours from now. I could handle twenty hours without my phone. I had my iWatch, after all. Might as well take a walk down to King's, I thought, on this early spring day, and check in with my advisor. Mum was right—I'd been distracted from my thesis, and it was high-time to get back to it. Take a break from Tik Tok, Instagram, and YouTube. I strolled down Piccadilly, over to Trafalgar Square, wondered if there was any music going on at St. Martin-in-the-Fields, and then when I found there was not, walked down the Strand to King's College.

The exterior of the university never fails to raise the hackles on my back. It is truly hideous, a bland, concrete exterior next to one of the most beautiful palaces in the world—Somerset House. Whomever it was that greenlit the exterior that faces the Strand should be required to write a 40,000-page paper on why any other building design might have been more suitable.

It's not until you go inside the quad that you see King's older, more beautiful buildings, hidden by that monstrosity. (I do urge you, if you are on the Strand, step inside. It's worth it.)

Alas, the humanities, and more specifically the English department, is housed within the modern building. While one dreamed as an adolescent of studiously raising one's hand to a lecturer's question in a wood-paneled room replete with oriental carpets, hushed tones, antique bookshelves, and soaring ceilings, we had cinderblock walls, 1970s tiled floors, and acoustic-tiled ceilings. Delightful and inspiring, it was not.

I rapped on the door of my tutor, Ellie Hartford. Ellie's two girls, Sophie and Abby, were sitting at their mother's worktable. "Well, hullo, Hartford girls!" I said.

"Hello, Ms. Palmer," they said, greeting me with polite little waves. Too adorable, the pair of them, perhaps eight and ten years old. One blond, one brunette, and their mom a redhead. Like Charlie's Angels maybe, although my only real knowledge of that show is the way girls now pose like them for their formals' pictures, holding up imaginary pistols.

"Gabby, hi," Ellie said, indicating I should sit on the chair next to her desk. "The girls are with me this afternoon. Teacher workday, and no help at home. We're going to do a bit of shopping after I just answer a couple more emails."

"Oh, how delightful," I said. "Though too bad it's the wrong time of year for ice-skating at Somerset House. I don't do very well at ice-skating as you can well imagine. It's like Las Vegas imploding an old casino when I fall down. *Kaboom!*" I winked at the girls. "I swear it cracks the ice almost in half."

The girls' eyes widened. "Will you come skating with us when it's open, Ms. Palmer?" Sophie asked. "I'd like to see that!"

"Wouldn't you just?" I poked a finger near to her tummy, faux threatening a tickle. "No, I'm afraid I've had enough humiliations. I'm here to talk to your mum about my thesis."

Ellie leaned back in her chair one eyebrow raised. "I'm elated to hear this news. It's been quite some time since you've darkened my door. How are you getting on with your paper? Your research?"

"Yes, well, I'm afraid I'd gotten distracted by the lure of easy money and fame. But the door has been firmly closed on all that. Add it to the dust bins of history, along with my love life, and there you have it, little old me—ha ha—hell bent on finishing my thesis at long last.

"I think I need to go on a fact-finding mission. When I was auditioning for the BBC show, I was reminded once again on how many notebooks of da Vinci Her Majesty has, thanks to the shrewd acquisitions of Henry Howard, in 1620. It made me start to wonder. So, do you know of any good sources into the time of young King Henry VIII? I wanted to see if I could find a connection between him and Leonardo da Vinci in any way, shape, or form. Acquaintances, influences, knowledge of the other, and whether the literature of England ever came across the desk of da Vinci." I paused. "You know, he was an inveterate book collector."

Ellie smiled, not at me, not with me, but up at the ceiling. I followed her eyes up there. Nothing but a bunch of old ceiling tiles, many quite moldy and likely a health hazard.

That's odd, I thought. Sometimes Ellie seemed to have inner jokes to herself, or looked off in the distance, like something was triggering a memory. Rumor had it that she and our chair of the department were waiting to release some sort of new finding from 1344, but nothing had ever materialized. Quite mysterious. Even more so, she was always vague when asked the specifics, and tended to steer the topic elsewhere.

Ellie came back down to earth to engage in conversation again. "Well, as you know I've uncovered quite a bit about Edward III—not really a whole lot about Henry VIII, and as for Leonardo, no—nothing at all. Not in the literature, of course. Hold on, I've got an idea."

She picked up her mobile and dashed off a text. "Maybe we'll get lucky," she said.

I peered at the family photos on her desk: the girls, her jaw-droppingly handsome husband, an ex-soldier named Harry. Then there was a photo with our department chair Jane Percy and Ellie and some fierce-looking sheep.

Her phone pinged with a notification and Ellie let out a hoot. "Woohoo!" she said.

"What is it?"

"I think we need to have a more private conversation," she said. "But first, I want to hand you a copy of a very special manuscript I've found. It's highly classified, but I'm ready to share it with you." She unlocked a drawer, and pulled out a folder with bound pages inside, and scans of an illustrated manuscript. "Look it over tonight. I'm about to make you an offer I'm hoping you won't want to refuse..."

WITH THAT, ELLIE had tabled our conversation for the next day, so I took off for home. On the Tube, I retrieved the copy of the manuscript Ellie had handed me. As part of my training in Middle English, I had to learn paleography, which is identifying the hand-written scripts of the age, as well as translating them into the language of the time, and then into modern English. The scripts somewhat resemble letters that we recognize today, but there are a few letters and phrases which would confound you unless you knew the habits of the time. So, what looked like hieroglyphics to the passengers on either side of me, actually reads fairly easily to me though I skipped over the odd word here and there that I'd come back to later.

The story started out about an innocent young knight who was headed to the Crusades. But before I could read more, it was my stop.

Disembarking at Goodge Street, I stepped off the train at the same time as a small man, wearing a pair of headphones who got off farther down the platform. I wouldn't have otherwise noticed him, but my safety sensors went off as he was muttering profanities to himself. Every city dweller knows never to make eye contact with a fellow traveler, especially if that traveler is crazy. Unfortunately, my gaze met his, and he immediately focused his attention on me, walking closer to me, cursing me. I averted my eyes, looked straight ahead.

I could hear him calling after me, something like, "I'll crack your skull in and eat your brains for dinner."

Yes, lovely stuff. I looked around for anyone that might help me; I was phoneless and could not ring for help. And, of course, there were no police available when you needed them. People just continued to stream by with no one stepping in to assist me, protect me. I was reminded for the 340th time that year that chivalry was well and truly dead.

I had half a mind to tell him off, while the other half of me warned, "Never engage!! Never make eye contact. Hurry!"

Finally I reached the top of the stairs, and when I looked over my shoulder, he was gone. Where had he gone, though? Was he in waiting, ready to push me in front of the next lorry or speeding car? I kept twisting around, looking, looking, to see if he was there, as I kept to the main road. When I finally felt as though it was all clear, I started on the road to my flat.

My sweet sanctuary, my safe place.

There is a time and a place to talk about unaddressed mental health issues, how our system fails those most in need, and the state of policing in this country, but at that moment, all I could see was his pure hatred of me—I had been a target of his ire for no reason that I could discern, except that maybe he didn't like the fact that I *had* made eye contact with him. My hands shook as I inserted my key into the front door, taking one more final glance that no one was behind me when I swept into my building's small lobby, nerves atwitter.

Then the thought struck me—in this modern world, nobody had come to my aid. Nobody had wanted to make a fuss or possibly shift the crazy man's focus from me to them. Maybe someone would have stepped up had he escalated and actually attacked me physically, but the thought both gutted me and made me irate. Where was the decency—the chivalry—for people to help one another?

Would I have stopped and helped another? I had no answer, just a vague feeling of overall *ick*. It clung to me like slime. What I needed, I decided, was a cup of tea to restore my spirits, so I hurried to my home.

The flat is in a nice neighborhood, overlooking a small, gated garden square, just two rooms, three flights up. The house was once a grand manse owned by an old relation of His Majesty's mother, but many years earlier it had been divided up into twenty flats. Mine had a living room/kitchen in one room, and a bedroom with an attached bath.

You might be wondering what I live on and might even assume I'm a wealthy heiress. Dear me, no. I'm extremely privileged to be the recipient of a "Grace and Favor" apartment courtesy of the Crown, but it's not as grand as a flat owned by the monarch might sound; I still pay rent for it, albeit at a below-market rate. Far, far, below it, thank goodness. Otherwise, I'd be commuting in from a small, windowless hut somewhere hundreds of miles from the city because of the cost of real estate in Britain, and cycling in, because of the cost of the trains. So, I'm extremely grateful that my connections have made my life as a student far more comfortable than I truly deserve.

While my 2nd cousin thrice removed—the king is the largest landowner in the country, my own line of the family, despite Mum's posh title, is decidedly humble. Turns out my great grandad bet his fortune on railroad stocks in 1927 and lost it all during the Great Depression. With that foolish gamble, the large houses, the servants, the cars, the trappings of being cousins to monarchs, all but disappeared. My grandad got given some sort of government job in the 50's, my father somehow parlayed his love of horses into a career training them, until his tragic early death when I was fourteen, and my mum is an administrator at a posh girls' school. It helps admissions to have somebody with a title on staff, but nobody at the school makes a lot of money, except for the headmistress.

Titled or not, we're the only ones in the family, for instance, who drive to Buckingham Palace in a Ford Fiesta. Luckily the guards know it's us, otherwise we'd get told to drive around the back to the delivery gates.

When I wasn't working on my PhD, I worked part-time at a frame store. You could classify it, if you *really, really* stretched it, as though I worked in an "art gallery"—but that's merely because we had art that was temporarily stored there, and some of it was hung, and some of it was on display as samples. Most of what we got in would make you weep, and not from envy, but from the fact that people have absolutely no originality. I felt like I was forever suggesting frames for the same thirty prints from the National Gallery, or from posters.com. Maybe I could put a lovely frame on it to make it look a little more original, but I despaired when I thought of all the many deserving, starving artists out there who deserved our patronage. Sure, it takes a bit of poking around to find art you liked, but when you do, you'll love that piece forever, and it marks you as a person with singular tastes. I, for instance, had a lovely painting of peonies in my bedroom, done by my dear friend's mother. She's an excellent painter, and I treasure how she captured all the many folds and layers of these beautiful flowers.

Finally home, I turned the large, filigreed key into the lock, and with some wiggling, the door finally gave way, and bliss. Home! My own space, mine, mine, mine. Decorated exactly the way I wanted it, minus the large budget to do it properly. But it was a good start. Robin's egg blue in the entry hall, a deeper marine blue in the living room, and a sky blue in my bedroom to help with waking me up in the morning.

Paint, thankfully, is inexpensive. What was harder to change was the hideous mustard yellow kitchen cupboards, stove, and fridge. That was #1 on my list to switch out if I'd gotten the job at the BBC; but still, best not to dwell on missed opportunities.

For now, Ellie had given me some sort of opportunity with this interesting little manuscript. I got to the part where he'd learned about the mysterious power of labyrinths from somebody, to bridge the veil between the worlds, and how it cured a broken heart.

Strange. Must be a work of fiction, I thought.

CHAPTER TWO

T HE NEXT DAY, my mum kindly returned my phone to me, asking if I'd learned any lessons. I had: I could use Messages on my laptop quite easily, as well as Instagram.

But she did prove her point. I *did* sleep better, and couldn't hit my snooze button on my phone three times the way I normally do because I couldn't do it on my iWatch, especially through half-open, blurry eyes, or by jabbing repeatedly at my wrist. I had to set a timer on my kitchen microwave, which required me to stumble through the flat in order to turn the effing thing off.

Ellie and I were scheduled to meet up at the Greenwich Maritime Museum. I wasn't at all sure why she'd chosen a "destination" an hour away from campus, but she'd asked that I indulge her this request, and that I would soon learn of its merits.

Rather than taking the tube to Greenwich, I decided to take one of those touristy boats down the Thames, even though it was the middle of March and not entirely warm. I had an internet coupon because we were in the "off" season. I sat inside and ordered an outlandishly priced Styrofoam cup of hot chocolate (how have these cups not been banned yet in the UK, I wondered? So bad for the environment). When I wasn't looking at the sights on either side, I'll admit, I looked at my secret cache of photos. Yes, I'd sworn to every one of my friends that I'd get all traces of Albert off my phone. Well I had... except for the screenshots I'd taken of him online and then hidden on a willing app that no one ever looks at. So handy. I could just pull them out whenever I wanted to…

The man was no good for me. That debate had been decided a long time ago. So, so handsome, but really, so inappropriate. No college degree. Failed jobs. Two kids out of wedlock. A slew of ex-girlfriends haunting him so much so that he was afraid to look at his phone when it rang. Did I think *I'd* be the woman who could settle him down at last, make an honest man out of him?

Laughingly—yet sadly—yes. My egotistical self truly believed my ardent love (and let's face it, *desire*) could arrest his roving eye, focus it exclusively on me, tame the never-ending stories of himself, and open him up to the wonders and glories of books, art, and culture. (Have you stopped laughing yet? I'll wait.)

The whole time I was dating him I'd had the nagging fear that he was just too good-looking for me. And being exactly one inch taller than I, one of the very few men who is, I kept trying again and again with him when he disappointed me in not returning my calls, not wanting to meet my friends, not ever planning anything more than an hour in the future. My logical self kept shouting in my ear: "Enough! You've given this ridiculous man enough of your precious time."

Well, I'm not the first woman to be disappointed by a man, and I certainly won't be the last. All the women who have traveled along these very shores of the Thames that I was passing by, from the Celts, the Brits, the Angles and Saxons, the Vikings, the Normans, and then… fewer invaders, more traders, explorers, travelers, emigrants, from all over the world. All the people of the world surely had suffered at least one instance of unrequited love in their lifetimes, went to sleep every night, wondering what that person was doing underneath those same stars. Probably only when they died did that tiny flame go out in their hearts.

Boy was I in a morose mood on that cheery little ferry. Must have been reading too much of de Lane's tales of lost loves the previous night.

After a speedy journey on the boat, we passengers dutifully queued to depart, the Old Royal Naval College looming up over the river, I admired the beauty of Christopher Wren's architecture, two domed buildings perfectly aligned opposite the other, imposing white columns forming a portico, the queen's old palace at the center. Truly lovely. It's funny, but when you live in a city like London, you really don't see the sights, do you? You think that you'll get there one day, but never take the time to do the things that people spend their life savings to come over here and do.

There stood Ellie, looking as lovely as ever in a long green wool coat, tied at the waist, and a pair of knee-high black riding boots peeking out underneath. The green coat highlighted the red color of her hair, and made me wish, once again, that I had red hair, and not this ordinary brown. Maybe one day I'll shock everyone and dye my hair. Quite out of character, that would be, me who likes to keep everything the same, just a status quo Flo.

Ellie waved me over and held up an old-fashioned guidebook. "I hope you don't mind me giving you a mini tour?"

We strolled around the grounds of what used to be a naval hospital, and then the Royal Naval College, and now a maritime museum. I learned that poor old Duke of Wellington, after his death in the Battle of Trafalgar, was actually "preserved" in some sort of barrel of rum or brandy to return to England, and then put on display here so that people could see him lying in state.

I stopped in my tracks. "Ellie, if I go before you, please don't stuff me into a barrel and marinate me."

"Would that be any worse than being stuffed into a rectangular coffin, which also happens to be a wooden box?"

"Most definitely!"

"I don't think this will ever be something you need to worry yourself about. Now, let's go up the hill to the Royal Observatory."

We huffed our way up the steep hill in the park behind the old college and came to the famous dividing line between the

Eastern Hemisphere and the Western Hemisphere. "Don't forget about the fact that this is where Greenwich Mean Time comes from," Ellie reminded me, ever the professor. We took a few photos of us standing in silly poses straddling the prime meridian, and then found a bench to sit down on.

Ellie seemed to hesitate at first before she spoke, chewing on her lip. "I've got something big to ask of you, but I kind of want to take you on a journey first, through the history of this place, so I can set it up properly."

I perked up. I'd been, of course, curious with a capital C about why she had asked me here, and what this off-campus meeting was about, and what it had to do with Anthony de Lane's manuscript. Maybe she was going to ask me to be a member of the faculty? It wasn't unheard of for a PhD candidate to get hired before they finished their degree. A lot of the old professors had retired for obvious reasons during the pandemic, and maybe they needed fresh, if inexperienced, blood.

But my guess was as far from wrong as it could possibly be because she wanted me to do something far riskier than teach Malory's *Le Morte d'Arthur* to a bunch of bored and stone-faced eighteen-year-olds.

CHAPTER THREE

E LLIE DIDN'T LOOK at me as she spoke. Instead, she gazed out over the Thames.

"So of course I do know about your connection to the monarchy, and parts of your family go way back here in Greenwich, which I'm sure you know. For people of that day and age, it was a relief to get away from the stink of London and come out to the country. Generations of royals followed Henry V's lead to come out here, eventually leading to King Henry VIII, who was born here. Queen Elizabeth and Sir Walter Raleigh had their famous 'laying down of the cloak affair' right here in this park, the very definition of chivalry. But as literary historians of the medieval era, we are not so interested in what happened with Henry VIII, we're interested in the medieval folks who lived before him."

I nodded. Basic history of the time, but I didn't want to insult Ellie by telling her that she was insulting me, if you see what I mean.

She continued, "Here's where you come in. Your knowledge of both medieval literature—your skills are excellent at reading the language on the page, and out loud—as well as knowing art history, makes you the perfect candidate for what I'm going to propose. Also, please excuse me for bringing up your personal life as your advisor, but I know that—unless things have changed recently, you're single, no children, excellent health, fit as a fiddle with no underlying conditions....?"

"Yes, you'd definitely know about the children bit." I laughed. "And no, I haven't met anyone recently to take me off the market, so to speak." Sadly, thanks to my obsession with the handsome-but-absent Albert. I pushed the thought of him away. (If only I had done it many times before this moment, but I digress.) "'Always a bridesmaid,' as they say. Fit as a fiddle, of course."

Ellie put her hand on my forearm. "I don't mean to bring any of that up or make a judgement on the merits of being single or in a relationship. But for this particular project it's good to be single and kid-free. And—legally—I should state that what we are doing here is *absolutely* unaffiliated with King's..." She looked at me, waiting to see that I understood.

"Duly noted."

"This is definitely something I work on during my 'off' time. But it's unwrapped an experience and a world I would have never seen otherwise, and I think you'd be the perfect candidate to take a trip there."

"Ooh, a trip!" I clapped my hands. I love travel. I have the perfect wheelie suitcase. Packs everything you need for six nights, seven days. "Where to?"

"'When to?' is the better question." She stared up at me, as if she were willing me to make some sort of leap with her.

I could feel my eyebrows pressing up against each other. "I've missed a step, or a word in there somewhere..." I said, my tongue trying to form the words. "Would you mind...?"

Ellie breathed in deeply. "This is the reason why I've brought you to this particular place—I thought it might help illustrate this proposition. You see, time is a modern construct, right? In the 1800's, everyone had their own notion of time, each village using the time when the sun rose and set for them. But when railroads came, there was no set time to say that the train would arrive in Guildford at noon and Portsmouth by 1:30 in the afternoon. People needed to know when their train would arrive and depart.

So they started using the time they established here in Greenwich on the meridian, for Greenwich Mean Time."

I thought back to our hokey pictures from minutes ago. I'd made a "mean" face at Greenwich Mean Time. Would have made a perfectly hilarious picture for Instagram.

"Yes, I follow you there," I said, "but what do you mean when you said, 'when to'? You mean I wouldn't be using Greenwich Mean Time anymore? Is there some other measure of time?"

"This is why I wanted us to sit down. You see, Jane Percy, our chair at King's, and I, or more accurately, Jane's older brother, John Stafford, discovered a place where you could—" she looked over her shoulder before whispering—"go back in time. As in, time travel. I went back—by accident—to 1344, to be specific."

I blinked. Had I heard her correctly? *Should I call for help?* Either Ellie was losing it, or I was. But she continued talking as if what she'd said wasn't completely crazy, and I kept listening, mostly because I didn't know what else to do.

"That's how my husband Harry and I really got to know each other and fell in love, because he time-traveled with me. But I was in a constant race to get back to my children; I was unsure and afraid of how time travel worked. Now, thanks to a lot more research, we think it's perfectly safe for someone to go back, so long as they have no children to worry about. Because worrying about whether your children are missing you or wanting to get in contact with you really does lessen the pleasure of the whole experience."

A bird sang nearby, a couple walked on the gravel path pushing a stroller, an elderly man, stooped in the shoulders, carefully made his way down the hill. Time, funnily enough, seemed to have stopped for me, or at least slowed down. *Is this really happening?* Was my highly respected advisor, whom I had known for three years as being as straight an arrow as they come—*and* her best friend Jane, head of our department, winner of an OBE for her work in English Literature and a shining light to everyone who loved the written word—time-traveling professors? Surely this was a prank?

"Gabriella?" Ellie pressed, tapping my hand to bring me back to focus. "Do you have any questions?"

"About a million, but I don't think I can breathe," I said, hand over my chest to contain my heart from catapulting out of my chest. "So keep talking. Tell me the whole story."

And she did.

SETTLING BACK INTO my blue rooms at my flat, plopping down on the settee with a large gin and tonic (light on the tonic, heavy on the gin), I was still processing all she had told me, about her trip back in time, how they knew that the author of the manuscript, Anthony de Lane, had also built the labyrinth. She'd told me of the experiences she'd had, and how she'd brought back de Lane's book.

Ellie was the most trustworthy person—besides my mother of course—that I knew. And Jane too. So, to not believe them was just out of the question.

But to know that I lived in a world where time travel was not just the stuff of movies and books? That was taking a while to sink in. Hence the gin, the couch, my beautiful blue walls, my art. They were my touchpoints in what felt like a new and unsafe world.

I kept thinking about that line in Greenwich; on one side was the Eastern Meridian, and on the other, the Western. From what Ellie told me, if I walked across that one specific place in Jane's garden in Kent, albeit in a certain way, in a very one-of-a-kind labyrinth, then I would be stepping from one world into the next.

Ellie explained it to me this way: "The world is there, operating right next to ours, in a way that we can't see. The Irish call it the *Veil Between the Worlds*, like the veil between those that have lived and those that have died." I nodded, remembering that from de Lane's manuscript. She continued. "But it's not ghosts we're talking about. It's living, breathing people, who don't know that you're not from there. So, in a way, you have to cloak yourself by being like them, acting like them, talking like them. And, it turns out, you have all the skills and attributes we need to cloak yourself in that veil, and fit in. As well as none of the burdens of worrying about lovers or offspring."

And then, she tempted me mightily by telling me that by walking through that veil I might very well meet Leonardo da Vinci, the greatest thinker of all time, artist, inventor, scientist, innovator. And my hero.

Honestly, when she summed it all up, and knowing that I had the support of two other, absolute superheroes in my world, who had dubbed themselves, "The Ladies of the Labyrinth"—what did I have to lose?

CHAPTER FOUR

THERE WAS NOTHING to hold me back. I had no real job to report time (the frame store didn't count), no boyfriend, no kids. My dissertation I could pretty much complete whenever, especially when I had the buy-in from my advisor and my chair. But getting to see Tudor England and France...?

Ellie said I'd even have a bodyguard.

Mummy would never know I was gone. That was important to me. I would never ever want her to worry about me. I was her only child, and because she is that sort of mum that, when I am late immediately worries I've been hit by a bus; when I am ill, she immediately Googles every possible disease scenario. She's had her own life, of course, and a full and busy one it has been, what with the job, and the patronages, and the representing of the family. But she'd lost Daddy when I was young, and that took away a huge part of her sense of security.

So, I came up with an excuse for Mum that explained my radio silence. I would tell her I had met with my tutor and decided to go off-grid for a time—no cell phone, no internet, and to *finally* buckle down on my thesis at her house in the country-side. Ultimately, Mum was thrilled.

And my excuse was partially true. Where I was going, there was no broadband and no cell reception.

Within a day or two, I was at Professor Jane Percy's place—a modern manor house built next to Wodesley, an old castle. This was where I'd undergo training of all sorts and be given the specific details around my "mission." There was loads of room and—it was also the location of the labyrinth.

If you knew a time travel portal was in your back yard, and you had two tween girls like Jane's girls, Cordelia and Alice, what would you do? Five years after Ellie's accidental trip, the labyrinth had modern security. Besides a wall surrounding it and a key, it now had an alarm system, a closed-circuit camera that could be accessed via an app. And just in case those failed, the girls had been told in no uncertain terms that the place was indeed haunted. Having your girls be terrified of ghosts and carrying around that phobia all their lives was presumably preferable than them being sucked back in time.

Jane welcomed me in now as a pampered guest, as a member of a team, instead of as a PhD candidate she had to oversee. She had the look my mum would call "country chic," silk scarf knotted around her neck, light brown hair straightened with not a stray out of place in a French bob, ankle-length jeans, and a white, button-down shirt. She was the kind of woman who is admired but makes people slightly nervous because she radiates her genius with her intelligent eyes acknowledging and assessing your every utterance.

She showed me to my guest room, which overlooked the labyrinth. It looked beautiful, green grass, pebble pathway, quite harmless. She may have put me in that room on purpose, with a casual comment that the noises it sometimes emitted had grown quieter over the years, but I swear I could occasionally hear sounds from it. It freaked me out.

So that first night after a delightful dinner with Jane, her daughters, and her husband Guy, I settled into my four-poster bed hoping I could sleep, but still listening for sounds. I pulled up the soft, environmentally friendly bamboo sheets and sank into a seemingly endless number of down-alternative pillows. Jane told me, "I'm well aware that our energy usage is far beyond what it should be, so I try to minimize other ways we impact the globe. Planting trees, growing our own vegetables organically, composting, that sort of thing." Important things to consider for all of us, but it was hard to concentrate on the state of our planet, when all I could think of was the year 1517, the year I was going back to.

As I stared at the coffered ceilings, counting the tiles, wondering if I was mad, the occasional sounds of horses neighing rose from the garden below.

Jane kept no horses.

Surprisingly, I fell asleep, even with the labyrinth's shadows seemingly casting its powers over me.

LANGUAGE WAS AT the forefront of all my lessons. Meeting downstairs in the Great Hall, Jane and Ellie sat opposite me, and we attempted to have a conversation, circa 1517. I needed to be able to speak both French and Middle English; during the year I was going back to, English was evolving into what was almost the more Modern English of Shakespeare. (Yes, to all who struggled with Shakespeare as teens, the language of the Bard is considered almost modern English by academics.) While we did some reading out loud of Middle English for my master's and course work in my PhD, I wasn't what you would call fluent. But I was fluent in French. I had studied it for years in school and spent many summer holidays with my best friend Beatrice at her parent's vacation home in the Loire Valley. Riding our bikes into the local village, we'd flirted with the local boys, bartered at the markets, ordered baguettes and other goodies to take back home with us, and were corrected in the proper pronunciation time and time again.

Even though the language of both the English and French of that time was not much different from how it is spoken now, it is just different enough to require a bit of translation, creating the opportunity for misunderstandings.

Beyond that, there were manners to perfect, food etiquette to know, prayers to learn (Catholics stopped to pray—even waking to pray—multiple times daily), and dances to master. It seemed like an impossible amount to memorize.

Jane's brother, John Stafford, the discoverer of the labyrinth's secrets, would step in to advise me when appropriate. He lived in the older castle next door and was a frequent traveler back to the past; he and Ellie had been "an item," but that was very much ancient history.

That first day after my arrival, Jane made us tomato soup and chicken salad sandwiches, and the three of us ate in the stunning kitchen that was the heart of the house. After I finished my soup, delicious with hints of basil and parmesan, I asked, "Does all this time travel have an effect on John?"

Jane blew out a sigh of exasperation. "I fear it does. When he came back with Ellie five years ago, he had a sort of heart condition and was left very weak for a while. But with the proper medical attention, he's rallied. He's better about letting me know when he's coming and going, and he appears strong physically. But mentally?"

Ellie gave a nod, looking downcast. "He's much changed since I first knew him, that's for sure. So—" she put a hand on mine—"we wanted to add another person to the mission. Just as Ellie had Harry, you will have Graham."

Ooh, I thought, if he was as dishy as Harry, this journey back in time would be a further wonder. I'd met Harry several times before at university Christmas parties as well as in Ellie's office when he came in with the girls, and obviously I had seen pictures of him on Ellie's desk. He was a gentle and quiet man, blue eyes, and a military bearing.

He was a big part of the reason I had agreed to this mad escapade. Not because I ever thought that I could be with him, obviously—it's part of the Sister Code to never even think about stealing another woman's man from her—but Ellie had revealed to me that her trip back in time was how she and Harry had met.

In fact, she'd told me the whole story of their love affair, from the time of him freeing her ex-boyfriend John from manacles, to him rescuing her on the labyrinth, and from her rescuing him, to them being reunited. Such a love story! After they'd returned and started dating formally, they'd gotten married soon thereafter, and he'd become became an amazing stepfather to those precious little girls who were now not so little.

I set my heart on something like that happening for me too. My life so far had been one dull, tedious run. Every time I went out in search of adventure—zip lining, whitewater rafting, alpine skiing, even crewing on a racing yacht—I'd been surrounded by women! Or one very odd man. Honestly, where *were* all the men? So if lightning could strike for Ellie, why not me? Who knows how appealing this Graham fellow, a sort of bodyguard, would be?

Besides the potentially hunky bodyguard, my mentors—and this included Harry—were giving me the skills to attend to my own safety. For the purposes of my training, Harry had converted the cabana/pool house/spare guest room. It was behind the house, at the end of the formal gardens where the pool was. As *if* Jane's family needed any more housing to go with their already numerous bedrooms, there was this extra bedroom suite in the back. But hunky Harry, ex-soldier that he was, made this space a war room of sorts to teach me the art of self-defense.

His idea of teaching did not come from having me sitting down, taking notes, and watching a video. Harry was hands-on; he even had a real sword that he'd brought for me to work with. Nothing at my gym had prepared me for how much one of those weighed. It seemed unlikely that a modern man, who spent so much of his time in a car, sitting at a desk, and watching TV, could carry one of those around all day, let alone fight with it.

Harry showed me how to use a knife defensively (though thankfully we had a rubber one instead of a real one), how to get out of a stranglehold, and how to elbow somebody's nose into their brain. As you do, you know.

Three hours later, sweaty and bruised, my bum had been seriously kicked. The day's lesson reminded me that I needed to spend more time utilizing my gym membership and less time reading at my desk. But at least if I were attacked in a dark alley, I now had a better idea of what to do.

Harry called Ellie over after our lesson and wanted to address something. They sat next to each other, an easy rapport between the two; Ellie had a hand on Harry's knee, and Harry's arm was draped across the back of her chair. I could tell that with these two, they always had each other's back, and the way they smiled when they saw each other...? It was seriously goal worthy.

"Ellie," Harry started, "I noticed something with Gabby that you may not have caught."

Uh oh, was he going to kick me out of the program? What had I done?

"What is it? I've known Gabby for a couple of years now, and—"

Harry looked at me and tapped his upper lip.

"Ohhh," I said, "do you mean my teeth?" I'd removed the veneers for my training, lest they fly out when Harry was demonstrating a defensive move. I flipped them out for Ellie.

"Wow!" Ellie exclaimed. "Those are remarkable! I've never noticed that those weren't real. What happened to your front teeth?"

"Typical Gabby story, I'm afraid. Most people who know me would have assumed it was from horse riding. But oh no—far less sporty accident than that. Broke one in half and chipped the other when I fell up the stairs coming up from the Embankment one day. To do proper veneers would cost a lot of money I just don't have right now. That's part of the reason I was hoping for the job on telly—it would have helped me pay for it."

Ellie looked at Harry. "So you're worried that it's going to give her away?"

Harry crossed his arms over his chest, unconsciously accentuating his gorgeous biceps and pectorals. "It might," he said, pursing his lips.

I shook my head. "No one needs know. I can sleep with them, ride with them. I won't take them out, I swear."

They both looked at me and shrugged. "Well, I have to say, I have never noticed," said Ellie, "and I've spent all this time with you. So please, please, please be mindful of not alerting anyone to your teeth. In fact, it would probably be more historically accurate if you *did* have broken teeth, though."

"Ellie, no! That would make me feel so insecure. I'd be covering up my mouth the whole time. With these veneers I feel so much more confident. And that's what you want in this role, right? A supremely confident woman."

"I completely understand," Ellie said, reaching out to pat my hand. "You're going to dazzle every last person who you meet, just as you did me when you first knocked on my office door."

The two of them got up and left the room, arms entwined, Ellie leaning her head on Harry's shoulder.

They were all the inspiration I needed to keep going. I was convinced love was going to find me in 1517.

CHAPTER FIVE

I F YOU'RE 60TH in line to the throne in the British monarchy, you're going to be damn well gifted on horseback; that was part of the time travel curriculum as well, but one I thankfully didn't need because I already had enough on my syllabus. Instead, I spent my time listening to recordings of six different readers of Middle English and French, trying to ascertain what they were saying without the text in front of me. It was akin to watching a foreign movie, with no movie. And no subtitles.

I wanted to cry.

Instead, I envisioned a horrible scenario of me just standing there, wildly and loudly gesticulating about what I needed...*A small crowd of villagers gathers to see this tall, crazy woman who can't speak the language. They decide to just put everyone out of their misery and throw rocks*...In spite of this dire, imagined scenario, I persevered until an hour later, when I threw in the towel (and not rocks), and went to Harry and Ellie's stables. They gave me the use of a giant horse, and went off on a cleansing ride—my absolute best remedy for anxiety.

Even though my mother and I had lacked the financial advantages of most landholding members of the royal family, we did have access to the stables at Windsor, Sandringham, and Balmoral when we visited. While the latter two were far away from our home in London, Windsor was a quick train ride away and I took full advantage of the privilege. Suffice it to say, I took advantage of the privilege here, too.

After a quick shower back at Jane's, Ellie sat me down in the library, which was a heavenly sanctuary painted in a dark green, including the ceilings, and lined with bookshelves stuffed end-to-end, and piles on top of piles of volumes. You could spend days in there and not uncover all the treasures: books on English history, English literature, academic journals, collections of essays, and classic literature.

But that day, it was time to learn about my 1517 identity. Ellie pulled up a Power Point on the desktop computer and pointed the monitor toward me.

"Have you heard of Rennes?" she asked. I shook my head. "It's a small town in Brittany. Up until this point in history, Brittany was considered a self-ruling duchy until the years just before 1517, when the last heiress to the throne married the heir to the kingdom of France, named Francis, or more exactly, *Francois*. At any rate, you now come from a landholding line of barons, and you have married Lord Dreux. By the way, this is a hereditary nobility that died out around this time, so it's conceivable there could have been a Lord Dreux. Henry VIII shouldn't be that familiar with all the particulars, nor should King Francois Premier."

Ellie had assembled a "who's who" of Rennes society, facts about the small city, places where one could visit at the time, local delicacies, etc. But the goal was to not go into depth about absolutely anything. I have to be honest, they'd done their homework well on both sides of the timeline, because who better to fill a role such as this than me, somebody whose family excels at small talk with absolutely everyone, from the dogcatcher, postal carrier, lorry driver, councilwoman, teachers, shepherds, IT professionals, line cooks, etc. The point is I could easily and comfortably give a few vague answers about me and my "husband," which would hopefully do enough to satiate a person's questions.

"I'll absolutely dazzle them with my questions about them, making everyone forget they were ever curious about me." I pushed my earlier worries about throngs of confused villagers with rocks. Instead, I told myself, I couldn't wait to meet the people of 1517 and chat with them.

"With that smile of yours, those deep blue eyes, and your happy demeanor," Ellie said, "I am quite sure you can pull a bait and switch. Why don't you go and study these materials? Your traveling companion/ 'husband' is arriving tomorrow."

My mouth immediately went dry as the Sahara. I was less nervous about journeying back in time than meeting my faux spouse. Jane and Ellie had spent days talking the man up as though he was the second coming of Mr. Darcy using terms like, "impeccable manners," "smart as a whip," "kind," "funny." It was as though I was being set up on a date, but instead, this was to be my pretend husband. Whether or not we could pull off the role of couple, we were placing ourselves in a time not known for its leniency should you put even a toe out of place; we needed to have each other's backs.

So the next morning, walking down the oak-paneled stairs, I stopped short when I heard a stranger's voice. Not Jane's husband. Not Harry. It had to be Graham.

It occurred to me suddenly that I was going to be fake married to a man who had the same name as a cracker.

I peeked into the kitchen to see Jane and Ellie talking with this man at the kitchen table.

From the back, his build was solid, like a rugby player's. Thick cords of muscles enveloped his shoulders, and his biceps nearly burst the tight sleeves of his button-down shirt.

"Hello everyone!" I said, my voice unnaturally high.

"Gabriella, I'm glad you're here," said Jane. "I'd like to introduce you to your new 'husband.' This is Graham." He scraped back his chair on the stone floor, and stood to his full height, two inches shy of mine. Certainly not an uncommon experience for me. His eyes were a piercing blue, almost like a husky's, and scanned me as though he was taking a mental photograph; I realized I was being assessed, not the way one is for romantic reasons, but almost like a job interview, or a threat assessment. It appeared he had done a lifetime of staring down people, eyes narrowing to sharpen his pronounced crow's feet. His close-cropped hair also denoted a somewhat traditional, perhaps military, mindset.

He gave a brief bow, and I stuck out my hand for a friendly shake. "Graham, delighted to meet you. So fun we'll be working together."

"Hello, Miss Gabriella," he said.

Jane gestured for me to take a seat.

"We haven't wanted to introduce the two of you yet because we were triple checking Graham's knowledge to make sure he's the 'real deal.' Being a member of the 'Civil Services,'" she said, using air quotes.

Having been around security agents and spies often enough with her majesty, I knew that meant he was something to do with an undercover agency.

Jane continued, "We were slightly reticent as he is not an academic by training, but his work on the early Tudors that he publishes online is top-notch. We set him off on a course for the last six months of learning to speak the language of the time, all under the guise that we'd like him to consult and act on a television series. We have also coached him on how to conduct one's self, etc. I'm happy to report he's an A-plus student, and his professional skills—he's assured me—will no doubt serve to protect you in the event of danger. During the past couple of weeks we revealed the truth of our labyrinth to him and given him a taste of what awaits in the past."

"So you've been training him and assessing him longer than me?"

Ellie and Jane both nodded. "But we've had our eye on you for quite some time, too, Gabriella. We just didn't know if your calling to be a TV star would steal you away first." Fair enough.

Graham was forty-something, built like he could tackle the best of them, and had probably killed people for who knows what controversial global geopolitical rationale. I guess we made a team, of sorts. But honestly, I had wanted a man who loved literature and romantic tales! Who could ride horses like he was born to ride bareback. Would make me swoon like Ellie does around Harry.

Maybe someone just a bit taller.

But this was not "The Dating Game." This was a real-life expedition back in time to meet Leonardo da Vinci. So who cared if Graham had a gruff face and demeanor, ears that slightly jugged out, and a name that reminded one of cello-wrapped crackers that tasted slightly like sand?

"We want to tell you more about your mission," Ellie started. "You two are to play a newly married couple. Gabby, you are Graham's second wife. His first, obviously, died."

"Did he kill her?" I asked and winked at him to see if he had a sense of humor.

"No," he said. "Childbirth did."

Nope—no sense of humor there so far. I was sure I could crack him.

Jane continued. "To make it easy, you'll keep your same first names, but be Lord and Lady Dreux. From Wodesley, you'll make your way over to the outskirts of Paris to find Da Vinci, who has been installed by Frances I in his own manor house, *Chateau de Cloux*, in the Loire Valley. The king is employing him as a kind of guru/teacher/art director for a royal city he wants Leonardo to design.

"As you know, Gabriella, Da Vinci was a perfectionist, never entirely 'done' with any painting he worked on; the world only has fifteen paintings by him. But he drew and wrote in his diaries, or notebooks. Her Majesty, I mean *His* Majesty—I just can't get used to that..." Jane shook her head sadly. "His Majesty has the largest collection of those notebooks of any other entity."

"Her Majesty was very proud of them too," I said. Her curator was one of the finest in the business. I didn't know if she was still employed by the new monarch, so many changes were going about. Maybe one day I could have the job.

"So let's be more specific about the mission beyond just trying to meet da Vinci. In the many documents that my brother, John Stafford, has retrieved from his time traveling," Jane said, "there was a mention of a painting that da Vinci was working on: *The Sunne in Splendour*. One that was unusual for him in that it wasn't a portrait, but more of a landscape. And it featured a phenomenon that scared the life out of nearly everyone who witnessed it."

"Really," I said. "Wow—may I see the letter?"

Ellie passed me a copy, which had her hand-written translation on the side. It was from Melzi, da Vinci's heir, assistant, and companion. A small line on the back read, "We have a prominent buyer for my master's landscape of the three suns." It was dated May 18, 1518.

"The Sunne in Splendour, from the Yorks versus the Lancasters—the War of the Roses?" I asked.

Graham spoke up. "I do know about the Sunne in Splendour from my reading about the War of the Roses. Before a major battle, when the sun arose that morning, there appeared to be three suns instead of one. Now, we know it's an atmospheric trick of ice crystals in the air. What's it called again?"

"A sun dog, or a parhelion. According to his biographers, DaVinci was fascinated by phenomena like this, speculating on whether they were nature-made, or signs from Heaven," Ellie said.

Ellie continued. "Here's where you come in. We obviously have no record that that painting ever survived, not even a sketch. All we have is this letter indicating it once existed. You could save the painting from disappearing completely. We don't know to whom Melzi is referring as 'the prominent buyer,' but we do know that after this date there is a strong likelihood it will be gone," she said. "If you get to them first—say two weeks earlier—*you* could offer to buy the painting."

Jane's brown eyes sparkled. "Just think of all the people who could enjoy a new da Vinci painting. What a discovery that would be! And how great for Britain."

In my mind's eye, I could see a battlefield, with the three suns hovering over the horizon like the holy trinity, a beacon of great things to come. Had Da Vinci used any historical knowledge of the event, I wondered, or had he just been inspired by his own imagination? Shakespeare, who was born after Da Vinci died, wrote of the scene in King Henry VI:

Three glorious suns, each one a perfect sun;
Not separated with the racking clouds,
But sever'd in a pale clear-shining sky.
See, see! they join, embrace, and seem to kiss,
As if they vow'd some league inviolable:
Now are they but one lamp, one light, one sun.
In this the heaven figures some event.

I almost recited the words aloud, but then decided now was not the time to wax poetic. Instead I asked, "So you think that if we could meet up with him in France, we could track down what happened to that painting? Yet it could be anywhere in Italy or France. It could be held by a patron of some sort, or even have been destroyed in floods or a fire, or on his travels."

"I think we can be fairly confident that it's with da Vinci in Amboise. Here. We've also found this letter to corroborate."

Jane held out an original letter for me, along with a pair of white cotton gloves so I could pick it up without damaging it.

Squinting down, some words stood out to me, but I had to work to make out others. "My eyes need to get used to the script..."

Jane pointed. "Do you see the name there? It mentions a Thomas of Egham being commissioned by King Henry VIII to seek this very painting."

My eyes flew open wider. "Oh my goodness, I've seen a picture of him! Yes, yes!" You don't forget a man like that, even if he exists only in a painting. A cross between the dark-haired and brooding *Portrait of Paul Victor Grandhomme* by Raphael Collin, and a painting of the famously handsome Sir Walter Raleigh by Hilliard. In it, Thomas had sharp features, chocolate brown eyes, and a gorgeous goatee so common of the time.

I had a collection of postcards of hunky young men depicted in paintings I'd acquired in various museums. Yes, friends took the mickey out of me for not having proper pop stars up on my wall, or film stars. But with this art, I could not only admire their good looks, but also admire the artists' skills. Thomas of Egham was one of my favorites.

I took another look at the letter. Oftentimes it takes dozens of readings to figure out the words in every script. The words are assembled like a puzzle:

> "to find artists of great consequences. DaVinci of Milano did
>   he reside
> In Loire, with Francis Roi of France for whom he did worke.
> I boutten a portraite of the famous penhailden for His Majestye."

"If you could get your hands on a Leonardo..." said Ellie.
"If you could *meet* with Leonardo!" said Jane.
My heart soared. "Oh my gosh, yes!"
She explained a very complex set of equations about how the labyrinth worked that quite frankly made my eyes roll back in my head just a smidge. Maths and particle physics and the like just don't compute in the same ways that art and language do for me. I just needed to know that it worked, and most importantly, that it could bring us back, especially if things went pear-shaped. The trip was to take three weeks' time as we had to go to France, far longer than Ellie's journey, but we'd be better prepared with what we'd be taking. Her trip was accidental. Ours was a mission.
"I'm saving myself for Chaucer," Jane said. "But we seem to

be moving forward in time with the labyrinth, not backwards."

"The Pearl poet for me," Ellie said. "But there's never been a single trace of him. Or her. Not one contemporaneous note. Plus, I have to wait until my kids are grown and safely through uni before I can go back. But in the meanwhile, you two—Graham, Gabriella—have quite the opportunity."

Graham and I exchanged glances. He had a kind, craggy smile. His eyelids were a bit on the droopy side, making him look slightly sad. Maybe a little like he'd been out on the range and had too much sunshine. Perhaps one of his assignments had him out in the desert, for years.

And years.

In any case, despite his "civil service" job, he also had a nerd's heart of wanting to know more about a past 500 years ago, and with that, I could completely relate. "What do you say, Graham? Shall we make a go of it? I mean, in a completely platonic way. Pretending to be husband and wife, yes?"

"Absolutely, and no offense, but I do have a girlfriend. However, I expect keeping our relationship PG will not be difficult for you." He was being modest about whether or not he was attractive to me, but it was true. He would not have to fight me off. There was unlikely to be any unrequited love here.

"I wouldn't dream of causing your girlfriend any concern," I said. "Now, how do we get to France to meet Leonardo?"

We hunkered down to study the maps Ellie began to lay out.

CHAPTER SIX

"I CAN'T TAKE a sandwich bag with me to 1517," I said. "Plastic, the little zipper thing? It would blow their minds."

Ellie looked down at the cubes of steak she'd just finished slicing. "Hmm, yes. No waxed paper, no parchment paper, no Tupperware, no paper serviette."

Jane walked over to a drawer and pulled out two cloth ones. "Here—a donation to the cause. I do not need these returned." Plain blue, worn, machine-made stitching, but still. They would do much better than plastic baggies.

"Remember to eat your meat as soon as you 'land,'" Ellie said. "Your symptoms shouldn't be too bad after that, and you will not get yourself into the pickle Harry and I did with me being sick for a day after going through the labyrinth."

I nodded, beginning to tremble. "Are you sure we're ready?"

"According to our calculations," Jane said, "it's now or never, the way our portal to the past works. It's got to be tonight."

My mouth and throat were so dry I felt like they would crack. And yet, I was afraid to drink water because… I didn't want to go to the bathroom in the Middle Ages. I thought porta potties were the worst, refused to go camping because of the lack of a bed, door, and locks. Worse, I couldn't figure out how to do the whole "squatting" thing without peeing on my underwear. And… well, there were simply lots of details about the whole process that I wanted to delay knowing about firsthand for as long as it was physically possible.

I licked my dry lips, akin to rubbing my tongue over sandpaper. Maybe just a quick sip of water? I grabbed a glass and drank enough just to wet my lips, and in a millisecond, my whole mouth went dry again. It was like a drop of rain in the desert.

"Where's Graham?" I asked.

"In the restroom," Jane said, sitting at the kitchen table, gnawing on one cuticle. It struck me that I'd never thought I'd grow so close to the head of the English Department that I'd be living in her house. But now I'd grown close enough to her to realize that dark circles had formed underneath her eyes, seemingly overnight. She was stressed.

As was I. "Well, at least he and I have that in common. I think I need one more trip…"

I scurried into a bathroom near the study. After I washed my hands, I laughed at myself. *What was the point of washing my hands? I'm going to live in filth from now on.*

I paused to study my reflection in the mirror; this new look of mine was early Tudor noble woman. Hair up, arranged in a wimple type of thing, pearls clasped at my neck, earrings dangling down my neck, I was donned in a blue silk dress with a square neckline and embroidered with bees. I hadn't been so formally dressed since the last state dinner when our dearly departed queen had invited my mother and me along; we were needed to circulate amongst the ambassadors. If they didn't get more than a handshake with the queen, at least they could spend time with the "minor" royals. Mum lent me a tiara that she had borrowed from a boarding school friend, while she borrowed one from one of her more well-off cousins.

The hand-me-down royals, we were.

But now I looked like I might be about to go on-stage in a production of *The Lion in Winter* or *Wolf Hall*. Tudor dresses didn't have as much a fairy-tale look as in the earlier medieval costume, where the style had been floaty, high waisted dresses.

And those infamous cone-shaped hats. Still, it wasn't about the clothing, now, was it? (Okay, maybe a *little*, but having a costume party would be far easier than this if it were just about the clothes.) This was an adventure. Time away from my real-life ho-hum-ness (oh, I know that you may think that going to a state dinner is really cool, but trust me, it's not. You cannot ever have a real conversation about anything significant. It all must be generalities about what puts the *great* in Great Britain!—museums, parks, historical sites, and of course, the royal castles and the monarchy). But what this meant was that I was getting away from my telly, my comfortable life, away from my phone with its horrible dating apps, and doing something that—until a few weeks ago—seemed only possible in a fantasy world.

"Well, Gabby," I said to the mirror, "I'm not sure if this is what people meant when they advised you to 'get out of a rut,' but I appreciate your spirit. Now let's see whether this labyrinth portal thingie actually works."

The architect of all the missions over the years, usually done on his own, mind you, John Stafford was to meet us down the hill. I'd thought it odd that Graham wouldn't meet the third member of our party until the time of departure, but Ellie shrugged. "He's best now in small doses."

Graham and I carried small trunks made from leather containing our clothes, and wool satchels, nothing that could be seen which should mark us as being different. Ellie had gold and silver coins fashioned for us, based on what John had brought back. Medieval folk used the same pound system as we, and schillings and pence. We were as ready as we could be.

Jane and Ellie stayed back in the castle, too nervous of being possibly sent through the labyrinth as had happened five years before with Ellie. So now, looming up in front of me in the moonlight, surrounded by torches set up for the occasion, was John Stafford. Tall, in his mid-40's, I could see why Ellie had fallen for him. Almost swaggering with confidence and spirit, hands on his hips, rising up on his toes like a ballet dancer ready to leap forth onto the stage. "Well, hullo, Miss Gabriella. Mr. Graham. Delighted, delighted to meet you. You ready for the ride of your life?"

Graham stepped forward, holding out his hand. "I understand you're the man responsible for all this. I commend you on your discoveries."

Stafford bowed. "Thank you, sir. And I commend you on your long career working for Her Majesty's government. I mean, His Majesty's government." He shook his head. "Can't get used to that. Anyway, your role sounds like perfect training for the travels on which we are about to embark." He turned to me, "Miss Gabriella. With your double PhD candidacy in art history and English literature, it seems like you have more than enough brains for us all. And I have the know-how." He gestured grandly at himself.

I tried not to guffaw at Stafford's Tudor outfit—it was the whole nine yards of poufy shirt, doublets (shorts), jerkins, big toed shoes, and best part of all, a clearly stuffed codpiece. How was one not to guffaw? I know it essentially acted as the flies on the doublets (shorts), connecting the two pieces together, but my God, this was silly looking. It's one thing to see a codpiece in a museum and paintings, but quite another to see one on a man, in the flesh. Luckily, Graham's outfit had such a long coat I was spared the sight of his, if he did have one.

I tried to focus my gaze anywhere else.

We approached a high wall at the base of the hill, and an imposing looking door. Stafford flipped up a plastic box on the wall and tapped in a security code.

"You ready?" he asked.

"As I'll ever be," I said. But was I really? Had I really thought this through? What was I getting myself into, and all over not getting a job I wanted? Spending too much time on my mobile? Because I still wanted to hear from a man I last had a relationship with years before? Who I clearly knew was awful for me? Deep down, I knew I had not had enough experiences in my life outside of books, classrooms, and riding rings.

I looked up at the moon, two thirds full, illuminating us three. No, I was not negating my life, I was confirming it. Confirming my abilities to do things, to take risks, and above all to see a different world, a luxury, and a privilege, that just a handful of people, as far as we knew, had had the chance to do.

I glanced over at Graham. "Fake husband? How about you? Ready?"

"I couldn't be more ready. I've been ready to go since Day One," he said, a big, boyish grin on his face.

"Righty ho," said John. He pulled out the key from a pocket in that enormous jacket of his, and as he turned it into the lock, he pushed the door opened.

I whispered. "It's beautiful!" as though I didn't want to disturb the tranquility. The winding paths of the labyrinth were made up of white pebbles, and green grass sprouted around each pathway. "How is the grass kept so tidy if you don't let anybody in?"

"We have one of those robot grass cutters," Stafford said, gesturing to the corner of the garden. "You know, it's like a Roomba vacuum cleaner, but it cuts grass. Jane lets it out of its pen once a week with an app, and it recharges over here." A little red light of a charger blinked on the far side of the garden. "We couldn't risk bringing anyone out here to do the job."

"Well, hear hear for modern technology says I," said I.

We all took in the labyrinth, but none of us moved. "So, you've done this how many times before?" Graham asked.

John scrunched up his nose. I could see he was making mental calculations, and then he gave a shake of his head. "I honestly can't say—seem to have lost count. Jane is worried that if you make too many trips it scrambles your brain, because she's noticed I don't seem to remember as well as I once did. But still, that's not a risk for you two with just the one trip, I shouldn't think. After all, Ellie's just as smart as she ever was after her one trip."

Great, add early dementia to the things that could go wrong here. But honestly, that was the least of my worries. I was more worried about short-term things, like long swords, bubonic plague, a lack of bathrooms, no baths, no deodorant...

"What do you say, Mrs. Dreux? Ready to be my fake wife in another century?" Graham said, reaching out to grasp my hand. His tone was light, as if to keep me calm. Like the whole thing was just a silly lark.

I matched his tone, determined to be brave. "It would be my great honor, Mr. Dreux. Will you be my pretend husband for as long as we both shall live in the 15th century?"

"I do." He was wise enough not to kiss the bride.

"So, now you go around the labyrinth like this..." John prompted us to start walking.

I started down the path, one bag slung over my shoulder, the case in both hands. I'd be happy to set them down on the other side.

Voices, singing, seemed to come out of nowhere. "Do you hear that?" I asked, craning my neck to discern where the noise was coming from.

"It's working," said Stafford. "Keep going."

Then, a pulling sensation on my feet, as though the very ground itself was sucking me down into it. "Help!" I yelped.

"Don't worry," Stafford's voice soothed. "It's part of the process. You're going to be all right. The next few mo—"

Then terrible screeching, high-pitched, straight into my brain, accompanied by falling. *How am I falling?* I had been on solid land, but down, down, down I went.

I was going to land at some point and I braced myself; I knew it was going to be the most painful thing I'd ever felt. I'd always had horrible morbid thoughts of what it would be like to fall out a crashing airplane, and how death would feel. This was it. I shouldn't have ever wondered—maybe I'd cursed myself.

But instead of a bone-crushing, organ-imploding smack, it was as if a puff of air gently held me aloft as I slowed, then came to a rest, down on the labyrinth, lying on my back with the trunk resting on my stomach, still clasped between my hands.

Relief coursed through me. I pushed the trunk aside to roll onto my stomach and start kissing the ground. "Thank you, God. Thank you, God! I'm alive!" I took a deep breath in, inhaling the scent of the earth, the grass. And then I waited for the odor of open sewage to hit me, like Ellie had described with her own experience. But nothing.

I was almost hesitant to look around, like when you are too frightened to open your eyes in case the noise in your room is really something to be concerned about. I held my breath, and then opened my eyes.

The castle, the one Ellie had described as being fully opera-tional and chock full of people celebrating, feasting, baking, jousting—had fallen into ruin. The walls were covered in ivy; grass and shrubs grew high and untrimmed around the building, and no smoke arose from the chimneys. The labyrinth beneath my hands and elbows was a meadow, with just the traces of the pebble underfoot to make the path visible.

"That was the worst thing I've ever been through," I heard Graham say from a few feet away. "I think I'm going to hurl." There was retching. I stayed down. I'm highly susceptible to feeling queasy at even the very thought of vomiting, and to see it within feet of me made the bile rise up to my throat.

Keep it down, keep it down, I thought.

After a few quiet moments, I said with a light tone, "All bet-ter, Graham?"

"Hrrrrmmmm."

"Okay, keep your head down, then, er, *husband*. You'll soon feel better."

I raised up into a sitting position, pulled out my steak from the cloth baggie, and started to consume it. "Yum." Char-grilled, garlicky, buttery. "Do you think you can handle some steak, Graham? Ellie said it would help. Right John?"

I got another "Hrrrmmmm" from Graham, who now was lying in a heap about ten feet away from me. But I couldn't spot John for the life of me. "John? Now where's he gone off to?" It couldn't have been more than a minute or two since we'd landed in this spot.

"What are you two doing over there?" A voice shouted from up on the hill. "Be ye hurt?"

*(My editor has kindly brought it to my attention that I should inform you, dear reader, that when you read my interactions with people from the Middle Ages, I am simply translating. While I do try to give you the odd bit of "color" in cadence, and the formality of the time, it is far easier for me to transcribe what they said in modern English. After all, spelling was not standardized back then, and quite frankly, it would take ages longer for you to read and comprehend. I do not want you to feel that you are back in your section on Chaucer in school, constantly checking footnotes and dictionaries, and cursing me. I'd far rather you be enjoying this tale than thinking this is a tedious assignment. So yes—back to the story—)

There was a man above us on the hill, near the castle, wondering what in the hell we were doing on his lawn, so to speak.

"Oh, hullo, good sir," I said. "My husband and I seem to have fallen ill and needed to lie down, but I am well now, and my husband will be up on his feet anon."

The man walked down closer to us, pitchfork in hand like an angry villager from the mob scene in *Frankenstein*. Being stabbed through with a pitchfork had not been on my list of things that might kill me on this journey. I clearly lacked an imagination.

"Madame, allow me to assist you and your husband. Please. Can you make it over to my house?" he gestured up the hill, back toward the castle where he'd come from.

"Do you live in the castle?

"Just the gatehouse, lady," he bowed. "I look after the castle for the family who once lived here, although I do not have enough help, and people take advantage."

"How many are you to take care of this great castle?"

"It is just me, madame," he sighed. "And I cannot write to let them know the others who used to assist me have either died, or left, as I am not a learned man."

"Well," I said, perking up with the notion that I could be of assistance, "your luck has changed. It just so happens that I can write. If you perhaps can assist me and my husband as we continue our travels, then I will assist you with your letter, and get the document on its way?"

"That sounds like an excellent plan, my lady, especially as I was going to offer my assistance regardless. My name is William of Wodesley."

"It is an honor to make your acquaintance. My name is Lady Gabriella Dreux. And this is my husband, Lord Dreux." We made our way over to pick up Graham, who was still lying in a fetal position.

I rolled my eyes—some bodyguard Graham was.

"Come on up, then, Graham," I shook him, reaching to pull him up. "Our new friend William is going to help us out."

Graham's eyes briefly opened, then rolled back in his head and shut again. I shook my head. "I'm not sure what has overcome him."

"He just needs some ale, some soup, and a warm fire." He put a hand around Graham's waist and pulled him to his feet. William was surprisingly strong for someone so scrawny. I picked up Graham's other arm and placed it around my shoulder, so we were both supporting him. "I'll come back for your belongings anon," he said. "Where are your men? Your horses? How did you end up here?"

"That is an excellent question. Our man Stafford seems to have disappeared when we fell ill. And we were going to ask about horses here."

William's nose wrinkled. "Oh, I know that man Stafford. Shifty fellow. Always coming and going in the dark of night, taking things that aren't his. I'm afraid you might have been hoodwinked by that one."

"So you think Stafford's a highwayman?" I struggled under Graham's weight; luckily William took much of it.

"No, not as such, but he might as well be with the way he seems to take things that aren't his. I've seen him out here before—I always try to get him to leave. You might want to make sure you're not missing anything."

"Thank you, I will, once we get my husband to his right senses. You are a good man for coming to our aid."

Much huffing and puffing ensued. Graham was built solidly—not a bird bone on the man. He'd need more than the usual six or eight pallbearers when his time came to visit St. Peter at the Pearly Gates.

"Graham, for the love of God I wish you'd cut back on the biscuit consumption a few weeks prior. You are killing me." He didn't acknowledge me.

"Aye, my lady, he is heavier than he looks. But do not berate him, I am sure he is doing his best."

I blew out a frustrated breath. "You are right, William. He did not intend to get ill. Are we nearly there?" The castle loomed up ahead, larger, much larger than the ruin that existed in the 21st century.

"The gatehouse is just here." We passed through the large gates of the castle, and once inside the grounds, there was a door to enter from the back. Inside was a small kitchen, with a fire going. We heaved Graham over to a wooden armchair and propped him up in it. "I'll get the ale," he said.

Sweat trickled down my chemise, and probably soaked into more layers of my beautiful outfit. Although it was spring, toting Graham had been the equivalent of hauling a trunk of a tree up a steep hill, and now that we were in front of a fire, I could easily have burst into flames at any moment. "Excuse me for a moment, William—I need to seek some cooler air."

I stepped back outside, dabbing at my face with a handkerchief I fished out of a pocket. Yes, pockets had been sewn into my gown. In fact, most gowns from this time had such conveniences, but I'll spare you from further details for now.

The moon had risen up over the castle, and I paused for a moment in wonder, when a newly familiar voice addressed me. "Ah yes, I thought William would take you in."

Stafford wandered up, eyes twinkling.

"Stafford, geez," I said, "I thought you'd abandoned us! Where have you been?"

"I had to get out of sight. I swear one day that man will run me through with whatever blade he has handy. He has seen enough of my comings and goings to know I can't be trusted."

I stood up taller but did not quite match him in height. "Well, frankly, I'm not so sure *I* can trust you, either!"

"You can't, but Ellie and Jane saw to that. They just asked that I hang around long enough to hire you a means of travel, along with the appropriate guards for people of your station." He made a mock bow, his hand twirling a flourish.

"How long will that take?"

"About a day or two. In the meanwhile, it looks as though Graham isn't going anywhere anytime soon. If you can't eat the meat, it's well-nigh impossible to feel better from that labyrinth fun-house ride for quite some time. I was quite kneecapped by it my first few times, but that didn't stop me from keeping up with the back and forth. Of course, the Dagworths, that kind couple who used to live here so many years ago, took me in and treated me like their long-lost son. I do miss them. Once they sold the place to a cousin of Edward III's, it never was looked after the same way, and it's fallen almost into ruins after years of neglect. It seems that William is all that stands between it standing or becoming a pile of rubble. It's been rather depressing to find it further and further declined, but then the fun of poking around in a new period begins once I leave the premises, and there's new people to meet, art to find, books to pilfer, armory, cloth-ing…Well, you've heard."

"Yes, and I'm not altogether sure that it's ethical taking these things away from the people." I crossed my arms over my chest.

He held up his hands in mock protest. "My dear Gabriella, these people are not equipped to take care of these precious works. Why, I'm bringing to light so many things that would have disappeared into the ether if I didn't rescue them. Look at you, by God—you are one giant hypocrite! Forgive me—" he bowed—"a giantess. Aren't you planning to steal a Leonardo?"

I put my foot down. I would not have the man insult me. "First, I am not stealing. I will be *buying* the painting from him; if he will not sell it, then so be it. But I am on a mission for the people of England, their heritage, and to save a painting by one of the greatest artists who ever lived. Don't try to compare what I'm doing to the kind of outright pilfering that you do, all in the name of ill-gotten riches."

Giantess, I thought, curling my lip in displeasure. *How dare he?* But I had to be diplomatic, and not go low. "Look Stafford, I respect the fact that you have done an incredible feat by discovering this time portal, but I feel sure that whatever it is that you are doing now is not what your younger self envisioned you would be doing. Would he be proud of the man you've become?"

That seemed to stump him. The boyish pleasure he held in his smile—a scamp you might call him—the kind that you get from stealing a candy bar from the candy store without thinking of the moral or financial implications of that action, evaporated. His mouth clamped shut. Until he said, "Well, I do try to be a responsible steward of this portal. I may not always succeed, but who amongst us is without fault? Maybe I do take too much advantage. Certainly Jane is forever on me about that."

"I know no one can fail to behave under Jane's stern gaze. Now, on to our business at hand. I hope you can track down Thomas of Egham and bring him and his party here when you're out getting horses."

His eyes perked up again. "Yes! I shall be back to pick you and Graham up. Keep pushing the red meat and fluids on him. He'll be right as rain soon, and I'll have your transport to France ready, as planned."

"Okay, and if you don't show up within two days?"

"Then something has happened to me, and you must move forward with Plan B. And don't forget about Plans, C, D, and E."

Ellie, a consummate worrier, had come up with contingency plans for almost every scenario going wrong. Just like my dear mother, who had trained me to be prepared for every weather event, carry along cash tucked in my bra just in case I'm ever mugged, to have three bank accounts just in case one is hacked or a bank goes belly-up (she doesn't quite understand financially guaranteed funds), to eat a snack before you go out, just in case you can't eat for hours, and to always visit the toilet before an errand. *Speaking of which...*

"Err, before you leave, would you know where I can find a toilet here?"

John led the way. He knew this castle—of course—like the back of his hand, and while it did not have indoor plumbing, of course, it did have toilets. And I'd brought my own paper, tucked into the folds of my skirts. Not a roll, mind you, but efficiently folded sections which did not add bulk.

I held my nose as I entered the garderobe. Let's just say it was dark. Dank. Smelled. And with no lights, I had no idea what was in the privy with me. I heard a scratch, or was it a branch scratching a wall? Regardless, I willed myself: *Hurry!*

The look on my face as I emerged must have been a sight. John doubled over laughing. "I'll thank you very much," I said, "to wipe that smirk right off your face. That was the very definition of unpleasant."

"Need I remind you, Lady Gabriella, that you will be expected to leave one of these toilets with a look of serenity, as though this is what you've been used to your whole life."

"Point taken," I said, holding my head high. "Then how about you do your best to not poke fun at me when I'm putting on this show?"

"Indeed."

"Lady Gabriella?" It was William calling across the courtyard. "Your husband is asking for you."

"I'll be there anon!" I said, and then whispered to Stafford, who had ducked in the shadows of an archway. "Thank God Graham's coming around. Now get a move on. Don't let William catch you lurking about, or you may see the sharp end of his pitchfork."

He bowed silently, and I rushed back to the gatehouse.

CHAPTER SEVEN

WILLIAM DID HIS best as a host, bless him. But the gatehouse was not built for three people to occupy. Two at most.

Inside was a rough kitchen for heating and preparing basic meals. During the heyday of the castle, William explained, the majority of the cooking would have been done inside the main part of the building and the food brought out to whomever was on watch. But William had made his situation work by putting up stands for a pot, a pan, and another for hot water. There was no spit—he didn't have time to sit for hours by the fire and turn it. That was a job usually done by small boys. He'd made a sort of oven over the fire for bread, which he was serving us now; he acquired butter from a neighbor in the village.

We three sat at a small, wooden table, William on a box, and Graham and I on stools. Graham had some color back in his face, but he didn't seem up to making conversation as yet. Instead, he sipped some mead out of a tin cup, and ate his bread, taking minuscule bites with the idea to see how it interacted with his stomach.

"How long have you been on your own?" I asked William.

He looked up to the ceiling, knitting his brows together. "That is a good question, my lady. The old family who used to live in the castle, well over a hundred years ago, moved to Italy, giving the place to his majesty King Edward III. Then the king gave it to an earl of some kind, but he was killed and left no heirs, so it went back to the king at that time...anyway," he said, scratching his fingers through his hair, "my head hurts thinking about it. The family who owns it now, well, they live mostly in France because of them being Yorkists. I think they never will feel safe in this country from all the bad blood. Neighbors fighting neighbors. Theys were dark times, or so my pa told me."

I nodded. The War of the Roses had occurred between different descendants of Edward III. The civil war dragged on for decades, with noble families taking sides and their men and money used as weapons. But people of this time didn't call it the "War of the Roses." It wasn't so named until the 19th century.

"I guess now that the country is at peace," William said, "they prefer their life in France. Even though they send us pay twice a year, the people who used to work with me, one-by-one, they either got called to France to serve the master, or they just got tired of nothing ever changing here, nothing to do.

"The place is built solid, but the roof over the east tower needs to be rebuilt. There was a flood inside a few years ago when the rain come down heavy. And with just me left, I try to keep people away from even entering the castle, so I sit in the gatehouse. But I'm just one man, and to keep the peace, I'll strike a bargain if strangers ask to stay a little while and then leave. Alas, they make a mess of the place." His voice caught.

A tear rolled down his cheek, and he swiped at it with his hand. "The money they leave behind don't make up for it. I feel terrible that the castle is getting ruined under my watch. But what is one man to do?" he sighed. "My pa told me stories of this castle in its glory days, that his pa had told him, and the one before that. Now I'm the last of the line, and I don't think I can do it no more." His head sank down to rest on his arms on the table.

Perhaps it was from the shock of witnessing this poor man breaking down, but Graham came to life at long last. "William, there, there. Surely we can be of help to you?"

"No, I can't ask you to trouble yourselves. You are too important to need worry about the likes of me," he sniffled, face still on the table.

I put on my sternest teacher's voice. "Stop that kind of thinking at once, William. I demand it," I said.

His head popped up and his eyes went round, still filled with tears. "Yes, madame."

"Now," I continued, "we will get in contact with your employer at once and let him know that you are no longer interested in serving in this role unless you have more help, or else he must find another person to take over for you. And we will assist you in finding a new job."

"But I do not know how to do anything else," he protested.

Graham piped up. "I disagree, because you are a man of many skills. You do *everything* here—you are caretaker, repairman, guard, cook, cleaner, overseer. You do the work of many men, and I know that a good family with a fine house or estate would be happy to employ a man of your skills."

William looked from me to Graham, and back at me. "Perhaps... perhaps a change might be possible after all, if I could trouble you to make introductions? I've never ventured farther from this castle than the next few villages near us. Hardly anyone knows of me. No." He shook his head. "But I can't leave the castle. What if something happens to it?"

"And what if something happened to *you*, William?" Graham said. "Would they even know? It is their fault that they have not taken care to aid you in your job. No one man can be expected to keep his commitment, day in, day out, year after year, and still be expected to be loyal. That is the mistake of your employer for not checking on your well-being."

Through our conversation, we were moving William from the feudalistic world into the capitalistic world. Since his lord of the manor had abandoned him, I saw no reason that he should be expected to continue on, no matter what. A person needs to be in control of their own destiny.

Our destiny that night was to sleep on the only beds William had. He insisted on it, and while I shuddered at the thought of what creatures lived in the bedding, I tried to distract myself by reviewing the words and phrases I'd heard William use. Graham had held up well—it turns out his brains weren't scrambled from the time travel. Once he started to feel better, I could see him attuning his ear to the language. It's kind of like when you go to Paris years after having learned French in school for a couple of years. You pick up the odd word here and there, and then suddenly that part of your brain is firing on all cylinders, making connections more and more until you *understand* very well, but you can't *speak* that well. That's when his training with Ellie and Jane kicked in, and he was sounding like a true native medieval chap.

Tomorrow, as we waited for Stafford's return, I'd make the most of our time and further explore the castle, then perhaps visit the village, with Graham and William in tow. Now was not the time to be a wimp, languishing in an empty castle courtyard, the safe and easy way. Now was the time to live.

THE VILLAGE? WELL, let's not say it would rate on TripAdvisor's top ten places to visit in Britain. Much as the castle had been left to ruin without the family there to maintain it, so too did the village wither without the benefit of the family's money, the visitors, the need for vendors. I wouldn't call it a dump, necessarily, but more like one of those ghost towns you see in westerns, tumbleweeds blowing through the center of the main street, where there's just a couple of stubborn families left in town after the gold rush who refused to move. No market. No pub. No shops.

"William, this is so sad. Where is the nearest market town?"

"About five miles hence," he said. "That's where I go with my cart for supplies." You would think that the caretaker of a castle would have a fine team of horses. Instead, William had just one.

"Is there anyone with whom you can socialize, tell stories, sing songs?"

"Well, I do visit with a couple of the tenant farmers. We break bread, but they do not have much to share."

The more time we spent with William, the more depressed I got for his living situation. No family, barely any friends, and not more than a sturdy horse to get him places. If anything ever happened to him, say he fell off a ladder, or became ill with a fever or food poisoning, who on earth would know?

I took Graham aside on the walk back up the hill to the castle. "We have to tell him about Stafford helping us. I don't want him to pull out his pitchfork and stab the man when he returns. Then, we have to get Stafford on board with helping him and bringing him with us."

"To France?" Graham's eyebrows went up.

"No, I don't think so, but we really can't go online and fill out a job application for him. If we happen to get lucky along the way to find him employment, then that's terrific, but if not, he'll have to come with us. I cannot leave this man on his own."

Graham shot me a look. "He has been on his own for years, Gabby, if not decades. He knows what he's doing."

"No sir, we will not pretend as if he's something we can just stroll on by. Where's your sense of duty? He's done his part in rescuing you, giving you food that is painfully hard to get, giving up his bed for you. He didn't have to do that. We could have been sleeping outside last night. Instead, we were warm, and we've been fed. The name of the game in this day and age is chivalry, and when you find someone who is down on his luck, especially when he's trying to do something noble and honorable, you help him."

"I get what you're saying, you've got a good heart. Maybe a wholly impractical one, but a good one. But if he in any way slows us down or endangers us, then we must cut him loose."

"Understood, 007."

He put his hand out to stop me, looking me in the eye. "I'm not a spy."

"Sure you aren't. Nudge nudge, wink wink. I won't rat you out."

"I'm just an administrator in the government," he said, presenting me with empty palms. As if that would prove he was not a spy.

"And yet Harry said you are skilled at weaponry, self-defense, and would make me an excellent bodyguard. Not that I need one." I stretched to my full height, peering over his head. "Everyone I've met so far is pint-sized. Pre-teen sized, even. Malnourished and weak, I'm sorry to say. Whereas I am far from being malnourished, have all my teeth, and can run up the escalators at the Angel line, and then run up to my 3rd floor walk-up, and then down to the basement where the laundry room is, and back up again. Fit as a fiddle."

"A city girl." He pursed his lips, further assessing me.

"I've got street smarts."

Graham turned to face me. "But do you know how to find fresh potable water? Can you make a campfire? Gather leaves and branches to make a hut? Forage and trap food?"

"Well, no, but if you do, let's say we divide and conquer. I'll be the one fighting off the pickpockets in town, while you can be the one to gather wood for a campfire. Deal?" I asked, hands on hips.

Graham put out his hand. "Deal. Besides, my Mandarin will do us no good here."

"Hmmm, an administrator who speaks Mandarin... Tell me more."

But my language lesson was interrupted when a cloud of dust appeared near the castle. "What the...?"

"It's horses," said William, shouting back over his shoulder at us. "Curses, and I've been away from my post. Let us hurry!"

Needless to say, thanks to my long legs and command of the Northern Line's horrific escalators, I got there first.

⇶⫷

NOT ONLY WERE there horses, there were men. Thankfully, it was not an invasion, but Stafford, back far earlier than expected.

William glared at him when he caught up, placing a hand on Stafford's horse's rein. "I hope you have not come to steal from us or these good people."

Stafford hopped off his horse. "William of Wodesley. It is good to see you again. You appear to have been through some hard times."

"And you appear to have not aged at all. 'Tis a miracle, or I wonder if the devil is at play?"

"No, no, good man. I eat for my health and long walks does a body good. Now, my Lord, my Lady!" He tipped his cap toward us. "I have brought transport as well as new friends to accompany us to France! I happened upon a party already en route, and they have agreed for the sake of safety against vile robbers, to join with us."

I took a look at the group, all men, but was struck dumb immediately upon my glance at one of them.

They say beauty is subjective, as is art. But unquestionably, there are people in this world who 99.95% of the population would say are beautiful, or handsome, and then there are the rest of us—those in the middle of the spectrum. Van Gogh could only sell but one piece of art during his lifetime, and yet ask any man or woman on the street now if they'd have one of his paintings on their wall, and they'd say *yes, please!* Therefore tastes change, and what is thought to be beautiful changes. My point is, and oh, it was hard to keep my point with this man around, he was unquestionably attractive, in this era or any other. Standing next to a horse and pulling off that early Tudor look of an oversized jacket (shoulder pads!) over tights, and yes, an impressive cod piece, *ahem...*

Where was I?

"Yes, please introduce us," Graham said.

"You will never believe how lucky I have been to happen upon Thomas of Egham, son of George Egham, renowned portrait artist," Stafford announced.

Not many people get to meet the man whose portrait poster graced their wall. Even though he was famous only for his looks and the pose that captured a certain romantic melancholy of the era, this was like meeting a celebrity for me.

There was no luck in this. We had done the research and Stafford was able to alert us to Thomas and the scouting party at this very day and location. He was *Plan A* in our scheme.

"Good sir, we are pleased to meet you. This is my wife, Lady Dreux. And I am Lord Dreux, of Rennes, in Brittany."

"The pleasure is mine," Thomas said, alighting from his horse as easily as one gets up from a chair, to bow over Graham's hand, and then, taking my fingers in his gloved hand, pressing a light kiss on the back of mine.

My character of Lady Dreux would think this greeting an everyday occurrence, and maintain her decorum, but a girlish giggle floated out of me when Thomas kissed my hand; I was so tickled at this man paying any attention to me. Of course, this was all good manners and had nothing to do with flirtation or any such thing, but my fourteen-year-old self was delighted.

Did Thomas notice my inappropriate giggle? A twitch of a smile was my only indication.

Thomas proceeded to introduce his party. Nobody traveled alone at this time in history, or, if they did, they were taking their life in their hands. Bandits lurked in hiding places, ready to strip you of any jewelry, coinage, fine clothes, and whatever else you might be traveling with, like tin cups, wine for drinking, even your food.

I'm terrible with names, and a trick my mother taught me at parties was to align somebody's name with a distinguishing characteristic, or just goofy alliteration. So as we were introduced to the other members in Thomas's party, I gave them nicknames.

Edward Edgy had an edgy cut to his jacket, making him look like a style icon. *Rockin' Robert*, as Robert had what looked like a mullet running down his jacket. *High Hugh* I'd dubbed because he was tall like me. Edward Edgy, Rockin' Robert, High Hugh. Say their names three times and the idea was you'd never forget them. All were dressed in clothes not of noblemen, who were often distinguished by their clothing and jewelry, but of the middle class, who had a few nice outfits, but none of the jewelry.

And Thomas's nickname, you ask? *Tasty Thomas.* Of course. Not that I'd forget his name, you understand. But just in case my brain short-circuited due to an overload of estrogen, I figured, I'd best follow the pattern and give him a nickname all the same.

"William, pack up your things, you're coming with us to find new employment," Graham said.

William clasped his hands together and rushed to gather up his few belongings.

In minutes, we were on our way.

CHAPTER EIGHT

M Y LITTLE MEDIEVAL horse had an untidy coat, a tangled mane, and a tail in dire need of a wash. But he did have a jaunty step, as though his pure pride could carry him past the neglect. "You poor thing," I said. "I'll spoil you as much as I can to make your life better. I'm sorry I'm so big."

Thinking back to meeting Thomas's eyes, they seemed to tell part of his story, and if I could have grabbed my sketchbook, I would have captured them, because they spoke to me so powerfully of hurt and pain. The eyes can communicate so much, and in his eyes, I saw that he was viewing life as though a dark veil covered the world, muting its colors and beauty for him. And with his tousled hair, aquiline nose, and pointed chin covered in a scruffy beard, I honestly wanted to envelope him in a hug, feed him chocolates, and make him feel loved until his misery evaporated, and he was back to being what he should be—a young man in the prime of his life.

But I could not. I was a "married" woman, though just in this lifetime of course. Still, just as my mum had taught, I tried to cheer him up.

I sidled over to him. "Thomas of Egham, how fortuitous it is that our Stafford has found you. You are just the man we were hoping to meet—this is remarkable."

"Indeed?" he asked. "How did you come to know of me?"

Good question, I thought. "We came to learn of you by reputation—as an art buyer with a good eye. I can't remember who it was that spoke of you so highly, but it came from more than just one source."

He sidled his horse somewhat closer to mine. "How very flattering," he said. "I am but a humble gentleman. It was my father who was the great artist. But whoever spoke so kindly of me, I am glad to know it, as it has given us more company. It is a long journey, and I am most pleased to have a woman's company. Without a woman in the party, the tone of the endeavor can descend quite rapidly into oafishness, lewdness, and base language. Women bring out the best in men; without them, we are truly beasts."

"I would agree with you there." I couldn't stop looking into his dark eyes, and I feared that despite the chill that was encroaching as the sun began to sink, my cheeks were a fiery red. *You've never been able to pull off that sexy flirt role, Gabby, blushing like a buffoon*, I thought.

Thomas said, "I am surprised I have never seen you at court?"

Another explanation needed... *Let's see if I can nail it.* "Yes, I have long been in Brittany with my family. I married Lord Dreux a few weeks ago, and he had some brief business here, and I have come with him on this adventure. But it's been a short journey to England, and now we must be away again. At least I have seen something of the land, even if my husband has gotten ill, and we've encountered misfortune in losing our retainers. Still, we are thankful we can join forces with you. You are very kind."

"My king would not have me back in his court if I did not help a beautiful English lady, even if she has been living in France. And of course, her noble husband."

"You are all goodness, sir," I said. "May I inquire, you say your father was a great artist?" I knew the answer, of course, but experience had taught me that asking someone about themselves was a great method of creating a connection.

"Yes, my father was a skilled painter of portraits, going from house to house of fine families to capture their likeness. When he had established his reputation, people came to sit for him at his studio. I grew up there, playing at first in the corner very quietly so as not to disturb his concentration. I know that some artists can have conversations while painting, and activity in the room, but my father needed quiet to get his work done. As I got older, he had me help with mixing his paints, his preliminary sketches, and framing. But I was never blessed with his talents. What I did have was an ability to find other talented artists when my father wasn't available and discovered paintings for collectors."

"His Majesty the King being one of your collectors?"

"Yes, one I'm honored to serve. Although his interests lay more in armory, and castles. But I have heard King Francis is much more interested in art, and I'm eager to meet him and scout out artists in France. Now, I must let you get back to attending to your husband, who I expect is long missing the quality of your conversation."

"Oh, well, I...uh..." but he was gone.

Darkness was rapidly falling, and my poor little horse's energy was flagging. Stafford led the way, so I nudged him up to find out how much more ground we had to cover before we could stop and rest for the night.

"How much longer, Stafford?" I let out a huge yawn.

"Tired? Not long. I have sent Edward ahead to attain accommodations at the inn in the next village."

"Good. This horse is not the hardiest."

"I shall attain a better horse for you for the next leg of our journey if I can, my lady, you can be sure of it." Stafford nodded, and kicked at his horse to gallop, and he was gone.

I was left at a halfhearted trot. Up and down, up and down, posting with both legs. Yes, two legs, no sidesaddle. Sitting astride. I'd read that Anne Boleyn, who Henry VIII would encounter in eight years' time, would hunt with Henry out in the countryside, galloping around. The special sidesaddle pommel was not invented until the 1800s, which permitted women to ride at full speed on sidesaddle without endangering their lives, so it seemed like it was possible that women of this time rode astride, especially if they were going at a brisk pace.

There was no means of conveyance that would allow for a quick pace in this day and age; no modern carriages had been made that had springs on them, and carts and wagons were heavy and slowed everyone and everything down on the unpaved and rutted roads. So baloney to those who think of women only on sidesaddle. Maybe that was for a trip to the village. But when women were on the go, it was astride; for this reason, Ellie and Jane had made sure that I had an extra stretch of skirting that I could pull across so as not to scandalize everyone who might catch a glimpse of my long, luscious (!) legs.

WE ENTERED THE village, a lively little place with two streets of buildings and a small church, and an odor of grilled meat wafted toward us. I sniffed with anticipation, quite famished, as always, and could have eaten an entire roast beef. And Yorkshire pudding. And mashed potatoes. I clutched at my stomach, worried I might be so hungry I'd mow down small children just to start smashing food toward my face.

The inn/pub seemed cheerily familiar, as it would to all folks British: half-timbered in black and white, with gabled windows on the first floor (which would be the second to Americans), a barn next door for the horses and other livestock, and the sound of voices, likely drunk, ringing out from the open windows.

I dismounted and William took the horses to the barn. "I'll just see to myself, my lady. No need to worry about me. Thank you again for bringing me along."

"Of course, William. I would not have been able to stand it had we left you alone."

I steeled myself for comments as I entered the pub, a tall

woman in Tudor England. Probably a giantess, as Stafford had called me, about which tales would be told for generations. So long as someone in my party bought me a drink or two and supplied me with a hearty meal, I supposed, I could handle it, as I've done innumerable times before when people jest, "How's the weather up there?" or "Hey girlie, can you reach that high shelf for me?"

I entered the room, and a hush fell over the crowd. Predictably. I looked at Stafford, as did Graham, hoping he would know what to do in this case.

The innkeeper hustled over to us and said in hushed tones, "You are most welcome here. I have a more private area behind these screens if you would like to follow me, my lady, my lords..." I felt a hand at my back, pushing me forward. Was it Thomas? Unlikely, as that would have been too forward of him, but a girl had hopes. I turned my head slightly to see that it was Graham.

Our party of seven sat at two tables. Graham, Stafford, Thomas, and me at one, and the other men next to us. I wondered, *How do we order? Were there menus? Did they just bring whatever they had out to us? How were we to know the cost?*

The lovely thing about having someone like Stafford in charge was that I just went along with the flow. It was like being with a parent who took care of all the details. Of course, that happens rarely as a grown-up so maybe it was more like having a sophisticated tour guide who knew the ways of the locals.

Graham was a man of few words. Perhaps he'd spent too much time in data-analysis (aka assassinating enemies of the state) to learn the art of conversation. Instead, he focused in on our surroundings, eyes flicking from one potential assailant to the next, and keeping an eye on potential points of entry and exit.

I watched him watching the same man who had led us to our table when he returned with wine all around, rolls, and butter. "Chicken, potatoes, soup?"

Stafford nodded, and the man left. Ordering moved fast when

there were no other options.

"We are lucky to find an inn," Stafford said. "The alehouses can be too rough for a respectable woman. There doesn't appear to be gambling here, at least as yet, and because they serve wine only, hopefully no fights will break out."

"The king knows something must be done about alehouses," Thomas said. "He fears not enough labor is getting done—too many working men don't show up for work because they cannot wake from their stupor, or feel too poorly in their heads. I much prefer a quiet night in front of the fire with a good book."

"Oh so do I!" I said, leaning over to him on my right. "And what kind of books do you enjoy reading?"

Graham interrupted before Thomas had a chance to reply. "I do wonder what the king might be planning," he said, stroking his chin. "Perhaps some regulations as to who can run alehouses. I once read there is an ale inspector who wears leather pants, and when ale is poured on them, if it sticks, that means the ale is no good!"

"I heard—" said Stafford—"of a woman who makes her beer with…" He stole a glance at me, and then whispered it to Graham, instead of telling the whole table.

"With what? Don't spare me the details." I patted the table three times, impatient.

"I fear your delicate ears would be too offended." He had puppy dog eyes on him, insouciant man.

"Believe me, I've heard more than you would believe."

"All right then. She flavored her beer with hen droppings."

"Ewwww!" I said.

"Why on earth," Thomas said, "would she think that would make her ale taste better?"

"I know not, but she was caught, and happily she is no longer employed in the trade."

It was at this moment, our food—including chicken, hopefully without droppings—arrived steaming, on platters. Besides the chicken, which had been roasted, were roast potatoes, some sort of orangey mash, carrots, and broth. As the lady of the table, thank heavens I was served first, and told everyone, "Please, eat! As soon as you are served, for I cannot wait a moment longer." Not the best meal I'd ever had, but far from the worst, especially since it did, in fact, appear hen-poop free.

We all ate until full. I finally pushed my plate away from me. "Put those potatoes on the other side of the table, far from me," I said. "Otherwise I shall keep eating. I do love my food, but enough is enough. I will not be able to fit into my clothes tomorrow!"

Thomas seemed to blanche. Perhaps this was too indelicate a topic for a lady to announce.

Graham patted my hand. "My dear lady does enjoy her food, and who can deny her? I prefer a woman with some meat on her bones, don't you, Stafford?"

I shook my head. I had no intention of being the center of a debate on women and weight.

"Now I must apologize," I said. "It was indelicate of me to speak so. Let us talk of something else." I thought of one of Mummy's guaranteed conversation starters: "What is your earliest memory?"

The evening wore on, and I could not conceal my yawns. I'd barely slept the night before. "Perhaps we should see about our rooms, Lord Dreux? I'm sure we have a long day of travel ahead of us tomorrow, and we should rest."

The men stood when I did. Ah, chivalrous manners. In my opinion, you could throw out a lot about Tudor England, especially the social repression and the patriarchy, but please— keep the chivalry. Why is it that was the first thing we eliminated, and not the last, in the name of female equality? *Civility and politeness to all*, is my motto.

And then, shouts erupted from the other side of the screen. It had been getting louder and louder on that side of the room, but now it appeared that the point in the evening had come, when the kind of binge drinking that the English are so famous for had come to bite our little inn at the butt. Chairs scraped, dishes and cutlery fell. "Hey!" somebody yelled.

"You'd better mind yourself!" yelled another.

And then our screen was pushed over, falling onto the shoulders and necks of Stafford and Graham. They promptly sent it flying back, which then set forth another set of "Hey!" Somehow in the very next moment, my fake husband was scrambling about the floor with a beast of a man in a kind of wrestling maneuver, legs and arms tangled. He had one leg around the man's neck, and the man with his arm around Graham's midsection. "Do be careful, Graham!" I shouted.

"You should not be here, my lady," said Thomas, a hand on my elbow. His voice in my ear gave me shivers.

"Yes, do let's go," I said, and together, we hustled up the stairs. Stafford and the other three men seemed to have fallen into the melee as well.

"I wish I knew where our rooms were," I said. "I'd lock myself in. But I'm sure the innkeeper is too busy with this fracas to attend to it."

"Let me see if I can find someone down the back stairs who could help. You stay here." He pointed to a bench in front of a window, in a corner between rooms.

"I won't move," I said.

The man was ingenuity himself—he found the innkeeper's wife, who knew the plan for our stay, and had all the keys on her person. She let me into a room that seemed like a refuge after the bar brawl downstairs. "Oh, it's beautiful," I said. "Thank you ever so much."

A canopied bed. Towels. A filled water pitcher. Even a toilet chair (yes, a toilet chair—like a toilet, minus the flushing). "Will you be all right here on your own?" asked Thomas, standing at the door.

"I will, thank you. Do you think you might be able to find our bags though? I am so sorry. I know you are not a servant. Or you can find Graham, and he can get them? I just really feel as if I should not go out there again. Too many drunks, and…"

"You are too fair a lady for that crowd, to be sure," Thomas said, shaking his head. "I am sorry you had to see that. My fellow man is not always as well-behaved as I would like, as we were speaking about earlier today."

"And that is why we have books. And art. To lose ourselves in other worlds."

A smile crept over his face. His face was wholly different—and so much more handsome—when he smiled.

"I'm off—I shall return."

I desperately wanted to use that toilet chair, but needed to wait until I was alone for the night. In the meanwhile, I could at least clean my face up of the day's dust and debris. But as I was reaching down to get the towel with my hand, I felt a scratch…

"Ouch!"

I looked down to see what had gotten me. A small nail, sticking out of the dressing stand. Well, some soap and water, and some of the antibiotic cream we had tucked away discretely in our bags would fix that. I'd recently updated my tetanus shot, so no worries there.

It did smart, though. It's shocking how delicate we humans are. One little scratch, and we fuss and bother. People in Tudor times wouldn't have any idea about bacteria getting into wounds, but did at least know to stop the bleeding. As did I. All I needed was a clean rag…

The door opened again, and I looked to see Thomas, holding our bags. "Ah good," I said. "Thank you so much. And now I just have one more favor for the night, and I promise I'll let you go, but I do need something clean to put on this?"

I held up my hand, with the bloody gash on it. It wasn't exactly dripping blood yet, but I needed to staunch the flow.

"Oh dear! Yes, of course. Let me see what the innkeeper's wife has."

And again, the poor man ran up and down the stairs for me, returning with a clean slip of linen. I guess with all the fights in her bar, the inkeeperess had to have a good stock of them. "Will you allow me?" Thomas asked.

As he stepped closer, he brought the most intoxicating blend of scents with him—a heady mix of almonds, rosemary, and lavender. If I could bottle it, I would be a wealthy woman. Like a love potion—you couldn't help but fall in love with a man who wore this scent.

Even better, Thomas and I were the same height, although the romantic in me thought maybe he was just a hair taller. I studied his concerned face as he first took a clean cloth and poured water over it, and then wiped the blood from my gash. Then, after dabbing it, he took the other piece of linen, and looped it twice around my hand, tying it neatly. Our heads bent over the task, nearly touching, and the feel of his hands on mine sent a shiver down my back.

Then he stepped back, quickly as though he was afraid of me. And with that, his heavenly scent disappeared.

"Please accept my apologies for being such a nuisance to-night," I said. "I don't know what could have happened to my husband; I trust that he is all right."

"After I leave you, lady, I shall confirm that the rest of our party is accounted for and in one piece."

I shuddered slightly, realizing the etymology of that phrase. This is a time when people were literally split into quarters for crimes. I placed a hand on my chest to calm my heart. But my heart was many layers underneath these ridiculous garments and though I could feel it pounding against my chest and hear my pulse thrumming through my ears, my palm couldn't sense any vibrations.

"I thank you so much for your kindness. I hope you have a good night's sleep."

"And you, madame. I am sorry you have no lady to assist you."

"I shall be just fine, after all we have been through."

And he was gone. I fell back onto the bed. *My God, that was* one of the sexiest encounters I've ever had, and that was just putting on a bandage. Imagine what an actual kiss might be like.

Don't be silly, Gabs, I chastised myself. You're a "married" woman, and Thomas clearly has a strong moral compass. There's no way anything will possibly happen.

With that admonishment, it was time to get out of these clothes and into bed. But my brain kept working anyway.

Even if I could never let on to him that I fancied him, I wanted him to at least have a crush on me. Bah, that would never happen. I was an enormous ostrich. A man like him wanted a delicate little lady. Perhaps a quiet one, obedient, not quite so forward, with not with quite so many questions.

Well, pretty boy, I thought, if that's what you want out of a woman, prepare for a lifetime of boredom! I reached around to start untying my clothes and undressing myself. Crap.

In the midst of trying to make myself cozy in this strange world, I wondered how I was going to get off all these clothes by myself, when all the ties were in the back? Jane and Ellie had not anticipated that I would be on my own. The previous night, Graham had assisted me by loosening all my ties.

Still, I managed to get my faux sleeves off, my slippers, stockings, and garters. I was able to get my farthingale off because I all I had to do was shift the laces to the front to untie them. But the dress's laces were up so high in the back that no matter how I tried to contort myself, I couldn't untie the bow. Even if I had been successful, there was still the kirdle underneath that, and it was also laced up. So I quickly did my business in the toilet seat and tossed the contents out the window (first checking to make sure there was no one about below), before Graham came in.

I crumpled into a heap on the bed, giving up. I was so tired. I heard men singing below. Maybe they'd all become friends again. Graham could always help me when he came up.

Except, he never came.

CHAPTER NINE

I'D LOCKED THE door for my safety, so if Graham had come up, he'd have to knock on the door and wake me to get in. No knock ever came.

Sunlight was shining in the room when I awoke. I had become aware of it earlier in my haze of sleep, but as no one had tried to wake me, I didn't think that I needed to get up. I stayed in that light sleep, prepared to arise but not anxious to when the noises in the courtyard became louder. A rooster called, chickens clucked, horses neighed, a person chopped wood. I could make out the smell of food of some kind. Still full from the feast of the previous night, I reached out to pat my belly, and found I was still in my stupid clothes, now probably horrifically wrinkled. If I'd had a lady's maid, she would have not only gotten me out of the outfit but would have hung it up to shake out the wrinkles overnight. It didn't really matter though; I'd be wrinkling my outfit anyway on horseback. Still, appearing disheveled wouldn't do me any favors when I was trying to seek out the supposed status I had as this mythical Lady Dreux.

Half-dressed, I wondered whether I should attempt to put on a new outfit and struggle with that, or try to replicate what I had on from the night before by getting on what I could? I decided upon the latter, and pulled on my sleeves, my hose, my hoop, etc., without being able to fully tighten the back of the dress. I'm sure I looked a fright.

And I felt like one. I'd been sold on Graham as being responsible, eager to help, a bodyguard of sorts, who would at least act as a husband. Instead, he'd been out all night, leaving me to brave this strange place on my own. Not even curious about how I was doing. Not even caring. Perhaps he'd taken up with a saucy barmaid or some such and spent the night rolling in the hay.

And where was Stafford? He should be organizing this expedition, rallying us all for a long day's journey ahead.

I stepped out into the hallway and carefully made my way down the stairs, wary of tripping on my dress.

As soon as I stepped back into the bar, the mystery was solved. There was Graham, curled under a table, eyes closed and mouth agape, while Stafford, belly up, stretched out on a bench, hands clasped over his chest. Hugh and Robert were curled up near the fire.

"Well, well, well." I slow clapped. "I so love to see honor, duty, and responsibility at the forefront of your male brains. Graham, I can't tell you how uncomfortable I was…"

I stopped. Graham had raised himself to a seated position, and I saw not only his black eye, but how carefully he was holding his forearm, the way one does when it's—

"Broke one of my bones, I think. Can't see out of this eye."

"This is not what we came here for—for you to get in bar brawls! What is this, your college years reenacted? We are on a mission, please remember!"

Graham held his head with one hand, the other lying sadly on his lap. "Yeah, yeah. We get it. We screwed up. But that fight was no joke, all right? If we didn't get in there when we had, well then the whole place might have been torn down to the studs."

"Hyperbole at work. The room looks just fine, but you two, well…" I peered at John. "Actually, Stafford here looks like he got away with nary a scratch."

Stafford shrugged, grinning like the pesky little brother who gets away with everything.

"Robert, Hugh!" I said to the two men by the fire. "Wakey, wakey. Where's your friend, Edward? Let's get ourselves sorted with some breakfast and get a move on. We've miles to go today, and we're already behind."

I thought I was acting at the height of restraint—acting with dignity befitting a woman of my nobility for our backstory. But what I really wanted to do was to take off my wisp of a slipper and start hitting them, lightly of course, for fun, you know. Yes, a good old swatting with a slipper would give these sad excuses for men an excellent lesson... Yet, while I was fantasizing about that happy moment, it sank in—

Graham has just one usable hand.

Who is going to help get me dressed and undressed? Will he be able to ride?

I hustled myself over to Stafford's side. He could do something. I said in a hushed voice, "I need for you to find me a lady's maid, immediately. Graham can no longer assist me. Please, muster up all your charm and find me somebody. I'm a complete disaster."

"My dear," Stafford said, pushing back his floppy hair, "we were lucky to intersect with Egham's party at all. But a good lady's maid, who knows all the ins and outs of hair, dress, toiletry, and so forth, well, you could only find those women at a great house, and we are in just a village. A village where the women are either employed here at the inn or work out in the fields. I highly doubt..."

"What is it that you doubt, Monsieur Stafford?" Thomas asked.

I turned around to find him looking as if the angels had descended upon his room last night to ensure that nothing could awaken him, so that his beauty would once again be refreshed. I took a step toward him, subtly, I hoped, to see if I could catch the faintest of whiffs of his perfectly intoxicating scent.

"I doubt I can find a lady's maid for Lady Dreux," Stafford repeated. "I'm afraid Lord Dreux has injured his hand and cannot assist his wife, which frankly, was not even a good idea to start with. But since their retinue has left them...?"

"We had been abandoned by our party! It wasn't our idea," Graham cut in, finally able to contribute something, and thankfully, remembering the backstory we were going with.

"No woman of Lady Gabriella's stature should be without a maid to assist her," Thomas said. "The idea is shameful. I've thought so from the start, and now I see that it is an even sorrier state of affairs. She holds herself with great grace, however—" Thomas bowed slightly to me—"but I demand, as an agent of the king, that this be rectified."

"Very well, sir! Consider it done," Stafford announced. "As Lord Dreux is not in the experienced in these matters, it falls to me. I shall return shortly. In the meanwhile, please take your breakfast, and do save me a roll if you please."

And he strode out, with all the confidence in the world. I shook my head. This would not end well.

STAFFORD, TO GIVE him credit where credit is due, was a go-getter. We gave him a mission and he succeeded. Because before long I had a teen-aged girl named Anne riding behind me with her arms around my waist. When I asked, she didn't know her exact age, but I guessed around sixteen. Even though I was a lady and nobody in our party thought I should have a servant ride on my horse, I refused to put a young girl on a horse with a man. I could easily envision a scenario where an untrustworthy man might take advantage, and that would *not* happen on my watch.

I had assured the girl's mother, a woman whose life was likely so hard she looked like she should be collecting a pension but was probably only in her 40s, that I was *in loco parentis*, and I meant it. I told her mum we should be back within the month, and Anne would make more in that time with me then she would at home helping her mother.

"Your accent is very funny, my lady," the girl said into the back of my dress, her skinny fingers resting lightly on my hips.

"Yes, I have been told as much by a great number of people. You see, I have lived in Brittany these many years, and so my English is not very strong."

Anne couldn't keep still. "I'm excited to travel farther than Willowshere. That's the farthest I've ever been away from home. I never helped a lady before. I wish to do a good job for you."

"You are truly Heaven-sent," I said. "All I really need is an extra pair of hands to help me with my clothes, my hair. We women need to stick together. You travel with me and help me, and we will see some sights, then I'll get you straight home in no time."

She rested her head on my back. Perhaps a sign of trust? "I am sure I shall like it more than mucking out the stalls in the barn, fetching water, and helping with all the cooking and the cleaning."

Yes, Anne was Heaven-sent. I could get in and out of my clothes and not look a sight for whomever we might encounter. Who would've thought that clothing would have been such a hiccup on this trip? If Jane had only known, I'm sure she would have gotten me dresses with laces up the front that I could manage on my own. I'd make sure to tell her for next time she sent someone into the past.

Thomas was ahead of me, at the pace of a moderate trot; he had a good seat on his horse. (That, friends, is a riding term, and I was not referring to his backside, except...well. In a horse-riding type of way. Of course.)

Watching him made me think of things that I find appealing in a man:

Must be able to ride a horse—ably.

Must be helpful and not prone to the over-consumption of alcohol.

Must be interesting—beauty fades.

Can't be lazy.

Has to stick up for what is right.

Has good taste.

Would get along well with my mother.

Well, this was the 16th century and not the 21st, but I did quite wonder what Thomas's flat might look like, or if he even had a permanent place of address. It was so much easier to judge a man if one has seen his home. In modern times, I ask: Does he have posters up of models and films, or does he have actual art? Is there a full fridge of goodies showing he can cook, or is it like one of my unfortunate friends found on upon looking in a beau's fridge that there was nothing but strawberries and champagne? (What a poser!) What is his bedding like—if one ventures that far. Is the bathroom neatly kept? Are there proper rugs and furniture?

Oh yes, so much with which to judge a man when you see his flat, but there was so little to go on here with Thomas, except for the cut of his clothing, his comfort in riding on a horse, and the few interactions I'd had with him so far. Still—by that measure, he was far superior to Graham and Stafford.

He'd asked about my finger earlier. It had healed nicely, but he insisted on putting another bandage upon it, and once again, I could luxuriate in his magical cologne and warm touch. In the meanwhile, Graham fashioned himself a sling from a dishtowel in the kitchen and insisted that he'd had far worse injuries.

Knowing his profession, I'm sure he was right. Although I hadn't seen him without his clothes on, even though he was my "husband," I felt quite sure there might be a few scars, and maybe an old wound from a bullet.

This was pure idle-mind chatter to pass the time on my part. Thomas was out of reach, out of my century, and I was just bored. It occurred to me that Anne smelt of the barnyard still, not having had time for a bath. I would make sure she remedied that tonight.

"TIME TO REST the horses!" Hugh, the lead man called out, and steered us over to a meadow next to a river. On the opposite side, a shepherd guided his flock into the water. We got off our mounts.

"Do they like to swim, do you think?" I asked Graham.

"What I know about sheep, my dear, you could write on my thumbnail."

"Don't they look so much smaller than what we're used to?" I whispered, thinking of the aggressive-looking sheep in the photo with Ellie and Jane.

"Is there such a thing as miniature sheep? Decorative, maybe?" Graham asked, poking Stafford in the side and pointing in their direction.

He leaned down to us. "This—I it looked up—is due to the lack of additional feed over the winter. Our sheep have supplemental food when the grass dies, whereas these sheep do not. Therefore, they don't get very big."

"Just like the people, I daresay," I said, and I cast a glance at little Anne, who was busy fussing over something for me. It was nice to be fussed over, but the girl could have used a few sleeves of biscuits, some bangers and mash, and a few trips to the chippie to put some meat on her bones. Maybe she might even grow a couple more inches.

"My lady," she said, coming over to me and dropping an adorably bad curtsy, "I've fetched some wine for you." She handed me a little cup.

"Oh, how delightful, Anne. Many thanks. And what a beautiful cup!"

Anne backed away with a happy nod.

I held up the cup to admire it. "So pretty," I said, admiring the shine of the pewter and how it reflected the light. "I do enjoy a good cup. Doesn't it make life that much better if you can drink out of something delightful? I have my favorite red mug at home. It's really a Christmas mug, but it says, 'Be Bright' on it. I take that as a sort of motto, you see. Bright at uni, bright on a dark day."

"What did she slip in your drink for you to be this cheery?" said Stafford, making a face. "We are sitting in a damp field with a bunch of unwashed men, with miles to go before we eat properly. This is not the way I'm used to traveling." He stalked away.

"What did I ever do to him?" I asked.

"That man is a piece of work. But you *are* far too cheery for this group, I think," Graham said. He paused. "You realize that pewter contains a high lead content and actually poisoned people?"

I ignored that comment, though I did—discreetly—set the cup aside on the grass beside me. "Well, forgive me for having a good attitude. Dickens wrote that 'cheerfulness and contentment are great beautifiers... famous preservers of good looks.'"

Graham put his hand on his chin, giving me a puzzled look. "I don't quite understand you, 'dear wife.' Forgive me for being an ordinary chappy who wasn't born into great privilege the way you've been, with your cousin the king, your great-grandfather a king. It must feel good to be you, with the time to admire cups and be a lifelong student. But most of us must fight really hard for things. I didn't always sound like this, you know. I had to make my accent seem more posh in order to fit in with those Oxbridge boys around me. I have to commute quite a long way in order to get into work every day from a part of the outer boroughs of London you've probably never seen before. There's clubs I don't belong to, outings I'm not invited to—all because I didn't come from a certain class. So while I'm enjoying playing the role here of Lord Dreux, it hasn't quite imbibed me with a sunny personality where I take delight in shiny cups, or sheep swimming, or things like your 'jaunty' little horse. Forgive me, Gabriella, but sometimes your pure happiness can seem like a slap in the face to a guy like me, who's been swimming upstream my whole life to get even 1/10th of the things you've been given solely due to an accident of birth. I truly wonder—if you were not a sort of princess, would you still be so damned happy all the time, with little bluebirds dancing on your shoulder and all that?"

I shifted in my seat. "I, uh, I'm sorry you feel that way." What else could I say to the man? He clearly had every right to be upset with my privilege. "If it's any consolation, my mother says that I've always been a sort of 'sunny side up' type of a girl since birth. Hardly ever cried, always a happy, gummy smile from the beginning. She said no matter where she took me, even if it was to run the most boring errands, I could stay transfixed by whatever it was that she handed me—keys, a tube of toothpaste, a sensory toy with buttons to push and shapes to squeeze. So if you want to do a sociological study on me, yes, being born into some kind of privilege made me healthier, loved, secure, whatnot—but I don't believe it gave me my personality. And you could count the amount of pounds I have in my bank account by using your fingers and toes."

Thomas's ear was bent toward our conversation and he seemed to have heard a thing or two that perhaps he should not have. He strolled over and made an *ahem* noise. "Pardon me, my lord, my lady, but might I enter into your conversation? I couldn't happen to have heard but a snippet."

The man could talk about the price of dirt, as far as I was concerned, or the complexities of calculus, and I would be happy to hear his voice. A warm flush flashed through my body.

"You were speaking of Lady Gabriella's privilege in her birth, and through that, her happy spirit, and linked the two. Having been at court these last two years, I wanted to present you, my lord, with my observations, in that they might help you." He made a thoughtful expression, one that only made him far better to look at. "It is my belief that being born into greatness, such as a royal king or duke, does produce obvious delight with the benefits of power and wealth, great houses and clothes and other luxuries that the ordinary man will never get to appreciate.

"But I have also observed that even with these people, it does not make them happier. They still have worries, albeit different ones, from the laborer who must toil before sun rise and go to sleep cold and hungry. The powerful and privileged still worry about love and position, reputation, the threat of illness, their families, and even good looks. I noticed this even too as a boy at my father's knee, as he painted the great families at court, and they complained so often as they sat still." He looked at me with those great brown eyes and I'll admit, I would have melted on the spot if it were a thing. "I think it is a sign of a beautiful spirit if you can find the splendor in the ordinary, especially if one is privileged. For often, one's eyes get dulled to the beauties of a blade of grass, of a cloud set against a blue sky, of a bird enjoying its bath in a puddle. To know the best of everything and still take time to notice only what the poor have, well…" he paused, looking for words, "one should appreciate that in a person's nature."

Now normally I do not enjoy being debated about, especially when it's done right in front of me, but in this case, I adored that Thomas came to my defense.

I clamped my hand over my heart. "Thank you, Thomas. I very much appreciate your generous thoughts. There, Graham," I said, nudging his foot, "what do you think of my ode to a shiny cup now?"

He shrugged, seemingly not impressed. "The fact is, my dear wife Gabriella does not know anything about hardship."

"And shouldn't you want to keep it that way?" Thomas asked. "Isn't that the role of a good husband?"

"Well," he blustered, "of course, when you put it like that. And I did make a vow to her. But would it not be good for her character if she *did* encounter some rainy days, some harder times?"

Thomas shook his head. "It is truth that everyone experiences heartache, but I would never desire anyone I loved to go through pain merely to build their character. It will come soon enough for us all."

"All right, all right." I stood and put my hand up. "Let us end this debate and have peace, please. My humors are going to be put off by this very talk." I took my cup and walked away.

Debate was ridiculous. *So I'm a glass half-full person. What of it? I can't help it. Would encountering more stress make me a pessimist? Hard to say, but as Thomas said, why wish that on anyone? I simply don't get Graham.*

Oh and indeed, just to make Graham happy that a little rain needed to fall in my life, it started to rain for real. I found Anne to help me retrieve my hooded cloak from my bag after she'd tucked the cup away. She already had her hood up, a cloak being part of her few belongings that she'd brought with her. Gray, woolen, probably scratchy, but water-resistant, the rain beaded up and pilled down her cloak, while the pellets of rain were soaking into my silk over-dress.

"Oooh this is miserable!" I said, crouching under her cloak with her.

She dug around and she dug around, and I about lost my patience and my dignity in the second before she shouted, "Here it is!" She fluffed out the green material and then immediately whisked it onto me.

Sweet relief! It was still not so nice being rained on, but the hood made sure the dripping rain fell well in front of my face. "We shall have to make sure my gown doesn't get wet when I get up on the horse. Let's make sure the cloak covers my whole outfit, yes?" The National Theatre costumer was going to have a fit when I returned the dress with water stains on the silk, for sure.

"Yes, madame!" She had to shout in the downpour. "You get up first, and I'll arrange the cloak, and then come up behind you."

The rain was already starting to saturate the ground; small puddles had filled up almost everywhere. We hopped over one after the other, and when I finally got to my horse, Graham was there ready to help me mount up. "I did not mean to bring the rain!" he said, in a kind of apology. But now I knew to be wary of him.

Although he surely didn't want me dead, he did want me to feel pain. That was not comforting.

He pulled his arm out of the sling and immediately grimaced when he positioned his hands to make a step for me.

Thomas jogged over and said, "Allow me." Rain beating down on his face, he cupped his hands together and easily launched me up onto the horse, and tucked Anne up with me after.

Anne did her best to spread my cloak over my dress, and off we went, down the muddy road.

I sighed. Where was that shiny mug when I needed it? Even if it would kill me over the long-term, for the here and now it wouldn't hurt me at all.

SOME THINGS WE modern women have that late-medieval women didn't: zippers, buttons, and multiple changes of clothes. Because the cost of cloth was incredibly expensive in this era, you would swap out pieces of your outfits—sleeves, the front of dresses, skirts, etc., instead of changing altogether. Then, these were pinned, to hold them on to you. It's been estimated that medieval women had a thousand pins in their clothing on a daily basis; to fit in, I had some too. Thankfully it wasn't a thousand, because my dresses were in my size. But, I have to point out, even twenty were too many.

The more we rode, the more I felt those pins sticking into me. Maybe it was the wet, maybe it was the addition of Anne clinging on to me for dear life in the pouring rain, but I was beginning to feel like a voodoo doll being poked in a harmful spell.

And the mud that splashed up didn't feel great, either. The rain had brought a definite chill in the air.

The clopping along of horses suddenly became noisier. More horses and people were joining us—a great many more.

"Aha! Well, here they are!" Thomas shouted, throwing his fist in the air.

Our party of eight was rapidly overtaken by a group of dozens and dozens. Perhaps over a hundred. It was hard to say with the sheer numbers.

Flags preceded the group, and it was clear that this was an important party. As a great big dollop of mud splashed upon the front of my cloak and over my hood, the young Henry VIII himself rode by alongside his wife, Katherine of Aragon, and tipped his hat to me. Anne immediately slipped off the horse next to me and scurried away somewhere, perhaps too scared to even be seen by the king.

Can we just have a brief word on the tragedy of this young couple? Six pregnancies, only one resulting in a living child—Princess Mary (later Mary 1st), who had been born earlier that winter. The pressure upon this duo to produce a male heir was so tragic. My seeing the two at this time in their lives, before Henry's horrible jousting-related injury changed his personality forever, was astounding. He was fit, handsome, and completely dashing, not at all like the portraits of the unfit and overweight Henry who would later decide to found his own religion so he could divorce Katherine of Aragon and marry the infamous Anne Boleyn, and then acquire and eliminate three other wives before one survived him to be his widow. Not all at the same time of course. I'm sure you know the story. But my point is that it's bizarre knowing what's going to happen to people in their future. When you're the king and queen, your life is very well documented.

Henry was going to go from the trim young man before me—slim, athletic, handsome—to an oversized caricature of himself with a vast girth bedecked in gold, jewels, floppy hats, and garments that would make him look even wider.

And poor Katherine! Short, somewhat stout, but with a ready

smile on her face, was—if I had my facts straight—still recovering from her first and only pregnancy to bear a live child. Perhaps she was still hopeful that since she'd had a healthy baby girl, she would one day give birth to a boy who lived past infancy. But she was already in her early 30s.

I can't even imagine the pain of everyone knowing your sad story, talking about you, and seeing whispers shared in front of your very eyes. *What's wrong with her?* they might have said, and she might have overheard.

I knew about whispers, though it was nothing like this scale. Whispers about me were common at school. Peers, knowing my heritage, muttered, *Can you believe she's cousins with the queen? She doesn't look like a royal. Look at the scuffs on her shoes!* Then there were the whispers, or outright bullying, over my unfeminine height. *"Off to the basketball courts, eh, Gabriella? How's the weather up there?"* That was oh-so-smashing and original. And then there was the time I was presented with a stuffed giraffe by a trio of girls, all sniggering, who declared, "We found you a boyfriend, Gabs!"

Empathy for nasty whispers? Oh, I had it in spades.

I had to feel empathy, even for Henry VIII. His suffering in later years, due to that jousting accident, was said to be excruciating. And because he could not participate much in physical activities thereafter, he ballooned up to almost 400 pounds, or 28 stone.

Soon, Henry would take a mistress, impregnate her, and the baby would be a boy. It was then he knew *he* was not the issue, but it was Katherine. She would be divorced, banished from court, and while comfortable for a while, she ultimately would die—probably from a broken heart.

I wished I could tell him that science had proven it was the man—and not the woman—who determined the sex of a child.

"Thomas—we have caught up with you," Henry said, "and yet you left before we!" Ah, one person referring to themselves in the royal third person was on full display, although to be fair,

Henry was traveling with a large party. "Why be you so slow?"

"I was asked by this man Stafford, here, to assist one of your lords and ladies. Lord Dreux here and his wife Lady Gabriella Dreux."

Henry's eyes flew over to me again, widening in surprise. I'm not sure why he had this look on his face: was it my height, or the fact that he had nobility he'd never heard of?

"They were in need of aide, both taken ill and their party left them behind. They are also going to France, so we thought we would join together."

Henry sidled his horse next to mine. Did one curtsy from on top of a horse? Was I supposed to leap down from my horse and assume that courteous behavior toward a monarch? I wasn't sure. Still, I decided to attempt a theatrical bow, like one would do on stage, throwing my right arm to the side and bowing my head and neck.

This was a man you did not want to upset by showing a lack of respect.

In later years, after the head injury, he would direct orders to kill anyone who got in his way of turning the country away from Catholicism, or anyone who annoyed him, or who had only been rumored to be disloyal. Over 56,000 poor souls killed. Because of that, I had hoped to steer well-clear of the man and get straight to France without making contact. While we could pinpoint Thomas's journey because of the letter we'd found, we did not have records that Henry would be on this very road at the same time of day. Records of the king were numerous, but the roads were not numbered like the "A-1," for instance. We'd known approximately where he was in a given month, but nothing more specific.

Now, he looked down on me. At over six feet tall, with his auburn hair and that aquiline nose so well-depicted by Hans Holbein, he was a grinning, good-time Hal. "From whence do you hail, Lady Dreux?"

"We are from Brittany and have come to England to visit

some relations of my husband, Lord Dreux. I have never been to England before, but it is a beautiful place, and I am honored to meet the King."

"It is a shame we have never met until this day!" His horse danced around, antsy, but Henry kept him under control. "We would like you to join us in our stay at Leeds Castle. I do hope you can spare your king a night or two."

Graham spoke up, "It would be our greatest honor, to be so honored." Oh my goodness that was three utterings of the word "honor" between the two of us. Where was a thesaurus when we needed one? Clearly our minds were not very eloquent at a moment of overwhelm.

"Come then, keep up with us! We shall have a fine time this eve!" He turned his horse and swept away, his great cloak floating behind him like a luxurious, silken wave.

Graham poked me. "Gabby, you're covered in mud! You met the King, covered in mud."

"And yet," I said, reaching my hand up to my face to try to chip away at the dirt, "I still got invited to dinner. Did my privilege assist me once again?"

He held up a hand and smiled, perhaps an unspoken apology for our argument earlier. "No, this time I believe it was your beautiful smile."

I gasped. "Was that a... compliment, Graham?" I fluttered an imaginary fan in front of my face. *Coquette, c'est moi.*

"Nah, I'm just wildly happy. Imagine what Mum would think of me supping with the king—any king—in a castle?"

"I think she would think you've had a stroke if you told her it was King Henry VIII. So let's keep that our little secret, shall we?" I tapped my horse's rump. "Come on, little fella. We've got a date... with a future murderer and madman. How bad could it be, right?"

Anne scurried back to me, her cheeks red.

"Where have you been hiding?" I asked.

She nodded slowly. "My mum always told me to avoid being

seen by powerful men. Who was that?"

"The King," I said.

Her eyes widened. "Watch yourself, lady. My mum is always right about these things."

How true this proved to be.

CHAPTER TEN

L AST I'D SEEN Leeds Castle was on a school trip. We'd staggered off a school bus that stank of diesel, on the hottest day of the year. I was tortured by one Jonathan Wester, who continually threw pebbles at my back from the lined paths in the garden. Not a teacher or chaperone in sight as I got pelted. Eventually, however, I extracted my revenge by "accidentally" bumping into him next to a large, ornamental water fountain, complete with statuary Neptune and mermaids. My celebratory moments, though, soon turned into stoicism at having to sit directly behind him as he stank of the ornamental koi from the fountain, and whatever detritus molds and trash that had been thrown into its water. I still can't take a bus ride for very long without feeling quite queasy.

Leeds Castle in the 16th century still held that feeling of queasiness for me, but no longer could I blame it on that sadist Jonathan. This time, I approached the castle with muddy, wet wool, shoes and gown soaked through, and with a drenched teenager hanging on to my waist. By this time, the ratio of pins sticking in me—rather than holding my clothing together—felt like 2:1.

However, "mustn't fuss" as my mother would say. "Make the best of it." So I focused on greeting the castle staff in the oval courtyard of what has often been called the most beautiful castle in England, a true fairy-tale castle the likes of which Walt Disney could never replicate. Yes, that's a snooty thing for an English woman to say, but by golly, we can build damned good castles. And *this* one was, and still is, surrounded by a lake and not a mere moat.

Henry VIII had inherited the castle upon his succession to the throne and was investing money in making it more "modern." While I did care to have a good looksee to check out the differences in the décor over the last six hundred years, my first order of concern was to get out of my wet clothes.

Led by some sort of official steward, Anne and I were taken up to a wing where the "ladies" of the court were staying. "I can't believe I'm in the King's castle!" Anne whispered to me. She stuck to the sides of the hallways, ducking behind doorways as often as she could.

As we entered the large room which we were told would be our quarters, we found three finely dressed women enjoying some sort of beverage by the fire. Six beds lined the walls, along with pallets made up for women who were not ladies. I wasn't sure if I was going to make the "cut" to qualify for a bed, but I sure hoped I would.

Truthfully, I was so tired after the bad night's sleep at the inn, and the bad night's sleep at the gatehouse, that I wasn't sure I was going to even keep my eyes open for dinner. (But upon pain of death I would. I didn't want Henry to have me drawn and quartered for falling asleep in His Majesty's presence.)

We introduced ourselves to the women, and I met the Lady of the Bedchamber, the Mistress of the Robes, and a Lady in Waiting to the queen. With this high-ranking company, I was definitely not getting a bed, but the Lady in Waiting kindly offered that I should bed beside her, as she would not want me sleeping on the floor.

Stepping behind a screen with Anne, we commenced the strip-down. Sleeves pulled up and over, the cloak laid draped to dry, the gown, the kirtle, stockings, all the layers. Now, unlike at an inn, there was no hiding our complete incompetence at our lady/maid set-up, and our unfamiliarity with the finer points of Tudor dressing.

There was water to wash my face with, but during the time of the Tudors—lucky me—baths were not really a thing. The pores being open to potentially dirty water was considered dangerous, so hands, face, and feet were washed, but to get the body clean, you had to use your linen shift as a kind of body polisher/washcloth. This Tudor underwear was actually quite efficient at removing dirt, and it was rumored that the king changed his shift, as did the queen, multiple times of day. Linen was breathable, quick to dry, and soft. I had Anne turn away as I did the whole naked-me bit, as I'm actually quite shy, being raised as an only child. (Even at school, I changed in the closet.)

New clothing retrieved, shaken out, and dressed, I was now presentable for dinner.

It's hard to know when you're supposed to do things or meet places, without clocks. During this age there were sundials, hourglasses, special candles, and even early versions of clocks around. But the sun ruled life, as did the religious services at different parts of the day. Henry was still Catholic at this point in his life, which meant if you were really observant, eight times a day you might be in prayer.

The ladies had told us it was not yet "time" to go downstairs, and that we could have a rest, or talk with them if we wanted to come sit with them by the fire.

"We are not yet needed by the queen. We shall be alerted when she does need us," the Lady of the Bedchamber said to me.

"I am sure it is a great honor to serve the queen as you do."

She nodded. "Indeed, 'tis. She is a magnificent queen, and all those who see and know her believe the same."

The ladies were fetched in due course, and Anne and I had a brief kip. I was having a dream about dancing with Thomas at a bar, believe it or not, when a gong rang out, and trumpets. That was the supper bell.

I followed the noise to the great hall, set for dinner, while Anne went off with our clothes to clean them. I joined Thomas, Graham, and Stafford at the table, and we all rose when the trumpets sounded again, to welcome in the slim, young king and his wife. There was the usual recitation of prayers—in Latin— before dinner, then the King's table was brought food. Eventually, we all got served.

By *served*, I mean plenty of alcohol in addition to the food. Lots of wine—good wine. I'm sure the purity of the air and rain in pre-industrialized Europe had a lot to do with it, or perhaps I was just thirsty because I did not dare drink the water.

Still, the wine made me bold, and determined to uncover the reason behind Thomas's beautiful, sad eyes. I may have been slurring my words when I asked, "Pray tell me, Thomas of Egham, I can see that while you came to my defense today in my conversation with Graham, you seem to hold a pain inside of you. It is in your eyes. It may not be any of my business, but I do want to know if I can be of help. You seem like a good man, and I hate to see you suffer."

Thomas seemed to physically startle, his hands flaring upward as if he had awoken from a kind of dream, and he took a sudden breath. I immediately patted his hand.

"Oh, my word, I did not mean to scare you, I—"

"No, no you did not," he said. "I just must have been lost in a world of my own. You say you noticed my pain? I can assure you, lady, I am quite well."

"Not that kind of pain, you look hale and hearty, but a pain here." I placed my hand on my chest. "And here." I placed my fingers to my temples. "Has something happened to you? A young man of your age should be living life to the fullest, telling tales, joking with other young men, drinking, gambling, dueling, and dancing with beautiful young ladies."

He held a glass of wine in his hand, staring into it as he spoke. "Sorrows do haunt me, lady, but there is nothing to be done with them. When I wake they are there, not soon after I forget my dreams. When I fall asleep, I am plagued with thoughts of how I could have done things differently, and I get no comfort. Even my life's work, now, makes me think of it."

"Art makes you sad?"

"Aye." Placing his glass down, he pushed a piece of roasted chicken around with his knife. (Note that forks didn't come into fashion until the 18th century. I was told by Ellie, when she conducted her tutorial on dining etiquette, that spoons, knives, and fingers were the tools used in this time, and that finger bowls were on the table for us to dip into when needed.)

"Why?"

"I should not say. I do not want to make my misery yours. You are like a butterfly, touching on everything so lightly, and then going off to seek new nectar. I would break your delicate wings."

That was a beautiful analogy, but still, I huffed. "I have often been told that I am too delicate, and it raises my ire to such a degree—you know not! Look at me, I am as big as a horse."

"Please don't compare yourself to a horse, Lady Dreux."

"Well, maybe not a horse, but being tall renders so many eyes on me it is impossible to dance lightly on a flower's bud. I can't do anything without ridicule." I shook my head. "But, this is not about me, do not concern yourself about me. I am as strong as an ox. I am worried about *you*."

He smiled weakly. *Oh men. Why are you all so ridiculous?* But I couldn't lash on him about his mental health habits—even modern man is still having a tough time owning up to issues like anxiety and depression. Idiots. The lot of them. *Everybody* should be in therapy. It's truly a gift. I learned that after my father died.

"I know you have a good heart, Lady Dreux. How about instead of me speaking, you tell me about your family. How many brothers and sisters do you have?"

I resolved to be the one to open up. Sometimes, if you take the lead, others will follow. "There is only me, I'm afraid. I am sure my father would have preferred a son, but it was not to be.

Still, we had fun, the three of us. My father passed away far too young, and now it's just my mother and me. Oh—" I looked over at Graham—"and of course, my dear Lord Dreux."

When he heard his name—even though it was a fake name—Graham patted me on the shoulder without looking. Not exactly gazing at me with besotted eyes the way a real husband would if he were in love, but Graham was engaged otherwise with the woman to his left. Her hair was loose down her back, signaling she was a single woman, and her hearty laugh seemed to have loosened old Graham up quite a bit. I wondered what they were talking about. Surely not Graham's favorite topic—suits of armor, diplomatic relations between France and England, minor historical facts.

Thomas said, "I would think your father was quite happy to have a daughter as cheerful as you."

"Oh yes, he loved me dearly and I adored him. But his dreams of raising the next star…" I was going to say *footballer*, but that wouldn't have an equivalent in the times of the day, "jouster were dashed. Although, I do love horses."

"You're an accomplished horsewoman. Most women prefer to ride in carriages."

"Oh, not me. The roads are far too rough, and the carriages, well, they are not made to handle these roads. Maybe in time they might become more comfortable, but for now, give me a horse to ride out in the open air, and I am happy."

"Please, lady, do be careful, though. Will you?" His voice had a slight tremble to it. *Oh my, how am I making him even more sad?*

"You have no need to worry," I reassured him with a warm smile. "I was practically born on a horse. Despite my high center of gravity, I've never once fallen. My mother calls it a miracle, but I—" I rose straighter in my chair—"call it *talent*."

"Gravity? I do not know that. Is that a word from where you come from? If so, I must learn of the meaning."

Oops! Definitely not a Tudor word or concept! Yikes. "It just means that those who are shorter can stay on the horse better because they are more balanced with the horse. But I talk too much about being tall. Now you must tell me about your family."

He sat back and crossed one leg over the other. *Elegant.* "I too am the only child of my parents, or the only one who lived past infancy. I never knew my mother, she died before I turned two. I've heard she was a rare beauty, with dark hair and dark eyes. My father never remarried, though that seems to be what men do when they are widowed with a small child. Perhaps another woman could never impress upon him her worthiness. But he did not speak to me of that. Instead, we had great fun, me by his side as we traveled the country, visiting great houses, painting people."

Out of the corner of my eye, I noticed Stafford attempting to woo the woman to his left, and she got so disgusted with him she threw down her serviette and stormed off. I couldn't help but laugh, but covered it up quickly with a hand over my mouth to contain my guffaws.

Thomas had a twinkle in his eye too at Stafford's comeuppance. He said to me, "Did you know about your laugh—it is most distinctive."

"Ohhhhh," I said, "that does not sound like a compliment. Maybe I shouldn't laugh again."

"No, lady, pray do not misunderstand me. I like the way you almost start crying sometimes, you're laughing so hard."

"I used to get in trouble for that at school—with my governess, I mean—for laughing so hard. I know you meant it kindly."

The musicians—some fiddlers, a lute player perhaps, and a kind of piper—gathered up in the minstrel's gallery and started to play. At the same time, the tables were being cleared and taken away, so that people could have room to dance.

"I must have a dance with my lady!" declared Graham, looking slightly sozzled, but perhaps this was one of his spy tricks. (Pretend to be out of commission, lull them into a sense of complacency, and then pull out a shiv and take out a vital organ, rendering your foe as good as dead.)

"Yes, let us show these people how they do it in France!" I said. Oh, that didn't sound good either. Graham and I had learned one dance at Jane's, and whatever the people were doing on the floor all together in a line, mixing, turning, jumping, twirling— was *not* what we had learned.

"Perhaps we should stand on the sidelines instead, Graham. Maybe learn a few more skills?"

He scoffed. "Nay, I was born to dance."

Oh my, his inner Hamlet was coming out.

"Apparently you were born to drink."

"Was I?" He shot me a look, and said under his breath, "Relax and enjoy. Keep up appearances, Gabriella. We don't want to stick out. Blend in, blend in."

I growled. "You know how hard it is for me to blend in when everyone in this century is insufficiently nourished! I walk around a head taller than most everybody. Besides, your arm is in a sling."

"Well, hold up the walls then, Lady Marmalade. I have heard that chess is a popular pastime here; I'll see if I can find a game."

"Just be careful."

"Don't worry, I won't be far away." He wandered off.

I leaned against the back wall, a piece of drapery nearly blocking me from the rest of the room. In the middle of the dancing, Stafford was keeping up with his dance moves quite impressively, hopping from one foot to the next, twirling the ladies who hadn't yet been turned off by his flirtations. He had a broad grin on his face, and a kick to his step—he really had come alive. I know Jane worried about her brother and his escapades, but if she could see him now, she might see him in a new light. She certainly hadn't known he could dance this way; it would have been useful. At any rate, maybe there were people just born in the wrong time, and Stafford had figured out his way past that.

What if I determined that 1517 was the time I belonged? Would I be able to abandon my mum for a life here? I knew it would break her heart if anything happened to me, and I just disappeared off the face of the earth. Would it make news if Lady Gabriella Palmer went missing?

Actually, I wondered, would it escape notice *now* if I disappeared to my sleeping chamber? I could not stop yawning, hiding it behind my hand, and my eyelids kept sinking down. Bed was calling. Was the etiquette that one could retire before the king did? At Balmoral and Sandringham, the few times we've been invited for lunch or a weekend stay, you did not leave until the Queen left—it was considered rude. She had often departed early because she was cognizant of that rule and didn't want to keep people up who were tired. But as a result, she missed out on a lot of the fun.

My mind lighted on different topics to keep me awake. Henry was soon to convert—quite brutally—the population from Catholicism to Protestantism. A benefit of this was that he began to have the prayers for service in English, and that helped more people understand what was going on in church. Until 1539, it had been forbidden to translate the Bible into English, but after the law was abolished, the people of England who could read had their sacred book in their own language.

Another benefit was the creation of the dear old English hymns, like what has been called Britain's (and is definitely my) favorite, "Jerusalem" by Sir Hubert Parry. With lyrics from a poem by William Blake, and the organ stirring one's soul, and on Christmas and Easter, when trumpets are added...*Goosebumps!*

Still, did Henry have to kill so many in this conversion? And all because he wanted to wed Anne Boleyn?

There was an absolutely brutal story of Henry that I had learned years ago when I was nineteen, on a summer internship with an archeological arm of the British Museum. I'd helped dig around Glastonbury Abbey, looking for further outcroppings of the abbey, relics of the old monastery. Legend had it that King Arthur and Guinevere were found buried on site, and moved to a marble tomb, where they remained until Henry VIII dissolved the monasteries across the country. The monks and nuns ran away;

the Abbot was drawn and quartered and, if I recalled correctly, parts of his body were sent around the country on display.

I scraped my fingers against the stone wall behind me, reminding me of the sorry state of my nails after that summer. For the hours and hours spent on my hands and knees scraping up spoonsful of dirt, in the heat, rain, and chill of an English summer, I discovered a fragment of a piece of pottery, a possible bone fragment, (though whether or not it was a human had to be determined), and a scrap of leather. My frustration at my wasted time put me off pursuing archeology for ever and ever.

It was hard to believe that this was part of the future of these people before me, who danced and laughed with no idea of the horrors to come, or the upheaval of their beliefs held since birth. Some of these very people would be subject to choosing between their support of the king and the continuation of their lives and their devotion to their God and religion.

While I waited for a subtle way to exit, the men and women in the room continued to employ their best dancing moves and their wittiest repartee.

At that moment, my enthusiasm for this project just ran right out of me, like a light being switched off. Being at Henry VIII's court made history all too real. Yes, he looked like a well-mannered, handsome man, yet he held almost absolute power, and I was quite ready to be out of his sight, like Anne advised and practiced. I hoped that Thomas, who was friends with the king and had no foreknowledge of what harrowing deeds were to take place in the next few years, and Graham, who seemed to have been caught up in all the revelry and who might lose his head if he became reckless, would follow me out of the room.

I pulled away from the curtain, and just like I'd caught the eye of the crazy man on the tube by accident, so too did I catch the eye of King Henry VIII.

CHAPTER ELEVEN

W HEN YOU HAVE to make conversation with a person you really have no desire to speak with at a party, you try to make the best of it even as the whole time you are calculating, *What's a line that I can use that will extract me out of here?* Imagine that scenario, then add the eyes of over a hundred people, staring at you.

The king was the rare man that surpassed me in height, which would normally be a delightful feeling that helped me feel as if I didn't stick out in the world, at least for a few moments. However, here, and now, his height intimidated me.

"Care to dance, my lady?"

Once again, you can never refuse your monarch. But I explained I did not know the dance. At all. He told me it was one of the easier "country dances," which, when moved through once, could be remembered easily.

He was wrong. Instead of it being a line dance like—for example—*The Cha Cha Slide*, which conveniently calls out the steps in its lyrics—this dance included things like holding hands at different times with your partner, and being twirled around, and then, during one particularly rambunctious moment, the female partner being lifted up into the air by the male while he twirled. I'm afraid at this point in the dance I whooped out loud, "Whooo Wheee!" And the king let out a hearty laugh, and couldn't stop, as we continued our tour around the dance floor.

"I have never had that reaction before from a lady," he said, holding a hand temporarily to his chest as the mirth overtook him. I feared he was going to go straight into a laughing fit that would bring us even more notice.

I told Henry, "I'm sorry, Your Majesty, I could not help myself. It is rare for a woman of my height to be swept off her feet by a man—I am unused to the sensation."

"Well, lucky for you that your king is a man who is not only of great height, but great breadth, so that you can have fun as easily as the petite ladies. And I must say, I *like* a woman who does not appear like a child in my presence."

"It is true that I could not be mistaken for one. And yet your queen is the most beautiful and fine of women, she is what every woman would aspire to be."

"That is all true, and a good mother she be. She is also the more pious of the two of us, and after dinner she often will pray for hours. Whereas I enjoy dancing—with ladies who are sometimes taller than she. And here we go!"

And up I went, his arm around my waist and his hand pushing my hand up into the air, twirling, and I tried to suppress a small, "Whoa!" but one popped out anyway.

"We do like it when you do that. Thou are such fun, Lady Gabriella. And such a sweet, rosy face. You are a most jolly woman, by my troth!"

Peering down at me (yes, down!), he had that look in his eye. You know it when you see it. Be it love, or lust, or fascination, a man cannot disguise his interest in you, like a fox eyeing up a meaty chicken in the coop: *Dinner!*

You have become an object that must be consumed.

I've only seen that look twice before—apart from Albert— and once was from a fellow fellow (graduate humor!) who had a crush on me. We were having a lively discussion on a topic over beer at one of the college's favorite nearby pubs, and I caught him looking at me like that. I didn't return his feelings, and tried to put a stop to his by putting up every sort of barrier and wall I could think of, but in the end, I had to be blunt. "I'm afraid you're just not a match for me," I said, taking a line from an online dating site I'd been on once. The fox's look immediately left his eyes.

But in this moment, the most powerful man in the land was giving me that look, and there was no way a cliched saying from a dating website was going to put him off. There were other ways, though, surely. I am not a woman without resources in the brain department. After all, I had 500 more years of historical and scientific knowledge than he.

He took my right hand's fingers in his left, escorting me off the dance floor. A servant immediately showed up before us with glasses of wine on a tray; Henry took one and chugged it back. Meanwhile, I took a delicate sip from my glass. He leaned down to me and cupped his hand in front of his mouth to propel his words closer to my ear. "We must know what it is like to have such a woman as you in a romp."

I covered my mouth as I gasped.

Ladies did not swear then, nor did they slap someone who had gotten far too fresh; well, maybe they did with Stafford, but not their royal ruler. "That is not possible, Your Majesty," I said.

"When we want something, we get what we want. And *you* are what I want." He clasped my fingers tighter.

"You always have options," my mother told me throughout my life. If the kids at school were bullying me, we could always change schools. If my test scores didn't work out for university, we'd come up with a plan B. If I couldn't carry on and finish my PhD, we'd figure that out too. But what were my options here?

I couldn't knee the man in his privates—definitely the wrong move especially at his own house, with his guards around. None of Harry's handy self-defense moves would work, and running away would likely get me into just as much trouble. *What do I do?* I could stick my finger down my throat and vomit up dinner, but he'd know that was on purpose.

I wished I could call my mum. "Mum! Quick! Henry VIII

wants to have a romp with me. No, not a run, a *romp! In bed!*
What are my options?" But alas, that wasn't an option either. I
searched my brain.

My brain! Will reasoning help?

"Your Majesty, I am a married woman."

"Do not worry your head about that. I can make him happy
when I empty my purse. All men can be bought."

Oh, for feck's sake. "I am not for sale, I—"

A throat cleared, loudly, nearby, and both of us noticed the
presence of Thomas at the same time. He had broken into our
space. *Thank you, thank you, thank you...*

"Forgive me, Your Majesty. I must tell you of the most beautiful subject I have found for your next painting," he said.

Henry frowned and waved a ring-bedecked hand. "Go away,
Thomas. Can't you see that I'm with this lady?"

Thomas flushed, bowing, his eyes seeking mine, and I knew
he too sought a solution. Behind him, a server maneuvered
between bodies tightly packed together.

It was then that I remembered a trick my mother had taught
me once at a dinner for ambassadors. If a conversation ever
becomes heated between two diplomats, former rivals, cold war
opponents, former colonizer with the former colonized, it's best
to intentionally create a commotion that would loudly break up
the exchange. For example, you could raise a toast on behalf of
Her Majesty or try to grab an elbow of one of the participants and
steer them to a delicious appetizer, or introduce another party to
the group so that those at discord would naturally discontinue
that conversation.

Mummy would be aghast at the crude method I used instead,
although I think in the end, she'd be quite happy that I'd gotten
myself out of my predicament.

"Pray, I would desire a glass," I said, rather loudly, to the
servant beyond Thomas's shoulder, and then I pretended to trip,
arms extended, hurtling straight into the man with the tray.
There was a wet, tinkling crash as many goblets—no doubt some

of them made of quite expensive Venetian glass—filled with wine, clattered to the floor. This brought the eyes of the entire room on us, along with—thankfully, the ladies of the court, my roommates—who immediately arrived to fuss and mop at my garments. Attention was so focused on us that Henry had to realize he could no longer manipulate a discreet seduction.

I was whisked back to our room to change, and once there, I declared it a night for me, changing into a fresh shift with Anne's help, and tumbling down onto my side of the somewhat soft mattress. But before I could sleep I decided we needed to get out of this place before Henry was able to whisk me off for himself.

With that, I went to sleep, thanking my lucky stars for that well-timed handing out of drinks.

CHAPTER TWELVE

AFTER THAT INTIMIDATING moment of me nearly becoming Henry VIII's unwilling chattel, I reasoned that an early start back on the road away from Leeds Castle would be best. I'd sent out Anne the night before to find the members of our party and get the message out: "Meet as soon as the sun rises, in the stables."

Unfortunately, she whispered in my ear later during the night, that she couldn't find even one of the group and that she didn't actually feel safe herself wandering about on her own, so she cut her mission short, coming back to the room near tears.

I practically slapped myself—I should have been smarter about Anne's safety! I felt terribly guilty and apologized to her for not thinking sensibly. I was not doing a good job at the *in loco parentis*. That night, we held hands as she slept almost right under the bed that I shared with the snoring lady.

I feigned an illness the next morning, trying to avoid any possible encounter with Henry, and sent Anne out again on her errand to find the men, this time in the safe light of day. She only succeeded in finding William, who had been put to work erecting a stage for a performance later. "They might want to give me a job here," he told her. "Wouldn't be overseer, but it's a grand place, with lots of room, many jobs, and good company. Tell my lady I'd like to speak to her about it."

With sunlight streaming fully through the windows of our shared room, I was alone. The other ladies had left to go about their daily duties with the queen, while Anne went to continue sorting out our clothes. Sounds of laughter in the hallways reminded me that I was missing out, and especially that I did not have a phone to scroll through, a book to read, or even a copy of a medieval manuscript to translate to pass the time. I hated feeling stuck, but I was too nervous to leave my room.

I tried a meditation I'd once heard—trace the outline of your fingers, from your pinky to your thumb, inhaling when rising, exhaling when falling. Five times up and down, my belly rising and falling beneath the sheets, staring up at the brocade silk damask encompassing the bed.

I must have fallen asleep, because the next thing I knew Anne was back, seated on a low footstool in front of the fire and poking at it with a fireiron. As I lay watching her and idly musing about our predicament, the image of Thomas getting almost shoved aside by Henry came back to me from the night before. Did he get into trouble for interrupting Henry's moves on me?

I sat up. I was not suited for this lying about business. I didn't want to spend my time in 1517 locking myself away in this girls' sorority. I needed to put my big girl pants on, gather up the troops if no one else had the sense to do it, and make waves.

I could and *would* take on Henry if I had to. More of Mum's strategies must have been out there for dealing with "difficult" gentleman, before the *Me Too* Movement allowed all of us to call out a letch for what he was—a power-hungry guy who used his dominance to get sex from anyone he wanted.

Not today, Mister King. Not today.

I'LL SPARE YOU the details of me getting dressed with Anne's help, but once deemed presentable, or as much as we could fake it given Anne's and my inexperience, I had two orders of business:

one, find my gang of misfits, and two, while they were getting their act together, see if I could sneak a peek at Henry's library.

Henry was deemed the most learned of all the kings that England had had up to this point. He was fluent in English, French, Latin, and knew some Italian. But what I was after was his marginalia, which are the notes a reader takes while engaged in reading a book. This was a handy way to highlight and illustrate the ideas that resonated with you, or ones you wanted to dispute, and your thoughts behind why they hit a note. Studying marginalia is one of my favorite pastimes; although not directly related to my thesis, it was fascinating to know that Nelson Mandela, hero of the anti-apartheid effort in South Africa and eventual president, wrote his name next to a quote in Julius Caesar that read: "Cowards die many times before their deaths." That stuck with me. How many times had I foreseen my own death as a result of a scratchy throat, a love arrow gone astray, a humiliation in front of a group of one's peers, or a failed bid to host a TV show? Or, for example, an attempted seduction by and a spilled tray of drinks in front of one of the most famous kings in history?

Yes, to live without fear of one's death means you would not waste your life with the what-ifs, like—what if I hadn't been able to escape Henry and he had taken me to bed? I don't know, but I couldn't cower under the covers in fear of it.

Striding down the halls of the castle, I took my skirts in one hand and hustled down the stairs to the outside, where a whole exhibition seemed to be underway.

Jousting was clearly one of the featured activities of the day, with a stand of spectators, the *thunk* sound of two lances meeting in the middle, cheers, moans from the losing side's supporters, and shocked variations of "Oh!" and a clang and a thud when somebody fell off their horse. It's possible that's where William had been, constructing the stand, but I doubted it since I heard hammers coming from another part of the garden.

I was on my way to follow that trail when I heard the high-pitched, "Zing!" of a bow and arrow. I squinted and saw that even farther away was an archery competition. The king liked to keep his noble young men occupied with sports and fun, but also training, should they be needed for war. I immediately recognized my own "husband" Graham in the mix, in the sunny yellow tights he had that he'd somehow thought appropriate when looking at all the possibilities at the National Theatre's costume department. After a lifetime of gray and black suits, the man was striding about in bright yellow. Admittedly, his calves did look very good in them, which was the point: tights were meant to show a man's muscled legs.

"Halloo!" I yelled across the field. One man threw down his bow in frustration at my disruption; I guess he'd had just been aiming for the target and I blew his concentration. His arrow must have gone amiss. *Whoopsy.*

Graham held a finger up to his lips to *shhh* me and gave me that wide-eyed, eyebrow-raised expression that screamed, "Shut up!" I skulked over to the area behind the participants, all standing in lanes marked on the short grass. *Short grass?* I wondered. *Is there such a thing as a Tudor lawnmowing machine?* I vowed to put that in file to ask Stafford later.

The men in competition had unbuttoned their large, padded jackets, or doublets, so that they could move their arms more easily.

"What on earth are we still doing here?" I hissed under my breath to Graham. "We can't stay here."

"And we can't *leave* either. Henry invited me and Thomas out here to compete. Luckily it's this and not the jousting, as I didn't come with any armor."

"That was on purpose—you know what happened to Harry!"

Harry had done such a good job at competing when he went back in time that he got recruited by King Edward III and had had a hell of a time getting back to Ellie. As a result, they all warned us that the men should not show any great prowess in fighting if we were to ever encounter the King. "Where's your sling? I thought you'd broken your arm?"

"I realized when I was sleeping last night that it didn't hurt when I moved from side to side. Must have been just a strain."

"What about Stafford? You might have been too busy playing cards to notice, but the king made some major moves on me last night, and I nearly got conscripted into his bedchamber." I glowered at him. "You decidedly went off-duty as my body-guard."

"Don't worry, I was not far away if it escalated."

"If it escalated? What would you have done then? It's your job to stick with me and not allow people—like the king!—tell me that he'd pay you off—my husband!—if I slept with you."

"I wasn't but ten feet away and saw the whole thing. Good work on creating the distraction," he said.

"But I didn't even see you there!" I flashed back to the scene in my mind. *Where could he have been?* "You don't exactly blend in in those tights!"

"Ah, but I was wearing the more formal black attire last night. If you've read much of Henry's biographies, you'll remember that he might be a bit forward, but he insists on a court that practices the art of chivalry and courtly love. He wrote endless letters to Anne Boleyn seeking to woo her before they actually got together. He's very flirtatious, loves to banter, but above all is a man who wants his nobility to have propriety, be distinguished, pious." He leaned in closer. "The trick of being an effective spy is to know who you're dealing with. Do your research."

I wondered if I could do some research of my own and punch him in the nose to test his reaction time. "That may be true, but you'll remember, I read art history and late-medieval literature, so I didn't have as much time to 'catch up' and read all this about Henry. Plus, who can really know a man and his behavior, especially if his biographers at the time were always seeking favor?"

"I get it. I'm sorry you felt threatened, but as I said, if the situation got to be too licentious, I could have always stepped in as your husband and broken it up." A murmur went through the crowd and people turned to look at Graham. "Oh! It's my turn." He picked up his bow, pulled a quiver from the packet hanging off his waist, and lined up the arrow on the bow pointing toward the target. He narrowed his eyes, squinting at the target, and released.

Bullseye!

Cheers erupted, and I hugged him, as any good wife would do even though what I wanted to do was *thwock* him over the head with his own bow. *Odious man!* Meanwhile, he held onto me a beat too long, I thought, for what was appropriate. Especially for someone who thought I was spoiled. Probably because he could read my mind and wanted to hold my arms by my side before I really *did* punch him.

"Hey," I said. "Don't get any ideas there. This is strictly a historical mission."

"Yes, I know, but people were looking at us, especially your king."

"Ah," I said into his ear, and then—for the crowd—cupped his cheek in my hand in a fond way. His skin was surprisingly soft. I gave him a gentle slap—an affectionate cuff to anyone watching—before letting my hand drift back down into my pocket.

He grinned and whispered into my ear. "I know you have a crush on Thomas. I guess he is more appropriately your age."

"Perhaps I do, but that doesn't mean we could possibly get together. After all, I *am* married. To you, supposedly."

"Indeed you are, but this is the age of courtly love, where men seek unattainable women to do favors for, write love letters to, and generally pine after. I have seen how he looks at you, Lady Gabriella. And I believe he might have a crush on you too."

I placed my hand on his chest and pushed him back a little. "You're just teasing me now. I haven't seen him even looking my way. Where is he, anyway?"

Graham pointed down the row, fourth from the left. "*Erm...*I may as well wish him good luck, right?" I said.

"Seems like the neighborly thing to do." He shrugged, a grin spreading across his face, almost all the way out to those silly ears of his.

I sidled down the grass, as other spectators were doing, with some working their way to the viewing area that stood halfway between the targets and the shooters.

Thomas leaned against the wooden hut separating him from the man next to him; he was gazing into the sky.

"You don't seem concerned about your competition," I said.

He lowered his gaze slowly and smiled. "Aye. I have been competing for years, and learned how to shoot arrows when I was big enough to hold a small bow. It was something my father liked to do after a long day's work painting, coming out into the fresh air, practicing with me, knowing that little boys should be running around and having fun."

"You must miss him. I miss my father."

The sad look came back to his face. "'Tis true. I do not know if you ever recover from the pain of losing a parent. My father and I spent nearly every waking hour together. I knew what he was thinking, and he knew what I was thinking—without ever speaking a word."

"I'm most sure that he would not want you to spend the rest of your life in mourning, though, Thomas. The look of pain in your eyes shows that you think of him often."

"I do," he said, "but it is not from the fact that he died. Death is a part of life. It is the gruesome way in which he drew his last breath that haunts me to this day."

"Oh, oh my," I said. *PTSD.* It would take centuries before psychiatrists would agree upon its existence, and more decades would pass as they sought and continue to seek the most useful therapies to stop the images of war, rape, violence, car accidents, and more from affecting people's lives. "Would it be helpful to recite to me what occurred? Sometimes sharing your story can help."

"Nay." He looked as though he might vomit. "It is much too gruesome for a lady."

"Player number four!" the officiant shouted. Thomas jolted back into action, quickly assessing the scoreboard. He loaded his arrow, put up his bow to shoulder height, aimed, and...

"Another bullseye for player number four!" The crowd cheered. Thomas held up his hand to the crowd to acknowledge their cheers and gave a brief bow.

"Well done—you are very good at this." I gave him a gentle pat on the shoulder. "But pray, tell me—I have seen much in the world that is not pretty, I promise you. You may have no fear this will affect me."

He shrugged. "If the story is too much for you, just put up a hand. Or, if you feel faint, you must tell me."

I nodded.

"We were out hunting with the king. He likes to ride fast, as did my father. They were chasing after a boar, when Father's horse must've broken a leg, and crumpled up, and in doing so, trapped my father underneath him. I was riding behind him, eighteen at the time, and observed in horror. I jumped off my horse and made an effort to try to slide out my dear Papa from under the horse, but the horse kept rolling and kicking its legs in agony, crushing my father further, and every time I tried to get close, I had to pull back so I would not get kicked in the head. My father was bleeding from his head—he'd hit it on a rock—and was gasping for breath with the horse on top of him, his legs bent at horrible angles, bone sticking out. His eyes opened and looked around wildly, then found me. 'Do not watch, Thomas! Look away!' he gasped, with one last agonizing breath.

"And then he was gone. Father, who so loved the beauty in this world, would not have wanted me to have this dark memory of his last moments on earth.

"Yet they haunt me to this very day. I cannot get the images of his suffering, of the animal suffering, out of my mind. To put the horse out of its horror I cut its neck with my sword, and only then could I draw my father's body out, but it did get soaked with the horse's red blood. We buried him in Greenwich. I visit his grave every day when I am there."

If I'd been at "home"—back in the 21st century, that is—I'd have pulled him into a comforting hug. But here there was none of that hugging thing going on here, especially between men and women. Only behind closed doors. I could only tentatively give a pat on his forearm. "I'm so sorry. That must have been horrible to see and live through. How do you cope with your grief?"

"I do not sleep well. The king has taken me under his wing since my father's passing, which has been very kind, but every time he goes riding, I fear another accident. Although I do not blame the horse, I no longer find the rides as exhilarating. I prefer to walk now, but the king has me seeking art for his collection, claiming that I have a good eye, knowing that I have been taught at my father's knee to see the details in masters' work. In excellence in carving, for balustrades and frames, the depiction of hair and silk in a painting, or a wave on the sand, the shaping of marble, the filigree of a sword. So, I must ride. It pains me every time."

I took a deep breath, and let it out slowly. How could I explain modern psychiatric practices, mixed with meditation, in a way that didn't sound bizarre to him?

"I think it is wise to dwell not upon how your father died, but when you notice your thoughts turning to his death rather than his life, think to yourself, 'There I am, dwelling on that part of my father's life again. I must put that aside, for it is not serving me well.' Then turn your attention to either another scene from his life—a good one—or notice something that is going on in your own life at that moment. Some wise woman once told me to notice things in 5, 4, 3, 2, 1, meaning I can see these five things in my room, I can touch four things in my room, I can smell three things in my room, I can hear two things in my room, etc. This helps me greatly when I need to calm myself."

Thomas gave me a look, one that might have conveyed that I

had two heads and he didn't know what in the world to make of me, *or* that might have declared that I was the most brilliant and insightful woman he'd ever come across. Perhaps there was a good reason I was single, because I couldn't ever make out whether a man admired me, or thought I was categorically insane. Maybe Graham could teach me in Spy 101 school about how to read a person more effectively.

Thomas looked down at his fingers, counting down the numbers, it looked like. Maybe he was taking my advice!

Then he reached out to take my hand. "I see a pair of fine blue eyes, a beautiful smile, hair the color of a golden sunset, two rosy cheeks, and..." He looked upon my lips, hesitating.

I looked at *his* lips, framed by that trim beard. *Would it tickle,* I wondered, *to kiss him?*

"I must say it," he said, grabbing my hand, "for it has bothered me deeply. Your husband does not treat you as you ought to be treated, and this makes me angry, my lady."

This had taken a turn I was not expecting. "Do not be mad at him. It is not a love match, but he *does* protect me."

"How?"

I laughed. "Well, he *says* he protects me, even if I don't see it."

"I have yet to see him fulfill that role. Forgive me for saying this, but if you were my wife, I would put you upon a pedestal and see that you were never in danger, never hungry, never rained upon..."

You can imagine my feelings at hearing this. I was alternately bursting out of my skin with pure joy, and somewhat, just a tiny bit... smiling at his endearing sentiments. Who can stop the rain, after all? Perhaps not the best analogy of which a doctoral candidate would approve. After all, I would not melt in the rain, as my mother often reminded me.

But I swear, this was but a blip that went on fleeting foot out of my mind, as the one thought that stuck with me was: *He Likes Me!* Heat flushed into my face, and well, everywhere.

Thomas continued, quietly, so I had to get closer to him. "Would that I could whisk you away, and make you mine, that is—if you were willing. But I mustn't think that way. I cannot say such things or even think such things. I would never want to ruin you, Lady Dreux. But sometimes I wonder, is our good standing really worth our unhappiness? Should marriage be void of love?"

"What is that, friend?" said a deep voice. I knew that voice and I shuddered as it continued, "Should marriage be void of love?"

It was only then that I put together that the increasing noise around us was from the recognition and excitement that arose as the king passed through our section of archers. The king was known to hand out gifts, money, and even pay debts, so he was forever mobbed by people asking him for favors. Thankfully the monarchy stopped this practice not long after, and Henry eventually would build up enough jadedness that he could no longer bear the interactions after a while.

It's one of the reasons my distant cousin, the Queen, had never carried money in her lifetime, but I'm a thousand percent sure she would have had more grace about that mobbing than Henry.

Thomas seemed tongue-tied. "Er..."

"Is this a philosophical question? Because I don't believe that you would mean that, Thomas, about marriage being void of love."

"No, indeed, I was arguing the opposite. Marriage and love should go hand in hand. Along with a love and devotion to our King, and to the good Lord above."

"Ah, now, Tom, you are just being proper. Tell me what you really think." King Henry turned his eyes toward me. "Or perhaps Lady Dreux could weigh in."

Oh, dear Lord, I prayed, *give me inspiration!* Song lyrics ran through my head, everything from John Lennon to Lady Gaga and Dua Lipa. But no, it was the great poets who really had something to say. In fact, I realized, the Bard himself had said (or would say) it best. So, I recited:

"Love is not love
Which alters when it alteration finds,
Or bends with the remover to remove:
O no! it is an ever-fixed mark
That looks on tempests and is never shaken. "

Henry looked down upon me and appeared taken aback. "Can you repeat that?"

I did. I had had to learn that sonnet in school, and it sticks with me to this day.

"An excellent sentiment, dear lady. Excellent. Never shaken indeed. Ah, 'tis like my love for our dear queen. 'An ever-fixed mark.'"

I swallowed, knowing this was not true. He might have loved her, but that didn't mean he wouldn't cheat on her. But at least I knew for a fact that, when he fell in lust with Anne Boleyn some nine years hence, he continued to keep Katherine of Aragon safe. Even when he banished—or would banish-her from court in 1531.

So sure, Thomas might have adored me then as a shiny new object, but like those who had gone before him (or beyond him, in his future and my past), the texts would not be returned in a timely manner, the phone not picked up upon my calls, and plans not made—all indicating a distinct lack of interest. Whatever the Tudor equivalent was of "ghosting."

"Come with me, Lady Dreux," King Henry said to me. "I'd like you to see what a fine day's festival we have put on. Surely, King Francois himself would be impressed, would he not? Let Thomas get back to his competition, I am sure his nerves have been most distracted by your beauty." He took my elbow and led me away.

I exchanged a fleeting, panicked gaze at Thomas, who gave me a reassuring nod. Perhaps he'd be good to his promise?

Graham certainly wouldn't know that I was being led away. He was nowhere to be seen, in spite of his bright yellow hose.

As we walked over to a table laid out with trays of sweets, cheeses, fruits, and cakes, I took my opportunity. "You spoke of King Francis. May I ask whether or not you have heard of the artist Leonardo da Vinci, recently of Milano, and now residing with King Francis as his advisor?"

He narrowed his eyes at me. "My ambassadors send me word about everything, of course."

"Well then, Your Majesty, I have heard some intriguing news of a painting done by Leonardo da Vinci; it depicts the incidence of the three suns at the Battle of Mortimer's Cross. I believe that it has great significance for our country. I have heard from our friend Thomas of Egham that you are interested in the paintings and architecture coming out of Italy?"

"You heard right, my lady. What do you know of them?"

"I study art, Your Majesty. As well as literature. I believe that every noble home should try to attain the greatest artwork and books that they can find to reflect not only beauty, but history, symbolism. And though I love the written word, there is so much that paintings can do that poems and books cannot, especially for the illiterate to learn through story, as we do in our stained-glass windows in church, and murals, and stone carvings. But you know all this, of course. Do you have a favorite painting in your collection?"

"Aye, I do, and it is in Greenwich, or else I would show it to you this very moment. It is a portrait of our mother, Elizabeth of York. I used to admire it as a boy, and stare at it for what seemed like hours, trying to remember her better." He sounded melancholy, as would anyone who's lost a parent in their childhood. This gave him a hint of humanity in my eyes that he'd not had before. But then no man is wholly bad or wholly good. "Of course—" he stood up straighter—"I also spent my time reading, learning languages, and math, the geography of our land, the people. But that painting loomed over me."

"I am sure you have heard of the phenomena of the three suns, yes?"

"Yes, of course. It is a monarch's duty to know his history; surely you do not mean to insult me?"

Ugh—this man's temper could change as quickly as the weather on the South coast. Beautiful one minute, raining the next. "Young Hal" was easily offended.

I guess if you fancy yourself the best person in the whole world, and everyone has been telling you that since your father died, it's hard to even be questioned, even minutely, not even for the sake of rhetoric.

"By my troth I do not. I only seek to share my excitement, for I know that you will value that part of our history—the turning point for the Tudor rose—to be of historical significance."

"It was a wondrous, magical day, by all accounts," he acknowledged. "And Edward proved himself as the man who would be a great king, my grandfather. He died before I was born, but the fact that he managed to calm the nerves of the soldiers at the sight of the three suns, to persuade them that it was the Holy Trinity of the Father, the Son, and the Holy Ghost, and not some evil omen, was magnificent."

I nodded. "I read that he said something like, 'be of good comfort and dread not; this is a good sign, for these three suns betoken the Father, the Son, and the Holy Ghost, and therefore let us have good heart, and in the name of Almighty God go we against our enemies.' What an inspirational leader," I said, placing my hand over my heart.

His fox's eye returned again. "You are an unusual woman, Lady Dreux, with a fine head for knowledge."

I deflected. "I must be on my way, with Lord Dreux of course, back to France to seek out the painter Leonardo da Vinci, and see if the rumors are true about this painting. I should dearly love to put this painting I've heard about into your hands to celebrate this great battle, from the likes of such a painter, who surely is one of the greatest painters who ever lived?"

Henry VIII stroked his beard, momentarily lost in thought. "Aye, 'tis a journey that would be most expeditious. Thomas, my agent, of course, needs to accompany you—he was going to France on my business anyway, and now he shall make a detour to see this da Vinci fellow. He must acquire it for us. There is no justice if our piece of important royal history, a Godly event of the Trinity, is in foreign hands. Our sister Mary was in France last year, made Queen of France, but the king did die, and now King Francois is in power, and Mary is back in England. But of course, you living in France and an *etudiant d'art*," he said in perfect French, "means that you and your husband, along with my Thomas, shall have no issues in getting that painting for us. And if you do, you must report back to me directly. But I am sure that da Vinci will be delighted to make the sale to us, and who could deny that pretty, happy face of yours? Surely no man worth his salt."

I knew that Leonardo would have no sexual attraction to me, as we are fairly certain he had only male lovers, but I'd hoped Henry's gold would get us a painting from the artist who famously never parted with his art. Or if not Henry's gold, then mine and Graham's. But how would we bypass Henry's request to visit him directly instead of returning to the labyrinth at Wodesley Castle? Well, we'd have to figure that out... if we were lucky enough to get that far.

People had gathered all around us, eager to speak with the king. "Your Majesty! Your Majesty!"

Henry gave me a nod. "Now, my Lady Dreux, I must attend to my many other duties."

I was free to go.

THE REST OF the day was spent in full frivolity. Thomas and Graham did not win the prize for best archer but finished respectably in the top seven (Graham bragged that "this was out of a field of seventy-five, mind you"). Stafford gave me a tour 'round the place, having seen its evolution over the years and met the various owners, and pointed out many of the players in Henry's court. I spoke with William to make sure that he was happy staying at Leeds Castle, and he grinned from ear to ear. "My lady, you was right. It weren't healthy for me staying on me own. I remembered how much I like being around people. They'll pay me an honest wage for an honest day's work—that's all I can ask—and at the end of the day, me and my mates can have a pint. And to work for His Majesty, well now..."

For William, no more needed to be said.

Anne got some tips on being a lady's maid from the other maids in service, and they found her some clean clothes and did her hair up properly. She was glowing.

After a quiet dinner this night, the king taking dinner in his chambers with his wife as I was told he often did, we all went to bed early so that we could rise at dawn.

It was Day Five of our mission, and my brain was overtaxed and over-stimulated by speaking in a mostly-foreign language, in a very different time. Plus, I was suffering from a severe sleep deficit, averaging probably just three hours of sleep a night since I'd "landed" in 1517. These nights were spent, tossing and turning, filled with dread of Henry pulling me off the dance floor, face leering, ordering "Off with her head!" *Alice in Wonderland* style. Me, wandering in front of the targets at the archery competition, eyes flying open, realizing an arrow was coming directly toward my chest. Me, on the back of a horse with a lance in one arm, a helmet on my head, so that I couldn't see properly, barely able to hold the lance up as the crowd booed and I crashed into the target.

Yes, my dreams were no respite from the worry. Would that I dreamed of Thomas again, recreating that scene from the BBC version of *Pride and Prejudice* when Colin Firth played Darcy, emerging wet, his white linen shirt clinging to his bulging pectoral muscles, flat abs exposed. Nope. No such luck. And, unlike those who famously thrive on little sleep, I was punchy, yet still coursing with adrenaline.

Before we could bring our horses around, a servant directed Graham, Stafford, Thomas, and me that we first had to visit the royal kennels. Meanwhile, Anne went to say our goodbyes to William and pass along some money as a token of our thanks.

The Master of the Hounds told us, "His Majesty has different types of dogs for different reasons. The greyhounds are for short hunts when dogs can run at full speed, and the spaniels are for when he goes bird hunting. The beagles are for sniffing out game, and in general, making a big racket. The king has personally chosen many of our dogs for use as generous gifts to other rulers. But he has asked me to show you the ones that remain, and what you think this painter might like."

I knew from the subjects of his paintings and drawings that da Vinci certainly liked horses, which makes sense because they were an essential part of life, or even a luxury, for anyone born before 1920. I recalled one drawing of his of a greyhound, but I couldn't picture an older man with a dog who liked to sprint— he'd never be able to keep up. No, the best thing for an older person is a lap dog, and one that is soft to the touch, with an insouciant face and long ears. A spaniel. Plus, spaniels did not yap like beagles, who had a penchant for getting distracted by a scent and wandering off after it and getting lost.

I walked over to the pen holding the spaniels. "Are any of these available?"

My guide climbed over the fencing, and immediately the dogs jumped on him, happy, friendly, eager for a scratch. "Aye, my lady. This young lad here, the liver and white. He is scared of running with the horses to hunt but would make a good companion for an old man."

He put a rope around his neck, and came over with an iron collar, with spikes on the outside, perhaps to ward off any predator or foe—like a boar—that might want to chomp down on the little one's neck. "Does it have a name?" I asked, reaching over to pick up the pup, who wriggled and kissed me on the nose.

"I've been calling him Scamp, but you can call him what you like."

I looked at Stafford and Graham. "Ideas?"

"Chester," said Graham.

"Not respectful to Lord Chester, I should think," said Stafford. "How about Dickens?"

"Hmm, I like it." But it wasn't quite right. The little dog wiggled in my arms and tried to eat my hair. "Oh, I know!" I said. "How about Winston? I do believe he kept spaniels. Or at least, the Churchill family is famous for the Bleinheims. Yes. Little Winston."

"Be careful, my lady, that he does not soil your dress," the dog master said. "He could probably use a bath."

Graham held up his hand. "We don't have time for that. We must be off. Maybe we can put him in a lake along the way."

I put Winston down, and tail wagging, nose sniffing, and with an occasional leap into the air—spaniels leap to flush out birds, but also jump when excited—we got our horses and were off. Since the puppy was afraid of running with the horses, and too small to keep up, Anne and I fashioned a carrier for him that strapped across my chest.

Thanks to Henry's patronage, we now had a horse for Anne and our party—Stafford, Graham, Thomas, Anne—and Thomas's trio of Edward, Robert, and Hugh set out. And now Thomas was no longer on a general art finding mission, but one with a purpose: we were headed to Amboise to find Leonardo da Vinci. Thomas's pockets were stuffed full of Henry's money in order to make the purchase, and of course, we had our own gold to use as well.

We'd gotten off our schedule with the diversion to Henry's Leeds Castle. I am not so sure whether Ellie and Jane would have approved my *ad hoc* pitch to Henry VIII, but I was afraid that without his interest in our leaving his court, we would have been trapped with him for a long time.

CHAPTER THIRTEEN

TWO DAYS OF hard riding later, we arrived at Dover, seeking the first available ship that had room for all of us, minus the horses, which we placed in a stable to await our return.

I'd been to Dover before, but it was with my parents, to take the ferry to France. I was so chuffed to be riding on a ferry, until we were greeted by the English channel's typical choppy waves and high winds. Soon I was lying below decks on a round settee, which, I later found out, is the *exact opposite* of what you should do. One should not be below decks with its stale air, and the potential stench of vomit from fellow seasick travelers. No, one must ride the swells and stay put in the fresh air and wind.

While we awaited our transport, we stayed at a local inn. By now Anne and I had gotten used to each other and worked out our roles and responsibilities; it was my great joy to spoil that girl rotten. Food, food, and more food, and I gave her a clean kirtle to wear so she could wash the one that she'd gotten at Leeds. I told her I'd hoped she'd burned the old one and she assured me she had. "My lady, the fabric is so soft! I feel like a princess!"

She'd protested when I told her we must wash and comb out her hair, and that I would be doing the scrubbing. I feared lice, and since she slept close to me, didn't want to risk it. Thankfully her mother was vigilant about lice, she'd told me, but she certainly benefited from a dousing of my shampoo, which I'd brought in a glass bottle, courtesy of the 21st century. She smelled a whole lot better, and apart from needing a haircut, looked like a much healthier version of the girl we'd pick up a few days before.

Sitting in the inn's dining room after me having put Anne to bed (this time) after an early supper, along with the puppy (she said just to poke her awake when I needed my ties undone), I was given a seat by the proprietor and ordered chicken, peas, and a side of bread. The chicken was grilled by the fire and was delicious, but as expected, the peas were mushy, getting stuck in my veneers. Whatever nutrients had been in there initially were long since boiled away. The bread was hard, but filling. I ate alone; I don't know what had happened to my other travel companions, but I had a small book I'd brought with me from home, leather bound, nothing on it to indicate it was from the future, except that the language was slightly more modern. That was all the company I needed.

I read from *Pride and Prejudice*, "She was convinced that she could have been happy with him, when it was no longer likely they should meet." *Ah, Lizzie, if you thought falling in love with somebody who would no longer visit your village was difficult, imagine how hard it'd be if you lived not 400 miles away, but 500-plus years apart.*

People started moving furniture around to set up a little stage, and much to my astonishment, Thomas joined an unkempt band of misfits upon it. A fiddler, a tambourine man, a flautist. In his hands, Thomas held a lute, and I wondered where he'd found the guitar-like instrument. Perhaps it was packed in his bags on his horse the whole time? This little band must have agreed on a set list beforehand, because they launched into a ditty about lost and unrequited love. I'd rate the lyrics a D-, but the execution was an A+. My God, what a lovely voice Thomas had—technically excellent, never veering off key, but more than that, his voice was the kind that touched your soul.

A server took my plate away and filled up my goblet with wine from a pitcher, but I hardly noticed. Then again, one never knows where to look when one is being sung to, does one? Does one look up in the air, over the singer's shoulder, down at one's feet? While looking into his eyes would surely blind me, like getting too close to the sun, I had to, at least occasionally, flick a quick glance at him to be polite, after all. Anyone on a stage, whether they be singing or trying to make the works of John Milton's "Paradise Lost" palatable to the smartphone generation, wants to make eye contact with the audience. It acknowledges that people are listening, engaged, and interested.

And remember how one knows that a man is interested just by the way he looks as though he wants to consume you? For the briefest of seconds, I saw that look flash through his eyes. *Oh my.*

After the applause died down, Thomas was encouraged to perform another. This time he chose a more upbeat song—I didn't quite catch all the lines, but it was a "making hay while the sun shines" type of theme—with important lessons for us all. The audience clapped in time, stomped their feet, and some even did little jigs about the room. It was honestly the most fun I'd had on our trip.

After this, Thomas stood up and another man—I guess the original singer/guitarist for the group—took his place, and people went back to their normal conversations and milling about, which must have been frustrating for the regular singer. But my eyes did not leave Thomas, who was corralled by two older women, leaning on his sleeve, grabbing his hand, rubbing his back. They might have been enjoying their nights out rather too much and they got rather handsy with him.

Stafford—from whence he came I don't know—came over to sit beside me at my little hide-out table. Ale in hand in a tin mug, his eyes looked slightly glassy. Where had he been drinking this whole time? He leaned over to me and propped his head on his hand.

"You fancy him." Not a question, but a declaration.

I shrugged, trying to be nonchalant. "Perhaps. But there's nothing to be done, is there? He's a 16th century man, I'm a 21st century woman. Not to mention, a 'married' one at that."

"Indeed. 'Tis a conundrum." He leaned back, and took a big swig, wiping his mouth with the back of his hand.

I turned to look more closely at him. Stafford resembled Errol Flynn from his "Robin Hood" days, broad at the shoulders, slim at the waist, and sporting a goatee of sorts. "You seem like you could be a real heartbreaker, Stafford. Have you ever had a great love affair on your trips to and fro? Ever been tempted to take a young lady back through the labyrinth, show her the modern world, make her yours for all time? Or even stay here permanently, settling down with a family?"

"I'm the very definition of 'love 'em and leave 'em,' Lady Dreux." He held up a finger for me to wait while he took a swig of his beer. "And when I leave, I go very far away, so there's little chance I'll ever run into them again, which is a good thing. Because they've aged a lot when I come back, and it would be rather difficult to explain why I haven't."

"I can see that. So, no hope of you ever settling down?"

He seemed to sigh just a bit. "The closest I ever came was Ellie, and that was a very long time ago. She wouldn't take my explanation of my time-traveling adventures when I offered it, which indeed would be the case with most people. And by the time she finally understood, years later, she was saddled with children." He shivered, then continued speaking. "And Harry stepped in. Outshining me perhaps in every way, except intellectually. But then, I am no war hero. Just a man who figured out time travel." He plucked the flower from the vase in the center of our table and twirled the stem between his index finger and his thumb.

"And a bestselling author, at one time. But your greater discovery of the labyrinth must remain a secret. Does that frustrate you?"

"Partly, if I'm being honest. But on the other hand, it's of great importance to me, for what we are doing as a group, to keep this quiet. Imagine if people were queuing up to use the labyrinth, and who would destroy absolutely everything—

screwing up history as a result." He shook his head. "What we thought we knew about the world would be changed, every day, people unsettling things. No, time travel must stay quiet. And the people that were born in this time must *stay* in this time, no matter who we might become fond of, or fall in love with, no matter how hard it is to see them suffer in myriad ways or know that they face a perilous future with plagues or war, famine, and illness. We can't change that for them. But as with Anne, and William, you can make their lives a little more comfortable—and dare I say—*exciting* while you are here."

"I see that. That's why I must keep away from Thomas. I can't risk my heart getting broken when we go back in time. I must just keep looking from afar."

"Oh, I don't know about that. A little dalliance might do you good, though. Loosen up a bit. This doesn't have to be about *marriage*." He rolled his eyes. "Or even dating. You are attracted to him, clearly, and he is most definitely attracted to you. Why not enjoy that?"

"Believe you me, I've envisioned it. But I'm *not* a 'love 'em and leave 'em' type. My neuroses and hormones cannot help but be entangled forever more. I do truly know that men and women are different in that regard. You could bed 100 women, and likely never feel any attachment, remorse, or thoughts of 'what if?' It's enormously unfair."

He raised his eyebrows. "I *do* have plenty of thoughts about them, but it's all pleasure and no sadness. Each one had her own delicacies that were worth sampling."

I started fanning myself, fearing that Stafford was going to start naming his favorite encounters and giving more salacious details. "I beg of you, Stafford, let us end this conversation before you start recounting your conquests. Excuse me." I got up and hustled out into the fresh air, away from the lusty Stafford and his tempting thoughts of abandon. I stood alongside the muddy lane, examining the divots made from hoof prints, people, and dogs.

It occurred to me that these would all be tamped down in no time and made smooth once more or washed away into the nearest stream. Just as my imprint upon this time—or any time—would soon be gone, making way to new prints from others. So the impression I made on the world, wasn't entirely clear to me. I knew I wanted to be a force for good, a power in enlightening people to the way both literature and art connected humans throughout the ages. I thought of how many people had fallen in love with the story of Elizabeth Bennet and Mr. Darcy, inspiring movies and TV shows and endless sequels and retellings as we all reveled in how Jane Austen captured the slow burn of love unfolding between the two characters. That was worth aspiring to. Or showing students the power of capturing a face, a portrait, in a painting, how that person lives through the ages, despite their deaths centuries before. Who can forget Mona Lisa's wry smile, after all? But would any man ever truly remember *me* as more than a fleeting moment, a passing flirtation, a set of blue eyes and a smiling face?

"Should you be out here alone, my lady?" asked Thomas.

Oh, my sweet lord. Had Stafford sent him out here to tempt me?

I knew I must keep our dialogue brief and light. Not a repeat of our conversation at the archery competition. Luckily, on our journey here, we hadn't been alone since... or, more to the point, I hadn't allowed us to be alone.

"You played and sang beautifully, good sir." (Note the formality I used, not saying his name made us seem mere acquaintances, right?) "From whence did your talents arise?"

"Thank you, good lady," he said, also keeping a fair distance, language-wise. Perhaps he too had regrets over his previous confession of his feelings toward me. "I learnt at the feet of some of the minstrels who came to the castle, or the great houses where we stayed. They told me I had a fair voice when I was a lad, but when my voice got deeper, the praise became more rare. Still, when a chance comes to perform, sometimes the desire to sing floods away my reticence. And I become the lad eager once again for the applause."

"Oh, I do know that feeling," I said. We started walking down the lane, toward the seawall; we had to do something with the pent-up sexual tension that swirled around us. A quarter moon hung low in the sky, and the waves breaking onto the shore sent up a fine spray of seawater, turning it into a salt-scented mist that hung about the seaport. "When I was small, I had the ability to make everyone laugh with my mimicry. As I got older, though, I became more self-conscious, and shy, and ceased wanting the attention in my 'awkward years' as a young lady. Now I regret that."

So much for my plan to keep it light.

"For such a beautiful lady, I cannot imagine you had 'awkward years,' as you claim."

Oh, we are in the danger zone, now! Back away quickly, Gabby!

"You are too kind, sir. But oh yes, you can imagine how much I stood out even at a young age. Most men agree that they do not want a lady towering over them. It looks untoward. Unsightly. Anyway…" I needed to switch topics to something less personal. "Have you traveled much by sea?"

"Aye, often have I visited the lands of the French, and I have been to Greece, but not yet to Italy. Once I deliver the king's painting, I shall be setting forth on a journey to Florence, and Milan. Perhaps Master da Vinci can help with introductions to other artists."

"Oh, there are so many you must visit!" I detailed the ones I knew. One of the earliest classes I ever took in art history was a vast survey of European art from "caveman" times to the Renaissance. So many dates, over 10,000 years of history. But one brilliant artist came after the other in Italy during this period: Michelangelo, Raphael, Donatello, Titian, Tintoretto. I practically swooned at the thought of being able to visit these artists in real time. "We must make you an itinerary."

"Could you and Lord Dreux be my guides, perhaps? You are so learned."

"Oh, uh, I am afraid we have family business we must attend to after this journey. But I do like helping other art afficionados with their plans. So much to see."

I thought I had cleverly steered the conversation away from

anything too personal, but it was at that moment that Thomas took both my hands in his. "Gabriella," he started.

He said my actual name! I'd been so used to the formal address I'd forgotten how romantic it sounds when somebody says your name, someone on whom you have a massive crush, with his deep voice, slightly scratchy from singing.

He continued, "I know it is far from mature to want what you cannot have, but there is nothing more I'd love—" his voice caught—"than to travel the world with you, hear your thoughts on every subject, look into your eyes, hear that joyous laugh of yours. You are a burst of sunshine in my days. I fear the pain of losing you in my world will be too much to bear."

He looked around, as did I, to establish that there was no one about. He moved closer and closer so that I could see, even in the darkness, the desire in his eyes, and feel the heat from his body. He placed one hand on my back, where I was tied into my dress so tightly; he grasped at the strings, pulling me in closer, so that our cheeks now touched.

Yes, he is just hairline taller than I, I thought.

My breath grew ragged—I'm not sure whether it was from the tightness of my dress or the anticipation of what might happen between us. "You know I cannot express my feelings to you without being disloyal to my husband but were I someone who was not attached to another, I should gladly return those desires to you. You are a—"

His lips met mine, silencing me with a soft kiss. I swooned, and would have staggered back a little had he still not had my laces gathered up in one strong hand, while his other hand cupped my cheek. "How can you be so soft?" he said, tracing a finger around the bow of my lips. "Impossibly soft."

His lips descended on mine again, and we became entangled in each other, my arms closed around his waist, our bodies pressed against each other's. Long days spent desiring him had pent up all this adrenaline mixed with longing, and now that we were in it, I was reluctant to act like a real lady and let go. Not to mention the matter of how long it had been since I'd been with a man at all. I was seconds away from ripping his clothes off.

When we finally came up for air, I managed, "Thomas, we mustn't."

I thought he'd stop briefly and start kissing me again, but instead, he fell to his knees, and pleaded, hands pressed to each other in front of his chest. "I beg your forgiveness, Lady Dreux. I don't know what overcame me."

"The same thing that overcame me," I said, shaking my head. I pulled him to his feet. "I have deep feelings for you, but you do not know my circumstances, you do not know about the relationship I have with Lord Dreux. Please know that you are not betraying Lord Dreux in any way, nor am I."

His brows knit together; he was clearly confused.

"Now let us return to our inn. We shall talk no more about the subject and pretend that this never happened." A chill wind whipped up, and I felt a strong need to burrow back into his body. *What would be the consequence, anyway, if we became lovers? Who was on this trip that would even care?*

Him. He would care. He, and his morals, and his view of himself and what a good man he was—these were the only things holding me back. Stafford had encouraged me to pursue him, but he had the morals of a bull elephant. Graham didn't give a hoot, I was sure, except where it concerned his own safety. Anne, well, she was likely an innocent, and I didn't want to corrupt her worldview, but on the other hand it's hard to say how much of life she had seen already in her small town.

The point was, Thomas was a good man, religious, raised in a world of chivalry that required a strict code of etiquette and behavior. Those who didn't stick to it were banished.

Or worse.

We didn't say a word on the walk back to the inn, even if my hand occasionally wanted to sneak out and grab his. *Oh, Gabriella, what mess have you gotten yourself into?*

I was worried about his heart, his reputation. But what I had forgotten to do was worry about mine…

CHAPTER FOURTEEN

I STOOD STALWART near one of the three masts, wind on my face, lungs filled with clean, salty air, the air wiped clean of the stink of what was stored and housed below decks. Dolphins jumped through the wake on either side of the ship, and since I was not seasick, I could happily enjoy their antics. I wondered, did they spot us from afar and swim over for the wake, like kids going to a wave pool? Or was there some other plan?

Whichever it was, I let out a yell or two of "Yippee!" and "Yahoo!" as they surfaced and resurfaced.

Graham, Stafford, and Thomas had all enjoyed the views as we left port, but had gone below to eat, and they took the puppy with them. We all worried Winston was going to fall overboard. I waved off their entreaties to come down with them, and insisted I would be fine on my own, but asked if they could bring up a bread roll. By now, they all knew of my insatiable appetite, and my irritability if I didn't get fed regularly. Thomas and I exchanged glances as he headed below decks, but I bit on my lip, hard, to not throw myself into his arms in order to recapture that euphoria I had felt last night. *Be studious and stalwart. Never waiver from your duty*, I entreated myself.

The crossing could take anywhere from a full day in good winds, to a couple of days in poor ones. Since high tide was in the morning, we were able to leave early the day after "the kiss," and nine hours later, I was still hanging on to the mast.

Graham was the one who'd brought me a roll and—bonus!—a hunk of cheese, wrapped in a cloth. "What happened to your friends?" I asked, biting off a chunk, ravenous. I'd need about three more of these to put a dent in my hunger.

"They're both asleep. Thomas said he didn't sleep well last night, and Stafford had a fair old portion of wine, called it his 'cruise cocktails,' and fell asleep at the table."

Thomas hadn't slept well, he'd said. Same here. I'd tossed and turned next to dear old Graham, who was busily snoring away. He was hard to sleep next to at the best of times, ten times worse when my brain was ticking over and over, willing for another encounter to happen again with my crush, sad that it couldn't be Thomas sleeping next to me instead.

Don't ever forget those precious moments together, Gabby. Hold on to them.

I'd thought of how I inhaled his scent, so different up close, how his beard scratched over my face, how I'd felt his eyelashes tickle my skin as he moved to kiss my neck. How I longed for his hands on me again, the feel of his body pressed against mine…

"You seem lost," Graham said, patting the deck beside him after he sat down. I still couldn't get used to the look of the codpiece making up Graham's pants, for God's sake. What were they thinking, to just walk around with a big old bullseye on their private parts? Figuratively speaking. Yes, they may have made fun of Katy Perry's whipped cream bra, or Madonna's conical bra, but this just did not compare. Breasts are beautiful, and well this area, while extremely useful in many ways, is not. At least, not on Graham, I was sure. On Thomas, well…

I moved my skirts aside so I could sit down without making the hoop skirt bunch up oddly. The skirts still poofed out a little, but I could sit on the back of them to tame the tendency they had to pop up. As much as I enjoyed playing dress-up here, I couldn't wait for a hot shower, a pair of sweatpants, and a comfy sports bra. Oh, and my heavenly cloud of a mattress, and pillows. Just the way I like them.

But for now, I had rolls. Cheese. Fresh air.

"Lost, you say? No, I'm not, just enjoying the seas, though I'm a little tired myself. Hoping we don't have much longer to go. Quite frankly, I'm looking forward to speaking exclusively French for a while. The language hasn't changed that much, and I feel as though I'm not speaking as poetically as I should with the Tudors."

"No kidding," Graham said. "My ears can't seem to catch up to what they're saying, and when I speak, I'm horribly slow. Like a kid in his first year of a language. And I've been studying this for years. Still until I found you, Ellie, and Jane—or to be honest until they found me—I mean, who could you practice with?" Graham was sounding more and more like his Estuary roots. I expected an "Innit?" to ring out any second.

"*C'est vrai, c'est vrai,*" I said, in French. *So true, so true.* "Well, I appreciate you having my back here, even if I've complained at times. I must admit my nerves have been a little fraught trying to fit in, but I feel like I can breathe a bit better now that we are away from 'Good ol' King Henry.' You're a big fan of the era—what did you think of him?"

"He's a piece of work." Graham shook his head. "Quite frankly, I don't know how he does it. The running of the kingdom, looking after all those people at court and beyond, taking all those requests. Not to mention the politics at home with the church, landowners, and abroad with France, the Holy Roman Empire. Maintaining and training an army. Worrying about a male heir. Kids these days—if they had that sort of responsibility—would choose to hide instead, or become an addict, or who knows what? The fact that he's doing it all and not complaining—at least, at his age—is remarkable."

"I'll give you that—it is a lot. But he has been trained for the role, knew that there was no shirking it."

Graham ran his hand along the groove between the decking. "Speaking of parents... I know I'm a few years older than you—

too young, I'd like to think, to be a parent to someone your age—but maybe you can look up upon me as an older brother type. What I'm trying to say is that you know how I've said I'd keep an eye on you?"

"Yes, I remember. Oh…" I took a sharp intake of breath, realizing what he was hinting at. "Oh no, you saw… Last night!?"

"You two art majors going out for a romantic stroll, yes'm, I did. I wasn't being pervy, just wanted to make sure you weren't in trouble."

"But I'd looked around to make sure there was nobody there."

He batted his eyelashes, deadpan. "Remember who you're dealing with here, missy."

God, could that man disappear into the ether! What a skillset. Not that you could put it on a regular CV. Although, I suppose, for a certain sort of company, you could.

He continued, "And pray tell me, good lady," he slipped back into his proper Tudor voice, "what are the young man's intentions? Are things serious?"

"Geez, you and Stafford, both lecturing me. I thought I was being discreet."

"Then I reckon it's a good thing you are not a higher-ranking member of the monarchy, because the paparazzi could easily find you in our day. Where is this dalliance going? As your chief security officer, I need to assess the potential fallout."

At that moment, we slapped down hard on a large wave, and spray hit us square in our faces. We gasped and spluttered; I said, "I hope this doesn't keep up. I really can't bear it below decks. I shall heave." I wiped the droplets of water off my face, skirts, and dress as best I could. "As for where Thomas and I are going? Nowhere. He's a respectable young man who thinks that I am a respectable married lady, and he was full of remorse after our kissing session. He's barely said more than a word or two to me since…" I trailed off with a sigh. We'd been staying away from each other as if we'd get electrocuted if we got too close. But then

I said, "Stafford reckons I should just go for it, have no regrets."

"That fits with Stafford's profile on advice he'd dole out to any young person. Or older person. In fact, anyone in general." Graham rolled his eyes. "Ignore him. Remember our mission. We have to not only get the painting from Da Vinci—"

We hit another wave, and another lot of spray landed over us. Graham grimaced, took off his hat and gave it a shake before continuing, "But we also have to come up with a way to divert Thomas and his men, so when we land back in England, they aren't left wondering why on Earth we're not going to Leeds Castle with our treasure. I can see Thomas is mightily conflicted now just as things are, just traveling, but imagine when a priceless piece of art is at stake." He continued, mopping his face off with a handkerchief he produced from a pocket inside his doublet. "I fear without an adequate explanation for the king on what's happened to his painting, Thomas will have hell to pay."

I closed my eyes. That thought hadn't occurred to me, but I wish it had. I felt guilt. More than that, I felt fear. Thomas could be in a bad way when we disappeared. "I hadn't gotten that far with the plan, I must admit. I've been hoping, and pushing, that he could continue on to Italy from France." It had to work. I wouldn't be able to bear it otherwise. "Yes. We *must* send him to Italy, and maybe two of the men too, so we're down to just one. We can easily shake one."

"*I* can, but I'm beginning to wonder about you. You haven't been casting a glance at any of those other fellows now, have you? Somebody else you can't bear to part with?"

"Graham, for goodness' sakes!" I rolled my eyes. "I've honestly barely noticed that lot anyway." I thought about their nicknames and began ticking them off on my fingers as I spoke. "There's Edward." *Edgy Edward.* "Robert." Aka *Rockin' Robert*, "And ...oh, give me a minute."

"It's Hugh." Graham shook his head at my failings. "'Never get attached' is one of the rules of my 'data mining' profession, you know. You have a mission, you go in, execute it, then get back out, with as little damage—or attachment—to anybody in the vicinity as possible. You, on the other hand, are prancing about with your royal waves and your beaming smile, trying to meet and imprint on as many people as possible."

Once again, Graham did not fail to make me feel horrible. "I do not. I just am very tall—I stick out. And also, it's better to attract bees with honey, as they say."

Graham shook his head and started laughing. "Girlie, even with your double doctorate, sometimes I wonder if you have any sense at all. The expression is, 'You can attract more flies with honey than vinegar.' Would it make any sense that bees would be attracted by honey when they're the ones making it?"

If Graham needed a nickname, it would be *Garrulous*, which wasn't the best option but there's not a good G-word that means "persnickety."

"Well, I'm not going to debate you on historic sayings, Graham. I'm no good at them. I should just leave them alone." As if we weren't wet enough, rain started to pelt down, hard, and the wind began to roar. "I think I have to give up on being on deck. We might get drowned." The waves were getting larger, and the ship was being tossed in the high winds and swells.

A sailor was waving to us to come down out of the rain. Other sailors were lashing themselves down.

"Come on!" Graham shouted over the wind. I grabbed his outstretched hand, and we carefully made our way to the stairs, just as Thomas popped his head out. "My lady, my lord, I was coming to beg you to come down the hatch!"

"We're coming!" I assured him. But stairs below deck are steep, like ladder-steep, and if you add rain, and long skirts, and shoes with little tread on them, then *clonk!* It was inevitable that I slipped down the stairs, falling, pitching forward, bashing my skull against something hard.

"Ouch!"

"Oh my God! Gabby!" Graham called out.

Every piece of me hurt. But what hurt more was the sight of Thomas, lying unconscious underneath me.

CHAPTER FIFTEEN

T HE BODY IS so much like a well-oiled machine that you only notice its inner workings when things go wrong, if you're tired or stressed, ate too much vindaloo, or walked too far in shoes that didn't fit. But when things go horribly wrong, like clonking yourself in the head with another human's skull, the body is quick to react to attempt repairs.

My body's reaction was to immediately erupt an enormous golf-ball sized bump on my forehead. Anne, who had been in the galley to get me some tea when I fell, yelled, "My lady! Oh, my lady," before running off to get a cold cloth.

It was impossible to know what poor Thomas's body was doing to mend from the blow I'd given it with my skull. He neither groaned, moaned, or welled up in a bruise. I got heaved off him by some brawny lads that I couldn't see because I'd shut my eyes in response to the pain. I realized that I sorely missed ice. Oh, ice would have felt so good on the throbbing hot mass on my head.

I worried about Thomas. I knew I would survive, although the hypochondriac in me immediately worried about, "brain swelling; stroke; internal bleeding," while my mother's voice came down the line, "It's just a knock, poppet. We all get them. Now get back on that horse!"

As I sat holding a dripping wet cloth to my head, Graham,

Stafford, and another gentleman, perhaps a ship's doctor, hovered over Thomas. All seemed capable, but differently armed. Graham came with a modern man's perspective on medicine and checked his pupils and pulse. Stafford gently slapped Thomas on the face, trying to get him to awaken. And the third man called for his bag. If he pulled out leeches to drain his blood, I was going to lose my lunch.

It wouldn't be difficult; our bodies pitched back and forth in the storm, a sickening see-saw.

"Come my lady, over here. You will be more comfortable." Anne pulled on my arm, trying to lead me away.

"No, I must stay here, and see that Mr. Egham is all right," I said. And then, over the sound of the wood of the ship groaning and shifting against the weight of the churning seas, I shouted to Graham, "My lord! How does he fare?"

"I expect he will fare well, my dear. Perhaps he may be out a while longer, it is hard to say."

My clumsiness, or what the headmistress at my college deemed my "awkward horsiness," had taken a man down. And not just a man, but sweet, beautiful Thomas. Why hadn't I taken better care not to slip and fall?

Stafford came over to me, presumably giving up on the slapping therapy for Thomas. "My dear lady, come—we are going to move Thomas to somewhere more comfortable. And you too. Let's have a look at that bump." I removed the cloth, and his eyes flew open for a millisecond before going back to normal. "Oh, oh dear. No, it's not too bad, really. Just turning a bit, er, purple."

"It doesn't matter about me." A group of sailors was lugging Thomas under the armpits and holding him by the ankles, carrying him into an adjacent room. "Let's go," I said to Anne and Stafford.

The seas made walking forward difficult. With me between them, we lurched diagonally from one side to the other, finally making it into some sort of a small salon. Thomas had already been placed in a lounge chair, head lolling to one side. I must have cracked my skull against his nose, which was bloodied and swollen, and then the back of his head must have smacked the hardwood on the floor. I had marred his perfect profile!

"Lady Dreux, won't you sit here, and let's prop your feet up a bit," Anne said, putting me in a chair, and sliding another underneath my legs. She placed the puppy in my arms, who wriggled, giving me kisses and nipping at my clothes.

Now, in the close quarters, with no air moving in the cabin, seasickness was coming on quickly, aided by my terrible headache. I closed my eyes and felt Anne putting another cold cloth against my forehead. I patted her hand with mine. "Thank you, Anne. That feels much better. But I fear I might be sick," I said, holding a finger to my lips. "Please fetch a bucket."

My retching only ended when we sailed into the harbor where the crazy waves abated, the rain stopped pouring, and I was finally able to escape above deck once more. Everyone but Anne and Winston had abandoned me and Thomas while we were below. I don't blame them—I was disgusting, but Anne once again proved herself as a stalwart companion. During that time, we had heard Thomas moan, laugh, and cry out, so I had hope that he was coming around.

I breathed in the fresh air as I stood with Winston, leash in hand, his fluffy fur shifting with the wind. Is there anything worse than vomiting? Yes, fine, there's lots, but you have to admit, it is pretty horrible. Still, it wasn't long before our destination— Calais—drew my attention and made me forget the wretchedness of retching.

Calais was under English control, first captured by Ellie's "friend," Edward III, not long after her encounter with him. It had been a brutal siege, with Edward threatening to kill the entire population, and when he'd finally succeeded in gaining control he'd demanded that the town leaders be paraded in front of him, one by one, with ropes around their necks. Only his queen, Phillipa, was able to beg for their lives successfully. He'd driven the population out of the city and repopulated it with English people. It was not at all a chivalrous act from the man who had founded the Order of the Garter with so much hope to be an example for all mankind of chivalry and honor.

In my opinion, in fact the way he'd used his power for ill was sickening.

From our vantage point on the docks, the walls of the small city loomed above, with watchtowers eclipsing them every fifty yards or so. A giant door in the middle of one wall, was now being opened as the sun rose above the horizon.

"I don't know how we're going to travel with Thomas passed out like that," Stafford said. "Perhaps we must leave him behind."

"No, we cannot," I protested. "He is the one who must negotiate on behalf of the king."

Graham shook his head. "We have our own money for this express purpose. Surely we can persuade da Vinci without Thomas."

But I couldn't bear the thought of traveling without him. Yes, call me selfish and perhaps even willing to undermine our mission, but I needed him with us. Otherwise, I would be pining away and pretty much useless—with my knowledge or people skills blunted. Or at least, that's what my heart told me.

"We need time anyway," I said. "I haven't slept in twenty-four hours, thanks to that storm. Can we find an inn, please, and spend a night here, and perhaps by tomorrow he will be better?"

Graham and Stafford both gave me a millisecond of eye-rolling, but they agreed. "Oh, all right, just one night. But not more than that," Stafford warned.

Some sailors placed Thomas on a litter; those of us who could walk continued to stumble about as though the waves were still in charge of our movements, even when we were back on solid ground. But we found a barn that had reputable horses for rent for the following day's use, and Stafford found us an inn where we could tuck Thomas into a proper bed. He was moving more, but still not opening his eyes.

Reluctantly, I left Anne to watch over him and then—at Graham's insistence (though it didn't take much convincing in spite of my worry for Thomas) we got ourselves a hearty breakfast.

French bread—you never fail to delight and sustain.

Unfortunately, neither coffee nor tea had come into vogue yet, so I yawned my way through the meal, Winston squirming alternately on my lap and at my feet where we placed a bowl of water on the ground for him, and a puppy-sized, hearty breakfast of cooked chicken and green beans.

After this, I made my way back into our room with some food for Anne so she could break her fast; she ate and then managed to get a few layers of my clothing off before we fell into our respective beds (mine a proper medieval mattress stuffed with straw, hers a trundle bed which had been hidden under mine. Graham got his own room this night, because he could. One of Thomas's men, Rockin' Robert, stayed with him to check him periodically and make sure to alert us if he had seizures.

With the dog curled up beside me, I fell asleep stroking its soft ears between my fingers, and slept the day away, still feeling the up and down sensation of being on the ocean, but every once in a while, I was sure bedbugs nibbled away at me. It could have been the scratchy sheets and an over-active imagination, but as I passed in and out of the waking world and sleep, I saw a vision: *The Three Sunnes* painting, each piece filling in like a jigsaw puzzle.

The first was the three suns, with one—the real sun—rising higher than the other two, in the dawn light. In the foreground were men, soldiers, distinctively painted in Da Vinci style, with their muscle definition outlined, their clothing realistic, and the horses all exquisitely conveyed. One horse was up on its rear legs, front hooves seeming to cycle in mid-air, a man on horseback in armor above, entreating his troops to not be afraid, his aquiline features noble, eyes shining.

I woke with a start. It was dark, and there was barely any noise about, so it must have been the middle of the night. Time was running out. Not only our time in the past, when we had to return by Stafford's calculations, but by the sixth sense I had that someone else was after that picture.

Anne was still sleeping, like a child, her arms raised above her head like she'd formed a goalpost. I slipped on my surcoat and went to check on Thomas. Guilt continued to gnaw at my conscience.

I remembered the location of Thomas's room, and found the door still unlocked. And yet I knocked anyway, to be polite. Rockin' Robert was asleep on the floor wrapped in a blanket, and I told him I'd take over if he wanted to go back and bunk with his friends in their room. He nodded sleepily and left with the blanket. "Thomas?" I said. "Are you awake?"

Unlike Anne's peaceful, innocent repose, Thomas had shifted from how we'd left him on his back—he'd moved to his side, limbs akimbo. *That's a good sign*, I thought. *Not paralyzed.* I went to his bedside, and kneeled beside it, gently picking up one of his hands, hot to the touch, and pressed it to my lips. "Thomas, I know you can wake up. If you can move in your sleep like this, you can wake up. We've got important goals to accomplish. And I need your help. I need you to be with me. I can't do this without you."

I'd heard told that those in comas can actually hear the people around them, that they are just incapable of responding. "Thomas, it's Gabriella, Lady Dreux. Please, squeeze my hand if you can hear me." I asked, again and again, until finally two of his fingers squeezed around my fingers. "Oh yes, thank you! Well done, you!"

He still wasn't opening his eyes though. "Can you try to wriggle this foot?" I reached down and patted his left foot. "Thomas, can you move this?" He flexed his foot. "Bravo!" I said. "You're getting better. Now, how about you try to open your eyes? It's just me, Lady Dreux. You might remember that I fell on you right before I knocked you out. I'm a big, giant, clumsy oaf, and I'm so terribly sorry. But please, I've felt guilt the size of the mighty ocean for hurting you...." I paused.

Is guilt even a concept Tudors are familiar with?

"Great woe, I've felt… great sorrow in my heart. Now, on the count of three, you will open your eyes. One, two, three!"

They did not budge.

I blew out a great sigh, suddenly very tired myself, despite all the sleep I'd caught up on. Thomas had made some progress responding to my commands. He wasn't paralyzed. But he'd now gone a full thirty hours without opening his eyes, and it was truly, deeply, madly concerning, to misquote a film title.

All the energy left my body. I couldn't even muster the strength to leave the floor, and just closed my own eyes.

"LADY DREUX!! WHAT on earth are you doing in here! I been looking everywhere for you," Anne said.

Oh, my bones hurt. What made me think I could sleep on the floor like some kind of undergrad? I unkinked myself. The roosters were going mad outside, as well as the birds, the sun lightening the window.

"I was checking on Thomas's condition," I said, "and suddenly became so tired, I just fell asleep."

"Good morrow, my lady, young Anne," a deep voice said.

I shot up, my limbs unkinking all at once. "Thomas! How do you feel?"

He propped himself up on an elbow. "My head does ache; I'm parched. And oh, my nose. I think I would need a garderobe if you wouldn't mind?" He looked around the room.

"Oh yes, I'm sure you do!" Anne showed him the necessities, and I swiftly exited the room.

"Graham?" I said softly down the hallway. "Where are you? Thomas is well again!"

Stafford came out into the hallway in just his shirt. "Splendid! We should rally the troops, then, and be on our way after we break our fast." The puppy barked, and Stafford took him outside.

Relief coursed through me. Had the dream helped, the vision

of those three suns? Or would Thomas have woken up naturally without my intervention? *Probably.*

Anne and I got ourselves ready. The swelling on the bump on my head had gone down, and she'd found some sort of powder to cover it up. I hope it was not what Elizabeth 1st had used to cover up her pockmark scars—*that* was rumored to contain white lead, which poisoned her over time.

Anne and I made sure that Thomas could walk properly and get down the stairs; she stood behind him and me in front of him, making sure he took the steps slowly. Winston tried to kill us all by getting tangled with his leash between us, nipping at our skirts and shoes. But in spite of his efforts, our ragtag army of art seekers was on their way again.

CHAPTER SIXTEEN

I DON'T KNOW whether it was the Vitamin D from the sunshine giving Thomas life, the breakfast, or the longest nap in history, but he seemed right as rain, albeit with a bruised—but thankfully, not broken—nose. He was chipper, almost, whistling as we trotted along, breaking out into canters now and again, and even galloping on our rented steeds.

We were making good progress toward Paris. After a little while, I stopped watching him for signs of unwell, and started to just enjoy the beautiful spring in the French countryside, the trees in various stages of budding, wildflowers in bloom, and the birds busily feeding their babies. We alternated riding with little Winston strapped in his baby-carrier like pouch. The steady rhythm of riding was soothing to him, I think, so that he often slept, but he was also a complete rascal at other times, trying to escape, chewing on everything he could get his mouth on, and sometimes having an accident. When he grew to adulthood, I was sure, he was going to be the most spoiled, yet cuddly, dog in existence.

The route through France had been a hot debate between Ellie, Jane, and Graham, and then once back in 1517, we were joined in that debate by the larger party, adding Stafford and Thomas, and his three ad hoc guards.

Men love nothing more than maps and strategizing which

route would be the fastest. Was it better to travel back on the sea and farther south, where we could cut in and head due east to Amboise? I had vetoed that plan. No more boats for me until I had to return back to England. I was born to be on a horse, and if I were to survive, that needed to be the route. The road from Calais to Paris was well-traveled because of trade, as was the road from Paris to Amboise, the seat of the royal court.

Still, it was a long, hard few days of riding. Every twenty to fifty miles or so, we exchanged horses for fresh ones so we could keep up our pace. Fortunately, Anne, the only non-experienced horseperson, took to riding like a duck to water. A bit of a thrill-seeker, that one, not afraid at all of high speeds, jumps, and mixed terrain. What a trooper.

At night, we were all so worn down, we barely stayed awake through a supper at an inn. Thomas and I exchanged a few longing looks, some of which were intended to be seen by the other, and some which were supposed to be discreet and yet were accidentally caught by the admiree. But every night, we were too tired to even flirt. Some nights there were rooms for all, and other nights, some of the men slept in a barn with the puppy, where he could make a mess and nobody would care. Thankfully, I always got a room, even if I had to share it with Graham and Anne.

Even more encouraging, Thomas's nose started to look a little better.

PARIS HAD BEEN deemed "the city of love" at some point in its recent history, with the Eiffel Tower its famous landmark, wide tree-line boulevards, fashion, and outdoor cafes drawing tourists from all over the world, but in the 16th century there was no Eiffel Tower. In fact, Paris was quite gothic-looking, with towers and spires, shop-lined bridges, refuse-filled, narrow streets, with wooden buildings crowding the streets below and supporting a population of around 200,000 people.

At this time, it was still a very medieval town and—for those of us from the future—a little hard to recognize, if it hadn't been for Notre Dame towering above the city, and the Seine running through it. Even the Seine was unfamiliar, with raw sewage, garbage, and other nastiness floating on its water. And the smog from thousands of fires burning to bake breads, heat houses, and other industry made my eyes water.

"*Tres miserable,*" I muttered to Graham and Stafford. "Let me know if you notice Jean Valjean moping around. This isn't the City of Lights, it's one foul scent away from Hell."

To Thomas I said, "I never tire of the sight of Notre Dame."

He beamed. "Surely it is one of the wonders of the world. The rose window takes my breath away."

In comparison, the stench of the fabled city's streets took Graham's breath; he coughed and held his handkerchief up to his nose as we weaved through its streets, following Stafford to a stable he knew where we could board our horses overnight and have them fed, watered, and rested so they could go more miles in the morning.

"We simply must see Notre Dame since we are here," I said to the group.

One of my art history lecturers had opened my eyes to the changes that the reformation brought in Britain, not just to religion, but to architecture in churches and beyond. Before the reformation, churches, castles, homes, etc. were brightly colored with paint. But after the reformation it was as if all frivolity and joy were stripped away from both exteriors and interiors. We think of churches and castles as always having been made up of just gray stone, but that was not the case for hundreds of years. The Notre Dame of 1517 was painted, and we had no record in the modern age of what it looked like. Yet, I thought. I'd bring back some description with me; I'd brought a small notebook with me to record my observations. I also really, *really* wanted to take a scraping of the wall to show as proof to all my fellow art history buffs, professors, and students, to draw a more accurate picture of the cathedral.

However, as Stafford and Thomas settled the horses, I wondered. Even if I got a scraping, how was I to explain how I'd come upon it? Part of me wanted to save this knowledge for future generations, but another part of me thought that desecrating any historic site to "preserve" it was extremely problematic. I reminded myself of the Elgin marbles; a Scottish nobleman stripped the Parthenon in Athens of much of its artwork, and then sold it to the British government to put on display. The fact that it remains in England to this day is a national embarrassment.

One of the men—Hugh—knew of a decent inn nearby, and there we rested for a little while. Then I asked if anyone wanted to join me for a trip to Notre Dame, which was not far away. Thomas and Stafford seemed eager to join me, and we left Graham to rest in a room that would not overwhelm his olfactory senses, along with the dog, who was so overwhelmed with the city he was exhausted. Poor Anne had the unpleasant job of washing out our clothes.

"Have you visited the cathedral before?" I asked both men.

"Aye, when I was ten and six," Thomas said. "'Tis a glorious house of the Lord, and a 'house' is an understatement. It is easy to feel God's glory when the bell tolls and the choir sings."

"That's exactly what I think," I said. "I once heard a priest say in a sermon that people can and should experience the Almighty in different ways—through the beauty of the church, in the hymns, and the music, during the prayers and the sermon, or even in the ritual of the service."

Stafford cleared his throat. "I, for one, am inspired by the intersection of man and nature. You never know what mysteries might be unveiled. Have you ever walked the labyrinth, Thomas, at Chartres?"

I threw him a look, as if to say, *What are you doing??*

He continued, regardless of my alarm. "Many pilgrims go to

walk the labyrinth."

"No, I have not had the honor. My father and I were too busy with our work. But I do hope one day to see it."

"I would be fascinated to hear your thoughts if you do. It marries mythology with math, and the act of worship with an activity. I, for one, fully intend to see it."

"Hold on," I said, "I remember the story now. Is there not some sort of tablet in the middle of the rosette, but no one knows what used to be in that center?"

Stafford whispered under his breath to me, "It was pried up during the revolution, and melted down. I have seen pictures of the rivulets that once secured the plate. It's unnerving."

I shivered. Every once in a while, the magnitude of what had happened to get me 500 years in the past hit me. Stafford had uncovered something that went against the laws of all that we knew in the labyrinth at Wodesley Castle, and it was frightening to think if a labyrinth had the potential to do that, what other kind of mysterious forces could be out there? Why were labyrinths even designed in the first place—spontaneously, it seemed—all over the world? And what, if anything, had been buried underneath the one at Chartres?

As we neared the cathedral, there were more and more stalls and hawkers selling food, flowers, and religious relics: what Chaucer had so skewered in *The Canterbury Tales*. The vendors would tell you the relics were tiny pieces from anyone or anything to do with Jesus Christ, the Virgin Mary, the apostles, and any of the saints who could put in a good word for you with God and St. Peter to let you into Heaven. Even the containers that once held the relics were considered holy.

I'm quite sure that the last thing that any saint or disciple had on his or her mind was the glee upon which their body would be chopped up into fragments and sold to the highest bidder. And it's likely that there weren't enough holy bones, remnants, and containers to go around, and these were all fakes.

But that's just my guess. Religion wasn't and still isn't my area of expertise. At all.

As we arrived at the cathedral, I whistled in surprise. "Wow, wow, wow!" The church was painted yellow and red on the outside. Such a difference to the dour, dark gray building that greets one in the 21st century. "I was not expecting so much color!"

"See how it accentuates the stonework, my lady," Thomas said, tracing the arcs with his finger. "With each architectural feature painted in a different color."

Stafford stood to the side, looking bored as we aimed to make sense of why the different elements were painted.

"I'd like to climb to the top," I said, "and get a good view of the city. I always try to do that wherever I go."

"I like your sense of adventure, my lady. I know few ladies who would like to exert themselves up quite so many stairs," Thomas said.

"Well, you probably have already noticed I don't fit in with the mores of what most women do."

"Indeed, and 'tis most refreshing," Thomas said, grinning.

Stafford just appeared to be over having to listen to the two of us chatter on.

Once we got inside, the smokiness of the incense, candles, and torches assaulted our senses. I wondered if it would even be possible to make out the many famous sights the cathedral was known for in all the haze. But we got around the crowds inside and stepped through a side-door marked *"Ascent."*

Climbing the stone steps, I was soon trying to catch my breath. I might have underestimated how difficult it would be to climb stairs in long skirts while having your breathing restricted by a tight dress. "Sorry," I said, holding up my hand. "You two go ahead. I shall catch up anon."

"No, my lady. I cannot leave a lady unaccompanied in the stairwell." Thomas said.

"Look out for hunchbacks. *Ding-dong.*" Stafford grinned as he waved goodbye and continued on.

I shot him a dirty look as I held myself up against the stone wall. It was one of those round staircases where you keep twirling and twirling up in circles and getting the strange sensation of vertigo. They're not inherently dangerous, as the stairwell is narrow, and if you fell or tripped you wouldn't fall very far, but because you couldn't see farther up than the next five steps, you had no idea how to gauge how far you'd gone. Not to mention that the only source of light came from torches in intermittently spaced sconces and narrow windows built into the walls.

"Thank you for staying with me," I panted. I wasn't going to argue with Thomas's courteous inclination but having him stare at me while I worked to catch my breath was rather humiliating. After a few moments, we ventured on.

My mouth was bone dry by the time we reached the top, but I must tell you—the view was worth it. The city stretched out before us. Where else could one get such a view of medieval Paris? I brought out my notebook, an artisan one made by people who loved the ancient craft of making vellum, and a nubby pencil. I'd tucked them into my pocket on most days to sketch but had been ultimately too tired to on any days of our travel. It was kind of like bringing along a travel journal and only filling it out for the first day on the plane ride over.

"What is that my lady?" Thomas asked at my elbow.

My pencil. *Oh my God, how could I be so stupid?*

Jane and Ellie had not approved it, they'd given me a quill and ink, but I thought a pencil would be easier and had grabbed one out of my bag. "Ah, yes," I said, trying to act nonchalant so as not to attract any more attention to it. Crude casings for graphite had begun to be made in this century, but not to the level of finish as the typical pencils that schoolchildren use. "Um...'tis a wondrous invention that I have found on my travels. It takes away the need for ink."

"May I?" he asked, wanting to make a mark in my notebook. "And your paper, so thin, so uniform! What a high-quality product."

I nodded, gulping, as he held it up to the fading light to examine the miniature book, which even though done by hand may well have looked alien to his eye.

"I have a fine supplier," I said. "In Rennes. I will give you the name should you ever find yourself there."

"Yes, please. What a useful instrument for the artist, for letters, and documents. Rennes, how fascinating. I have visited before but never heard of such a vendor."

I knew by the time Thomas could visit Rennes I would be long gone, and he'd just have to endure a wild good chase. (As if a journey in the medieval world isn't fraught with danger and potential deprivation. At the very least—discomfort. *Where are my morals going?*) "Please don't mention it to too many people," I said. "I don't want my only supplier to have not enough for me."

"Yes, of course. The lady must be able to do her fine sketches." He bowed and turned to look at the magnificent view of the city.

I sketched a crude map of Paris from our vantage point, with the Seine flowing on either side of us, looking down to where the Eiffel Tower would be located, the *Champs Elysee*, the *Arc de Triomphe*. None of those landmarks were there, of course. The Bastille, which at this time was still a fortress, was behind us.

In modern times, the roof of Notre Dame is hemmed in by a cage to prevent jumpers, or terribly clumsy people, from falling to their deaths. But in this era, there was no such barricade. As a result, I stood farther back than the other tourists, afraid that a misstep or a shove might send me over the precipice.

"You do not like heights?" Thomas asked, raising his eyebrow.

"I do not. Scared to death, actually." I held out a shaking hand. "My sketch is not so good."

"May I see?"

I shrugged.

He pretended to admire it, with a few, "Oh, well dones," and, "I see that quite clearly." But when he came to a drawing I'd made of a man, his mouth started to twitch. "Is this... is this a *man*? And what's...that?"

I pressed my lips together, ready for the teasing to commence. "A horse."

"Oh, quite. Yes, yes, I see it now," he said, holding a finger to his lips, as if to quell the rising giggle.

I stamped my foot. "I didn't say I was any good! Why, look here, surely you can see his muzzle, his nostrils, his forelock?"

"Ohhhhhh, I thought the nostrils were eyes. Yes, that does make more sense now that I know what that is."

I started to giggle. He was trying so hard to be supportive that it was almost as hilarious as my drawing of a horse. Then he started to giggle, and finally, we both burst out into laughter, tears springing into our eyes. I snorted out loud, and then started to wheeze. I couldn't catch my breath, I was laughing so hard. Thomas bent over, slapping the roof of the cathedral.

"Oy!" called a guard. "Respect this house of worship!"

That shut down the obvious mirth; I covered my mouth, although I couldn't help but let a little laugh erupt from underneath my hands.

"Would you allow me to give it a try?" he asked, smiling, indicating my journal.

I loved this request. A 21st century man might just say, "You idiot, you're screwing it up. Let me do it."

Instead, this 16th century gentleman asked politely, "Would you allow me...?" He was not asserting his right, or his superiority, commenting on my stupidity or my ineptness, but instead offered his willingness to help.

Would you allow me? Four words that summed up the age. Ah yes, *now* I remembered why I had chosen to be here. Albert, the terrible boyfriend, would have swatted me. "Move aside, you cow." Teasing yes, but also highly barbed and painful, no matter how much you pretended to be cool, thought being called a cow was "adorable," and took it on the chin.

In this century, Thomas drew quick lines on a fresh page to

denote the streets, and then started on the buildings, the river, the boats docked, the market stalls. The sun setting from one angle. Then on another sheet, the gargoyles, or *grotesques*, that surrounded us, there to serve as spouts to drain water, and especially to protect the cathedral from evil spirits. Long necks, chests out, pointy-eared, they were sprightly creatures, ready to spring into action once their stony bodies became living flesh.

Thomas turned to me, and with a studied eye, started sketching me underneath the gargoyles on the page. Like da Vinci, he would not waste paper.

"Oh no, stop!" I said, afraid of what I would see.

He shook his head. "May I please, Lady Dreux? The sun is just right."

I'm not sure if I thought he would draw me as one of the gargoyles, or what he would do, but I knew I wasn't ready for what he saw with his own eyes, and whether that would look like some caricature, or at least be completely unflattering, with the dark circles I knew were under my eyes, the bruise fading on my forehead, my hair springing forth from my headdress, my clothes wrinkled from the long ride.

He turned the paper when he was done so I could see. Instead of capturing the embarrassed, self-conscious version of me, he'd created an image of the happy me, the one who saw the glass as half-full, even when standing on top of Notre Dame, slightly terrified of falling, but still appreciating the magnificent view that lay in every direction before us.

"Oh, Thomas. You flatter me—how lovely," I said, tears welling, this time from happiness and not from mirth. "This truly captures me the way I want to see myself. I was nervous when you started, but now...I'll treasure it." I swallowed, trying to compose myself, wiping an errant tear from my eye. "And look at this map—how brilliant. You said you were not an artist, but I see many skills at work here."

"'Tis but a map, not anything difficult. Put me in front of actual paints to try to capture silks, flowers, animals, though,

and…" He shrugged. "I fail. But for the basics, I can serve them
well. And I am happy that you like the little sketch I drew of you.
This instrument is most excellent," he said, holding up my pencil
to the fading light, twisting it. "I am unsure of how they made
this, but here—it belongs with you for safekeeping." He handed it
back to me.

At that moment a guard appeared to announce the closure of
the balcony. *"Veuillez descender les escaliers,"* he commanded. We
took a quick look around for Stafford, but he was nowhere to be
found. Lord knows where the man went, but we knew he would
find his way back.

"How well do you know Stafford?" Thomas asked, once we
got back to the ground and were standing outside the cathedral in
the gathering dusk.

"Not well at all," I said, which was true.

"Let us walk along the Seine. I think it will be safer, perhaps?"

Not in my day, I thought, but perhaps in this one? I nodded.

The river flowed downstream. There were no overpriced
tourist boats on it, offering questionable food like I was used to
seeing. Instead, it was a hive of industry: fishing, trading, cooking,
washing. Still so much activity for this late hour. Which reminded
me, I needed food, and lots of it. "I am famished!" I said.

He laughed. "I do not think that is true. You had rather a big
midday meal."

I nodded in agreement. "You're right. I'm sorry, I was being
needlessly dramatic. Something we do back in my hometown. I
simply meant *I am hungry.* Do you think the food back at the inn
will be good? What might we have tonight?"

"I do know of a place," he said, "that has an excellent lamb. It
is not too far from here, but it is not where we are staying. Would
your husband be angry if you did not eat with him?"

"My husband? He…" I thought about it a moment. According
to Graham, he was always following me, even when I thought he
was not.

"I think he knows I am safe," I said. "With you."

Indeed, he knew that Thomas likely had a thing for me, but whether or not he thought the king's curator had the ninja skills to keep bad guys away from me, well, that was another matter. Thomas did demonstrate his archery skills on the field. That did not mean he was skilled at the other martial arts, like hand-to-hand combat, or sword fighting. But he did have, like all gentlemen, a dagger at his waist.

As did I. Harry had made sure of it.

"How did you two meet?" he asked. "Was it an arranged marriage?"

I debated telling him a version of the truth, that it was very much arranged, a matter of convenience for the both of us.

"Yes, it was arranged, but I do not want to tell you more than that. If you only knew the truth of our arrangement, it would confuse you. So it is best that you do not know."

He closed his eyes, perhaps in frustration. "Please tell me that he treats you well, though, with the respect a lady like you so deserves."

I sighed. "Thomas, please don't. We promised each other we would not have this conversation again."

Just then, he gently steered me to the right. "Ah, here it is—just as I remembered."

Restaurants did not exist at this time, apart from inns. I'm not entirely sure when restaurants did become a thing; medieval studies completely engrossed my attention, but I from what little I'd read it would be at least two hundred more years before cafes and restaurants began to open up. But here, besides inns, which served weary travelers, there were market stalls. And, like the fast food stands and doner kebab places that stay open late in London after the pubs close, so too did these places serve the drinking establishment, to sop up the alcohol so it wouldn't make people sick.

"Here is the best grilled lamb in Paris," Thomas said.

Now, I am not a fan of eating baby animals, I'll say that for a start. It's cruel to cut short the life of something so young. Just cruel. I would have ordered something else, but that was the sole option on the menu.

So, we got two servings of poor baby lamb. I tried not to think too hard of all the Tik Tok videos I've watched of lambs, hurling themselves joyfully on the grass on their farms. Shear the fully grown sheep for its wool, but let's pass on the meat. Especially from the little ones.

We sat at a picnic table of sorts, next to the stall, with a dozen other folks. As we ate, I mused, as I do.

Thomas was a puzzle to me, whereas Stafford and Graham were easier to fill in. Stafford was a history and thrill-seeking junkie, able to grift in and out of this world with seemingly no ill consequences. As much as I was impressed with his ability to fit in, and his intrepidness in getting things done, he seemed interested only in himself, except for maybe a little gossip. Graham, as shady a spy as he might be, was essentially a fanboy of the time, much like me, I suppose. He fell in love with this era as a hobby and was now living it, and he too got caught up in the excitement. While I applauded his enthusiasm, I was always suspicious of those who dealt in the shadows, and could never reveal what they were truly doing. Was it for money, security, or was there some darker personality trait at work?

And Thomas. Besides the fact that he was not hard to look at—with even the simplest broad strokes of a pencil, an artist could capture his perfect symmetry—there was more to him than a pretty face. I did a quick review as he inhaled his dinner. He was intuitive, quickly garnering the fact that Graham and I were not truly bonded, and he somehow knew when Anne or anyone else in our group needed help. We shared a love for the arts, a common language, one that he'd come to naturally through his father. He sang. He sketched beautifully. He was a natural at archery. He got along easily with everyone, from a king to a serving girl who had never been outside her village. He came alive on horseback, one of my favorite things, even if the memory of his father's fall haunted him.

His father had been gone for a while now, and yet it followed him like a storm cloud that he was unable, or unwilling, to bat away. He seemed drawn to my happy-go-lucky personality, but would he, if we ever could be together, drag me underneath that cloud with him? Would I ever allow a man to do that, in the name of love and empathy? Or would I spend an unceasing amount of time trying to brighten everything for him, but in vain?

The point was moot anyway. We were just a couple of twentysomethings sharing a plate of food, in Paris, under starry skies. Not my era of study, but I could never come to France, seeing the burnt umber of the colors all around us, and the starry sky, and not think of Van Gogh.

Ah, Van Gogh and his starry skies. The most haunting and yet beautiful set of paintings of the impressionists. The man who never knew success during his lifetime, but could paint with such raw emotion, such optimism, such bold use of colors. Such sadness, and some said madness. I knew Thomas would admire his work.

"There's an artist I know," I started, "named Vincent van Gogh. He captured a night like this, with a cathedral spire looming up over the city, a moon on the right, the planet Venus in the middle, and other stars. At the time he painted it, he had an illness that he was being treated for, here." I touched my head. "While we don't know what was going on inside his thoughts, except what he put down on canvas, it's said he couldn't stop thinking thoughts that were negative, or controlling, or strange. But what he produced was magical—not realistic, but something that everyone could relate to. I wish I could show you what I'm talking about."

"Can you sketch it for me?"

I shook my head. "No, I only wish I could. But as you saw earlier on top of Notre Dame, I am no artist, just a student."

He grinned from ear to ear, remembering my horse, perhaps. "Do you like being a student?"

"Ha—that is something my mother asks me all the time. She calls me an *'etudiant professionale.'* She wonders if I will ever be properly engaged." What that probably meant to Thomas was being a housewife, and running an estate, and providing children for the lineage. But what *engaged* actually meant—to my mother—was to get a proper job. I think she'd hoped that I would be a lawyer, or a financier, or a doctor, and help lift us out of our genteel poverty. Instead, I couldn't have picked a worse profession for pay, that was clear.

I continued, "Do you ever have visions in your head that you'd like to capture for eternity?"

Thomas thought for a moment. "There is a landscape that I love—a lakeside, with trees, and a farm alongside and cows in the meadow—that gives me great peace of mind. Sometimes I go there with my imagination, and picture me sitting there, thinking of nothing else but how the grass stirs with the wind, how the clouds are moving, and the water lapping onto the land. That is when I feel the most connected with this earth and my place in it."

"Oh, that sounds lovely," I said, giving him a friendly pat on the back. "Have you ever tried to capture it?"

"No, as much time as I spent at my father's side, he was the master of the interior—the portrait. Not of the outdoors. When I've tried to paint a tree," he shook his head, "I just give up. *Quelle disaster.*"

I laughed. "As much as I love art, you've seen I can't draw people to save my life. They look like they're made from sticks. And faces—forget it! Eyes confound me, and noses? But I can draw a pretty decent tree if I want to give myself some modicum of credit. I certainly couldn't do a portrait of you as you did me today. Truly, your drawing is one of the few pieces I've seen of me that I wouldn't actually tear to shreds. It's funny how people have such a skewed idea of how they appear to other people."

"I don't even think about what I look like," Thomas said, taking a swig of his ale.

"Oh, come now. I find that hard to believe. You dress nicely, your beard is trimmed, your hair is combed and has a lovely wave to it. I'm quite sure that you've received many compliments about your handsome visage since you were a lad."

He shrugged. "Perhaps people did, back then. But since my father died, I've just gotten looks of pity, of sadness. As if they were attempting to anticipate my need for soothing because of it. It is as if I was carrying a sign on my hat that says, 'This man saw his father crushed to death,' and that's all anyone can think about. And if I do happen to let out a smile every now and again, they might think that I'm not properly mournful."

The two of us fatherless children continued to talk into the night, as the stars rose higher in the sky.

WE WERE THE only two left in the place when a man sprang one leg over the bench, then the other, right next to me, invading my space. "Hey!" I said in protest, until I saw who it was.

"I wondered where you two had gotten to," Graham said.

"My lord, I—" Thomas started.

"Oh, now don't be troubling yourself, young sir, over the fact that you and my wife have been out all night, and without Stafford, I see," he said, looking around for the negligent chaperone. "It does not look so fine, though, to the unknowing onlooker who sees a man's wife out with a younger, more handsome man, but—"

"Now, now, Graham, we are just talking as you can see," I said, glaring at him. "Need we be overdramatic?"

"Well, yes, in fact, Gabby, we must. We are talking about our reputations, and by that, our very lives."

"I am sorry, Graham. We did ask you to come out with us, but you wanted to stay at the inn. And we just needed a bite to eat and got to talking and lost track of the hour. And as for

Stafford, we lost him atop Notre Dame and never saw him again." *Insufferable man.* I pushed myself to my feet. "Shall we go now?"

"Yes, let's." Graham stood as well and gestured to the door with a sweep of his hand. I gathered myself and moved away from him.

Thomas walked with us, following a respectful six feet behind.

After about a block of this, Graham glancing back at him, stopped, and then turned to face him. "Would you mind giving me and my wife some space? I am perfectly capable of walking her back to the inn without you."

Thomas bowed. "Of course, my lord. Pray pardon the intrusion." He then walked ahead of us, and soon took a right to go another route.

"What on this good green earth has gotten into you, 007? Why are suddenly playing up the angry husband role?" I put my hand on my hips.

"The longer you two are together, the more you two will bond, or have already bonded. People who spend time identifying with each other have a more difficult time of keeping a mission central in their minds. *None* of this can be personal. We go, we get the painting, we go home, with no loves left behind, no man getting his head chopped off because he fell for a woman who ultimately does not have his best interest at heart. Wise up, your ladyship." He began walking again.

But I put a hand on his chest to stop him from proceeding. "Look, mister. If this was your fear, then why on earth did you let us leave together in the first place? In Paris—the City of Love!—of all places?"

"I admit that was a poor decision on my part. I thought an hour would be fine. And you were with that arse, Stafford. I took a wee rest but when I woke up I realized you weren't back, and set out looking for you. There are too many damned alleys and narrow streets in this place—it's like a feckin' rabbit warren.

Thank God for that bright yellow dress you're wearing, like Big Bird, right? Otherwise, I would have never found you."

"Gee whiz, Big Bird, thanks." I turned on my heels and walked away from him, as fast as I could, back to the inn. How could a night so wonderful be turning into one so insulting? It was *his* mistake, not mine. And it wasn't a mistake. It had been a perfect evening.

Until now.

"I can't believe I have to share a room with you," I said.

"I'll sleep in the barn."

"And what about your precious reputation? Would Lord Dreux ever sleep in a barn?"

"If they knew his wife, they surely would understand."

I was momentarily made mute by that insult, a real gut punch. "You, sir, are a piece of work. I rue the day that you and Ellie ever connected."

I speed-walked all the way back, left Graham outside, and climbed up the stairs to find Anne asleep in my bed with Winston. "Move over, girlie," I said, pushing her gently so she was not sprawled across the whole mattress, and then put the pillow over my head to muffle the sobs that rushed out of me. Winston circled around my head, and stretch his neck over mine, falling back into a deep sleep.

I must not have been very quiet, because I soon felt a pair of skinny arms around me, and Anne's voice said, "There, there, lady. It'll be better in the morning."

CHAPTER SEVENTEEN

I T WAS EASY to see why the French royals had chosen this breathtaking city of Amboise, on the Loire, as a place to reign the country, which they had only recently conquered as a whole. (Well, except for Calais.)

Amboise was 226 kilometers from Paris—about 140 miles, for you non-metric users on the other side of the pond—and even with my love of horse-riding, the past few days had been brutal. We rode at a breakneck pace, covering the distance in three days.

I put Winston down, and he twirled in happiness and peed at the same time, relieved in more ways than one to finally be one with the ground after a long day of being restrained. I might have joined him (at least, in the twirling part) except every bone and muscle in my body ached. As I stretched out my back, my shoulders, I realized that this journey had revealed that day riding was pleasurable, but long-distance rides could and would do a real number on your bottom as well as the rest of your body. Even my teeth hurt. Thankfully I had a lot of cloth between me and the saddle, but still, after sliding off my horse at Amboise, I wasn't entirely sure if my bum had any skin left on it at all.

We found an inn in the center of Amboise, on the bustling main street. Up on the hill, and over a rocky promenade loomed the royal castle. Da Vinci's house was less than half a mile away from there.

Our plan now that we were in Amboise was fairly loose. We did not know if we needed to visit King Francois to pay our respects, or to go straight to Da Vinci at *Le Manoir de Cloux*. Thomas had the most experience in our group with these kinds of art-buying interactions, and we had, as a group over dinner the previous night, formulated that he, along with Stafford, Graham, and I, would present ourselves as admirers of his. Thomas, being the one with personal connections through his father and his painting guild, would make the introduction.

We were all dead tired and sore, in need of medicines and creams for our aching muscles, or at least bandages for our bottoms, and as much of a bath as we could muster from a basin of water. We sipped bad red wine while picking at the skinniest roasted chickens you've ever seen, and some sad turnips. You *know* the food is bad if I'm not devouring it; this meal could have been packaged as a brilliant new weight loss program for people who've indulged in too many biscuits. Call it the *skinny chicken and turnip diet*.

But still, there was meeting da Vinci to look forward to—we hoped. From his diaries, reports from his colleagues and biographies, we knew that he got up early to work in his studio, surrounded by apprentices who would make his paints, observe, and learn from the master. Franscesco Melzi was Da Vinci's pupil and future heir.

After da Vinci spent the morning working in the studio, he then had a vegetarian midday meal, provided by his faithful cook.

Da Vinci was famously loathe to part with his paintings, never believing them finished and ready to be released into the world. But as he had—at some point during this time—been struck down by strokes and would at some point during these brief two years in France lose the use of his right hand. I had written down some quotes to help me learn how other fellow artists felt about letting go of their work. But most of them had come after da Vinci's time, so he would not have known them. In fact, he was the one who'd written the most famous quote of all regarding when a work of art is done: *Art is never finished, only abandoned.*

We were hoping that our secret knowledge of *The Three Sunnes*—or whatever he was calling it during this time—would also help serve as an entrée. And since da Vinci was known to appreciate a good-looking man, we'd hoped that Thomas asking him to buy a painting would capture his attention, along with his mission from King Henry, who was quite a stunning patron for a painter from Italy. But as he was now loyal to Francois, it was hard to know if he would respond well to an historic adversary of the French.

That's how Graham and I fit in, as private patrons. If a sale to King Henry was too politically fraught with complications, we could buy it as independent art lovers.

When our dishes were cleared, Graham said, "Tonight, let's all stick together, right?" He narrowed his eyes at Stafford, Thomas, and me, while giving little Winston a scratch on his ear as the puppy sat curled on his lap. "We can't afford to have anything happen to any one of us—we don't want gossip, we don't want mischief, we want to look like respectable folk."

We all nodded. "Of course."

Determined to rest before our big day with the Maestro, we all turned in early. By now, Graham and I had perfected the art of sharing a room without talking. Anne helped me to get undressed; with any luck I'd be in bed, pretending to be asleep, by the time he knocked. Then he let himself in the room, and arranged himself on the floor with a few pillows, or on the bed alongside me, if it was big enough.

Though really, it was never big enough.

Just hours away from meeting the great man, perhaps the most brilliant Renaissance man of all time, I couldn't sleep. Winston snored in my ear; his deep breathing (puppy-sized of course) was normally reassuring, but tonight, I found it irritating. Or maybe it was just that I'd tried not to get too attached to him, knowing we had to give him away and yet I'd already fallen in love with him, his floppy paws and ears, and his adorable long-eyelashed eyes that were almost human.

In my worries, I kept picturing scenarios wherein I screwed everything up, where we'd get thrown out of the manor house on our already-bruised bottoms. Then the mission would be over. I just didn't know how it would happen. Maybe it would be because of something I said, or because our cover story wasn't convincing, or because da Vinci had a complete disinterest in our offer. What if, when we arrived, he had a meeting with the king? Or worse, what if da Vinci had just had another—or the first!—stroke, or was truly tired, or—

I bunched up the pillow under my head, turned to one side and then the other before flopping onto my back to stare up at the ceiling. I did some deep breathing exercises, and finally, I'd started to fall asleep in some interesting half dream. Then Graham let out a snore from the floor, and my mind set to racing again. Over and over again this happened until, when the rooster crowed in the morning, my eyes were still wide open, and I lay there anticipating the sounds of the start of the day. Seconds after the birds started cheeping came sounds of people moving about in the other rooms.

I leapt out of bed, Winston following me. My eyes were scratchy and dry, still filled with dust from the road. I knew my heart was beating an extra few dozen beats per minute because there was no denying that today was going to be a monumental day in my life, and I had no intention of lying down for even a second of it.

Before Anne even opened the door to come in and ready me for the day, I was already turning the knob to let her in; her teenager's gait was well known to me now and I knew when she was galumphing down the hall.

"Out Graham," I said to the lump on the floor. "We'll be done in twenty minutes, and you can do your ablutions then."

Graham barely seemed to open his eyes, but he picked up a pillow, accepting Winston's leash from my hand, and went out in the hallway. I'm not sure whether this was a normal sight for people to see a husband thrown out of his own room while his wife got dressed, but no matter where we stayed, no one ever raised an eyebrow.

"Today's the day—I want to wear the red dress, with the blue surcoat." Just like the Virgin Mary wore in *The Annunciation*, my favorite Da Vinci painting. Maybe reflecting the colors of his Madonna would create some good feelings in his heart for me?

"Would it be a scandal, do you think, if I wore my hair down today?" I asked Anne. I'm not sure why I asked—she was no more familiar with French court etiquette than I—but she'd lived in this world her whole life.

Anne drew her lips in. "Lady Dreux, you are a *married* lady. I don't know any married ladies that wear their hair down, excepting when they sleep."

"True, true," I said. "But I brought along this hat that I think will allow for my hair to be mostly shown. I hope that the Master likes my hair color."

In doing our research, I'd found a painting of Mary Tudor, who wore her hair hanging loosely at the sides, and then tucked into a low bun, with a jaunty hat on the back of her head. Okay, yes, she was a queen of France, and therefore could wear whatever she pleased—to an extent. But I thought maybe... maybe I could get away with it? Because I thought maybe da Vinci would appreciate my effort to be different than the women I'd seen, with their hair pulled back so severely in these ugly headdresses. The Mona Lisa had her hair down, with a see-through veil covering her head. In fact the few women that he'd painted had minimal hair coverings. He preferred to show the texture of the hair, usually long and curly, in both his male and female paintings and drawings. I didn't have curly hair, but what I did have was a pretty shade of brown. I was determined. Whichever way I, or Thomas, or even Graham, or Stafford could attract his attention, we would seize the day.

I had been to *Chateau de Clos Luce* during summer holidays a few years earlier in my time. A friend had let a holiday home for two weeks nearby, and of course we'd had to stop at Amboise to visit da Vinci's home and grave. The place was filled with his inventions, which had only been sketched out on paper, but researchers and enthusiasts had built them to scale and filled the grounds with them. Children and grown-ups alike delighted in spinning a water wheel, turning an Archimedes screw, and—on a tour—seeing da Vinci's bedroom and studio.

Now, not two years later, but five hundred years *earlier*, the paying tourists were gone; still we were not the only visitors to his home as we wound our way up the drive to the manor house, Winston following us off-leash.

Compared to the other chateaux of the Loire Valley, it was a small chateau but nicely proportioned and built of pink and white bricks. Inside I knew the rooms were spacious, with high ceilings. A manservant met us at the front door, and after we asked for an audience with the famous maestro, he said, "My master is at work and does not like to be disturbed, but he will be taking his *dejeuner* at mid-day. Would you care to wait, or would you like to return another day?"

"Oh, we shall wait," I said. "Tell him that Lord and Lady Dreux have come, along with Thomas Egham, son of Walter Egham."

There was a scrambling at our feet, and I scooped our errant pup up in my arms, waving one of his fluffy, fat paws at the man. "And Winston!"

He raised an eyebrow at the dog, especially when I said, "And please tell Signore da Vinci we have a gift for him."

The older man bowed and sighed; I'm fairly sure he was thinking that if Winston was our gift for his master, it would just mean more work for him. He led us inside the great hall.

I was bursting to tell Thomas that I'd been here before, that I knew exactly where the master's studio was, where his bedroom was, his kitchen. Stafford, Graham, and I had discussed the layout of the place between the three of us, just in case. What that "just in case" was, I didn't know.

Da Vinci did not have much in the way of security, and even though one could easily walk away with even *The Mona Lisa* at the time, I had argued that we could never do that. It was a horrible thing to do to an artist—or anyone! Graham and Stafford had said they agreed with me, but I feared what they would do if we didn't get our way, or greed got the better of them.

Eventually, a serving girl brought in cups and a pitcher of wine, and we served ourselves. I could not keep still, nor could Winston, who was straining at the end of his leash, unable to bear being inside during the day.

But I couldn't bear being away from the house; the great man himself was below us at that very moment. I couldn't wait to meet him. Would he look as old as some of his self-portraits, or those sketches done by his students? Or were they exaggerated, as some had guessed, with da Vinci picturing himself in a negative way? It was hard to tell, without meeting the man; all I knew for sure that some artists try to make themselves look better, while others emphasize what they see as flaws.

He was only in his mid-sixties, which was not considered old at all in our times, with men and women that age running marathons, captaining businesses, and traveling all over the world. In fact, da Vinci himself had just crossed the Alps in order to get here too, so surely he must have been in good shape.

"I believe," said a scratchy voice coming from the doorway "that I have callers?"

We all scraped back the benches and chairs that we were sitting on to rise and see the Old Master. From what I could see, he was sharp-eyed, bearded, and wearing a floppy, somewhat ugly cap on the top of his head; he sported a long, oversized robe which flowed around his slender body, and thin, scarlet slippers that reminded me of the Prada shoes made for the Pope. He looked nothing like I expected—and yet, he was exactly every-thing I'd expected.

In short, I was overwhelmed. The moment had arrived! I was

meeting my hero, the one person who—if I could have dinner with anyone in history I would choose—Leonardo da Vinci.

Wowwww!!

I curtsied, and the men bowed. Leonardo tut-tutted that, as he stepped closer to us. "No need for such formalities. I understand we are amongst old friends? Which one of you is Egham's boy?" He then cast his eyes on Thomas, who was beaming. "Ah yes—*you*. You look like the son of a painter." His sharp, dark eyes twinkled.

I couldn't blame him for that. Thomas made my eyes twinkle too.

Thomas stepped forward to grab both of Leonardo's hands. "Master!" His voice was hoarse, as if his mouth was dry and his heart was pounding. *Oh...wait.* No, that's what I was experiencing. But then again, maybe Thomas was too.

"Dear boy, so good to meet you! I heard the sad news of your father's passing. I admired his work greatly, and although I never met him directly, I could see by the pride in your face that he was your father. His excellence shall live on in his work. And I daresay, in *you?*"

Thomas nodded, tears in his eyes. He blinked and smiled at the great man, and that's when I knew for sure he was unable to talk.

Not to be outdone, Winston emerged from under the table and hopped about on his hind legs, waving his fluffy paws in the air. "And who is this?" asked da Vinci, leaning down to greet him. Winston wiggled in doggie delight, obviously as overcome as the rest of us by this man, who had influenced and would influence so many.

Thomas said, "This is Winston, a gift from King Henry VIII of England, with his very special good wishes."

"Oh, how delightful!" said da Vinci, bending lower so Winston could lick his face.

"He is an excellent lap dog," said Thomas. "He can keep you warm and give you much amusement."

The older man smiled, eyes crinkling, perhaps both overjoyed at this new addition to his household, and making quick calculations as to how much care this lump of fur was going to need. After another moment of communion with his new companion, he straightened and said, "He is a beauty. I shall have to sketch him." He handed the leash to his servant, and asked, "Would you give him a good run and some water please?"

The servant—the same man who had greeted us at the door—took the leash and shot us a look that spoke volumes, mostly, *damn it, I knew this was going to happen, I should have told them to leave,* and he led Winston from the room.

Leonardo had once been extremely handsome, according to all contemporary accounts, but now he was stooped, prematurely aged by modern standards, felled by strokes and the inadequacy of the day's medical intervention. My eyes had lingered so long on da Vinci's face that I hadn't noticed the young man who stood behind him, except for a brief glance.

Now that my heart had stopped pounding I was able to really look at Leonardo; he had grooved lines etched into his face, showing that he smiled with his eyes, and two "elevens" between his brow, which indicated that he spent a good deal of time tinkering endlessly with projects, thoughts, and myriad details.

Now that I was breathing again, I noticed that his hair and beard were silver. His hair hung well down past his shoulder blades, and his beard extended to mid-chest. Though its length would put some hipsters to shame—or at least, into a state of beard-envy—the hair around his mouth and chin was slightly stained with a hint of purple, perhaps from red wine. His fingers were long, stained with ink and black paint, like the backgrounds of *The Mona Lisa* and *St. John the Baptist.*

Thomas couldn't stand still; surely thrilled to be around another great painter like his father, he fidgeted like a boy, especially when Leonardo asked him, "May I examine your face? Please, come sit over here. Extraordinary."

He sat Thomas down by an armchair near a window so he

could see him better, holding his face lightly between his two hands, running his finger down his nose. "The straight lines on your face, a triangular profile with the chin… Excellent planes. But such a dark, sad look in your eyes."

"That's what I've said!" I said, unable to contain myself. I was fangirling so hard, I sounded like a pre-teen meeting her favorite member of her favorite boy band. *Calm down, Gabby. Deep breaths.*

Leonardo looked at me, nonplussed. "Oh! *Bonjour, madame.* Pardon me for not saying hello, I was so distracted by seeing Thomas."

Of course, he was. *Who wouldn't be?* I curtsied again. Thomas distracted me all the time too.

Thomas—as usual, bless him—came to my rescue. "Allow me to introduce the Lady Gabriella, from Rennes," he said with a smile.

Now Leonardo was peering into *my* face. Oh no! I wondered what he saw and experienced a moment of panic. I shouldn't have worried, however. "My dear, would you mind? Putting your face close to Thomas's?"

Would I mind? Does an elephant have a trunk? Does a witch wear a pointy hat? Do I fall to pieces when I see a puppy?

"Of course!" I said. At least, I think that's what I said. I was kind of having an out-of-body experience at that moment; I'm pretty sure most of what I observed was done from a corner of the ceiling while my body stayed numb and not functioning properly, below.

I do know that Thomas half-arose to give me his seat, and that I put my hand on his shoulder. "Stay, you need a moment's rest." (Why? I have no idea. It just seemed like the right thing to say.) I leant my face down to be close to his.

Leonardo clapped his thin hands together and a delighted expression crossed his face. "*Bella, bello!* The dark is with Thomas, and you, Lady Gabriella, you are the light, the *bella luna.* Your face—it beams like the moon, shining light upon the darkness. Oh, you two make me wish I could draw or paint again, but my eyesight is not that good, my hands, not that strong." He looked frail just then and just like that his energy and body appeared to deflate, so that Thomas immediately got up so the elderly da Vinci could sink down into the chair.

"You like to draw contrasts," I said then. (Apparently and unexpectedly, my mind began working again.) "Young and old, the pure and the worldly."

The artist nodded. "How does an Englishwoman know this?"

"Your reputation goes far and wide, and I am certain it will transcend the ages," I asserted.

"Oh, I *do* like you. You have just the energy I need around me." He turned to the young man then and held out his hand. "May I present to you my son, Melzi? He is not of my own blood, but he *is* a son to me, and I entrust him with my whole world."

We all bowed to the young man, slim, dark-haired, and elegant. He returned our bows, elegantly, of course.

"How may I address you," I said, turning back to da Vinci, "Maestro, or Master, or Signor da Vinci?"

"The people around me call me *Maestro* now, which of course is a great honor."

"My name is Lady Gabriella Dreux, and this is my husband, Lord Dreux, and a friend of ours, John Stafford, a writer."

Stafford bowed.

"And what do you write?" da Vinci asked Stafford.

With a deference he bestowed only to the rich and powerful, in my observations of him anyway, he answered, "Adventure stories. At least, I used to. I am far too busy traveling now, alas."

Alas my ass, I thought. I addressed the great man once more. "I have seen your work when I traveled in Italy, particularly *The Annunciation*," I said. "Signore...Maestro. I cannot tell you what an honor it is to meet you. We have so wanted to visit and pay our respects." Tears began to well in my eyes, and my hand trembled when he reached out to me and clasped my fingers in his. Then he did me the honor of bowing over my hand to give it a kiss. *Swoon.*

"Dear Lady, *Bella Dame*. What a beautiful smile it is that you have. *Enchante*," he said. "Perhaps you would like to look at my studio after we enjoy a quick luncheon? My cook did not know that you were coming, but there is enough bread and cheese, and some…?" He looked at Melzi, who shrugged. "Ah, well, we shall find out when we get *dans le chambre*."

"Now, friends," said Melzi, "let us go in to eat."

Da Vinci, who hadn't released my hand (would I ever wash it again?) peered up at me from his seat and said, "Will you accompany this old man? You know we need all the support we can get!"

"It is my distinct honor," I said, helping him to stand. As we began to leave the hall, I noticed that he needed to lean on me a little, and he favored one leg over the other. Would this have been why he reportedly did not complete much work during this time? Instead, his time was spent planning the castle town for King Francois, which—as it turns out—would never be built because of fears over the health of the air around the city.

I had to remember that I did not know the way and let Leonardo lead me to the dining room. Like all the rooms in the chateau, it was brick-lined, with a few tapestries hanging on the walls for both insulation and decoration. On one side of the room, three tall windows overlooked the ornamental gardens and in the center a long dining table was set for a generous meal, although, upon da Vinci's orders, he told us, there were to be no meats served. "All living creatures can feel, and it is cruel that we eat them."

Again, future hipsters would cheer. Of course, I already knew that Leonardo was a vegetarian, a dietary choice unusual in an era and in cultures whose meals featured mostly meats. I'd read that Leonardo had a soft heart for the creatures of the world. He freed birds if he saw them in the markets, buying them, and then letting them go.

"These grow in my garden here." Leonardo gestured to the table. "Beets, *courgettes, aubergine, patate*. The cheeses are made locally, and the eggs are produced by our own chickens, of course. My cook does such a wonderful job—I am lucky to have the gift of this place. It is by far the most comfortable I have ever been, and for an old man, it is good to have comfort. Please, sit. Let us enjoy this repast."

We settled at the table. Because I'd helped the elderly genius into the room, I was able to sit in the chair closest to him and I hurriedly took my seat so he could sit as well; he wouldn't drop into a chair as I knew he wished to until I was sitting. Ah, chivalry. It was a blessing, and yet, a curse.

Once we were seated, he continued, "As you can see, the fireplaces here are enormous, to keep my bones and hands warm. There is little worse than being cold. Is that not true, Lady Dreux?"

I concurred, and with that we immediately set to talking over issues mundane, like the weather and drafts, which then led into issues slightly more controversial, like education for children, land wars, and then—finally—Italian artists up to that present day, like Bellini, and my favorite Botticelli, who painted *The Birth of Venus*. I told Leonard I preferred *Primavera* or *Fortitude*. We moved on to the sculptures of Donatello, like the lithe, adolescent David, or the absolutely downtrodden Mary Magdalena, which I was unable to tell him was so stark, I considered it almost modern in its bleak attitude.

The food was delightful, not overcooked, but one of the vegetables got stuck in the space between the veneers and my real teeth, and when I couldn't stand it anymore and thought no one was looking, I quickly snapped them off with a flick of my fingers, ran my tongue over the errant piece of food, and clamped them shut again.

When I turned back to da Vinci, I couldn't tell whether he was looking at me, or just past me, but his eyes were a little unfocused. He surely hadn't caught me flicking my veneers because I'd become such a ninja with my subtlety, nobody ever noticed. *Maybe he's just tired*, I thought.

Thomas interjected when he could, but when da Vinci asked him about his opinions on these artists, including his arch-rival Michelangelo, he did not have much to say. "I am afraid I have not traveled as much as I would have liked to in my youth. My father was exceedingly busy in the British Isles, making occasional visits to France, but since I have gotten to know Lady Dreux, and with my new commission from King Henry VIII, I am excited to travel to the Italian states."

"Excellent, excellent. Yes, let the news of the Italian Renaissance spread far and wide. I shall write for you letters of introduction to get you into the studios of artists that I recommend."

Thomas beamed.

"Speaking of Henry VIII..." I decided it was time to start the conversation about why we were really visiting da Vinci. You know, "the mission" and all that. I even shot Graham a glance to let him know it was "go" time. "You must know that he is very interested in preserving our nation's history and bringing to light great moments from our past. And we have heard a rumor," I said, lowering my voice and leaning closer to the maestro's ear, "that you might have a painting capturing such a great moment in England's history. That you were interested in the phenomena known as the *sun dogs*, or *sun angel*, or *parhelion*?"

He looked at me, his eyes growing even more curious. "How did you know of this? I have put that work away until I can understand the phenomenon better. I am particularly fascinated by water, and I believe the crystals in the water, when frozen, have something to do with it..."

"Yes! You are right." I held a finger to my lips. "Although some, including our king, like to think that it is a sign from God."

Da Vinci shrugged. "I equate nature with God's work in all its ingenuity. And speaking of which, would you like to see my beautiful gardens?"

"I would love to," I answered, but was unwilling to allow the subject to drop. Not yet. If Leonardo didn't agree to letting us buy the painting, the past few weeks and all the preparation would be for nothing. "But please think about what I said about my king's desire for anything to do with the three suns."

"I shall think on it, but as young Thomas is the king's emissary on the matter, I shall consult with him."

"I have complete faith in Thomas," I said.

And we strolled out to the gardens.

CHAPTER EIGHTEEN

I T WAS ALL going so terribly well. You know, that kind of wonderful where you're looking over each shoulder to watch out for the truck that's going to hit you to smash all your plans into pieces.

We had made plans to check back in with Maestro da Vinci the very next day. Thomas told us that while on the studio tour, he had taken da Vinci aside and negotiated a good price for *The Three Sunnes* that would please King Henry (using not quite all the funds he had advanced) and yet befitted da Vinci's genius. "I am but an old man, and have little to indulge myself with, but it shall greatly help my Melzi so that he does not have to work so hard as his papa has."

The rub? Nobody had actually laid eyes on this painting. I would have felt so much better if we could see it, if I could connect the dots between what I imagined in my dream with what was da Vinci's true work. But the maestro said that he had it in storage, rolled up, along with some other paintings and notebooks that he had yet to "air out" after his long journey through the alps to get to France last fall. He needed a day.

Oddly enough, "the downfall," (that truck) came with an invitation to a ball at the palace. Apparently after we had left the manor house, King Francois had come to visit Leonardo, as was his wont after having finished his daily duties as head of state. No doubt Francois was told of the visitors from England who bore a gift from their king and wanted to question them. I hoped that da Vinci had kept his lips sealed about the reason for our visit—to buy a painting for Henry—his arch-rival. No doubt Francois would like to keep da Vinci's work close, as his patron.

So, a message arrived at our inn inviting us to the ball that very night, with two hours to spare.

Graham had grown increasingly petulant, and as we dressed for the party, his cheeks appeared flushed. "Are you feeling okay?" I asked. "You're even crankier than is normal for you."

"What does 'okay' mean?" asked Anne. She shook out my dress.

"It's just short for feeling well," I said. "Something we say at home."

"I shall never get used to your odd way of speaking." Anne shook her head.

She was busy lacing me into yet another garment on top of the others, so I could not move. "Come over here, husband. Let me feel your head."

Graham shuffled over. I will reiterate shuffle, as Graham nearly always strode everywhere, with great purpose. But not tonight. Laying the backs of my fingers across his large forehead, I startled, pulling my hand back quickly. "Egads!" I said. "You could fry an egg on that—you are burning up!"

The man then fell into bed. "I thought so," he said. "I just want to sleep. If only I could get these clothes off." Together, Anne and I got his outer layers off, which were wringing wet as we got closer to the large undershirt that made up the final layer. It resembled a nightgown and was a garment worn by both men and women. In this moment, Graham looked a little bit like Scrooge in his long nightshirt when he was awakened during the night by the three ghosts and taken through time all over England.

"I'm freezing!" he moaned, grabbing for a blanket.

"Ugh," I said. "Man flu. These men are such babies when it

comes to falling ill."

"I don't know, my lady, it could be some bad humors," Anne cautioned me, putting a finger to her lips.

"Bad humors, you've got that right. Why don't you go fetch my lord some wine to drink, and we'll finish getting me dressed in a minute."

As soon as she left the room, I dug around in my secret hiding place, the bag I attached to my clothes every day (more pins!), where I kept money, some emergency medicine, and one other thing to help keep us safe if need be. Here, acetaminophen would be just what the doctor ordered to bring down his fever. "Here Graham, take these," I said, giving him a bit of water that we had not yet poured into the basin so we could wash our faces and hands. Surely the water would not do him any harm if it was just a sip, right? He needed to get the pills down before Anne came back.

I propped Graham up far enough so he could swallow just enough water to accompany the pills, and then he collapsed again. I levered his head up enough to slip a pillow underneath and pulled another blanket on top of the first one. His teeth chattered.

When Anne came back in, Stafford was with her. "Not dressed yet? Oh, good Lord!" He stopped in the doorway. "Whatever happened to Graham?"

"He's ill; I'm thinking I should stay home from the party. We can't leave him like this," I said.

"No, lady," said Anne. "You look far too pretty to stay at home. I'll look after him."

"Errr," I said, not so sure I felt comfortable with the entire situation.

"Lady Dreux, we need you tonight," Stafford said. "We can't let this deal fall through. Your absence would be taken as a dishonor on da Vinci, and especially his number one patron—the king. I hate to admit this, but it is you and Thomas who have won the man over this time—not me. I know words, but you know art..."

I corrected him. "I know both, actually." I held my head up higher. But he was right. I had to go. "Okay, Anne, let's finish the laces. Stafford, I hope you're not going to disappear as soon as we arrive at the ball."

"I will likely disappear," he said, a glimmer in his eye, "but not before I see you through a potential meeting with the king."

I pursed my lips together—I didn't like the look of that glimmer. But I quickly became reoccupied with attending to Graham to make him more comfortable.

IT'S BEEN SAID that my sorely missed second cousin twice removed, Queen Elizabeth II, with all of her royal palaces, the crown jewels, her personal fortune, her real estate holdings in London, and her artwork, used throw some pretty spectacular parties. But because the press endlessly detailed every penny that she spent for the state-run parties, frugality was the order of the day. Of course, things looked impressive in the grand rooms with the beautiful paintings, the china, the silver, the flowers, and the staff in their finest livery, but you might have noticed the nicks on the walls that need painting, the faded upholstery, and the very small band.

But back in the 1500's, the press had yet to gain a foothold in society, and the outcry over "Let them eat cake" would not come for another 250 years. So, if you were the king of the realm in France, you could throw some pretty epic parties using as much of your vast wealth as you desired. For this reason, Francois's ball was by far the most elaborate, fanciful party that I had ever been to.

Rows and rows of torches lined the drive up the steep hill to the castle which was a much grander one than I had seen in 2022, as little of the structure remains standing in our time. Just like

Wodesley Castle. Because these grand palaces—as any footballer knows who has overspent on real estate and then gets an injury that permanently ends his playing career—are damned expensive to upkeep. Fads come and go: one day it's granite countertops, and the next day it's quartz or marble. One day it's a jacuzzi tub and glass tiles, and the next, it's a free-standing tub and vanities. Imagine that on when you have a hundred rooms, with all those windows, fireplaces and chimneys, and then deciding to retro-fit the bathrooms and toilets and plumbing and electricity. And while obviously a constitutional monarchy is far more just—even as flawed as ours is—if you ever want to experience a real party, go back in time and party like it's 1517.

Swans floated in fountains. Exotic animals roamed on leashes. Banners hung from the rooftops and fluttered down to the ground. Three different orchestras played on various stages spread throughout the grounds. And while the weather could not have been better for such an event—cool but not cold—there were bonfires to keep you warm if you wished, or beautifully woven silken shawls you could use if you were cold.

Meanwhile, servers wandered about with trays full of food. There were buffets as well, and you could eat at one of the smaller tables set amongst the elaborate French gardens—so much more manicured with their conical bushes and trees, and their geometrically-shaped gravel paths raked into ornamental patterns. They were an art form unto themselves. Even now, Mummy says that she prefers English gardens because we luxuriate in the plants themselves, allowing them to grow wild and according to their nature, whereas the French want to tame them.

Here, Stafford stuck close to me and Thomas because the treasure was within our grasp; we circulated together, on the hunt for da Vinci. I feared an interrogation by Francois, or on behalf of Francois, but surely he must have been used to having his artist propositioned several times a month, or even weekly by this point. I'm sure da Vinci must have told Francois about our proposal as he would want to do nothing to endanger his relationship with his best-ever patron.

A crowd had gathered nearby. "Let's go see what they're looking at," I suggested. And my instincts were right. Just like the monarch gets mobbed during the summer garden party receptions on the lawn at Buckingham Palace when they let in seemingly thousands of people (I got to go once with my mother, but as minor royals, nobody would recognize us or care if they did meet us), the crowd, all patiently lined up behind cordoned off areas, all lean in to see the monarch. Francois dressed in bright colors, a beautiful peacock blue, that not many men of today's generation would be bold enough to wear. However, if you want to get noticed, you go for it.

Plus, Francois was as tall and handsome as Henry—and possibly taller. This made him extraordinarily tall for this era.

The crowd was eating up whatever it was that Francois was remarking on. People, it seems, are so much more of a wit when they are famous and powerful.

Leonardo was standing next to him, much smaller and so frail, leaning on a cane. He met eyes with Thomas, and a big smile came over his face. Winston the puppy stood beside the king and da Vinci, tinkling on the ground when he noticed us. Oh, I'd missed the little laddie! I went into full doggie-mom mode, crouching down, putting on my puppy-mom voice, and saying "Winston!" not caring what anyone else thought of me. The dog broke away from Leonardo's grip, and came running, leash and all, toward me.

The crowd laughed again as I swept the dog up into my arms and was promptly covered in kisses.

"I assume that it is you, madame, who gifted this beautiful dog to our Maestro?" Francois asked.

I curtsied, "Yes, Your Majesty. It was my great honor. Or rather, the honor of Thomas of Egham here." I did not want to mention Henry's involvement, lest that put him into a foul mood. "I have long been an admirer of Maestro da Vinci. And thank you so much for inviting us to your party. It is truly the most magnificent one I have ever attended."

"But of course!" He managed to appear proud and deferential all at once.

Leonardo made the introductions as a woman, surely young Queen Claude—a legend in her own right for her work reforming the church in years to come—approached the crowd, limping somewhat. I knew this was from a deformity of her hips; something that could have been fixed in our modern era, but a difficulty for her whole life. She was petite, dressed in a dazzling, gold brocade dress, with a tiara of diamonds, emeralds, and opals on top of her beautiful brown hair, and wearing cape of emerald and white around her shoulders. As it was said that Francois was a notorious hunter of deer and women, she was the victim of an unfaithful husband, just like Katherine of Aragon and probably most other queens.

Ugh.

I curtsied this time. "Your Majesty," I said. She held her arms outstretched, and I handed her the dog.

"He's so soft! Are you sure there is only one dog that you have brought?"

"I fear so, but if I had known that you loved dogs I would have brought one for you as well, Your Majesty. My humble apologies."

"I understand from the Maestro that you are most learned in art, so I do hope we shall a chance to talk about your travels. It is rare to meet a woman who has had so much education," she said.

"It would be my greatest honor."

"But I fear, for now, I must make sure that our guests are happy." She nodded to us all, handed the puppy back to Leonardo, and swept her husband away as well.

I blew out an internal sigh of relief. No bargaining, no arguing about a sale. Perhaps they did not know.

"I have a light show to attend to," said Leonardo. "Would you find Melzi and give him my little pup?" he asked us. "I'm sure he can find a servant to take him back home. I just wanted to wear him out a little before bed. It is quite a challenge for someone of my age to have a young pup, although he does give me great joy and for that, I thank you. Please, enjoy, have fun, and I look forward to seeing you in the morning to show you your art. I do hope you will be pleased with it. I do wish I could work on it some more, but..." He held up his shaky hands.

Leonardo turned away, his admirers following in his footsteps.

"Sooo—" I said. I put two thumbs up to Thomas and Stafford. Stafford smiled at this, whereas Thomas looked confused. "I guess Francois isn't going to interfere in our buying the work? Or maybe da Vinci didn't even tell him. Anyway, this has all gone really well! Looks like we're in the clear! But I'm feeling guilty. I wonder if we shouldn't get back to my husband," I said to Thomas and Stafford. "Now that we have fulfilled our duties."

"All except one," Stafford said, pointing to the dog, currently lying on his back with his stomach in the air, waiting for a belly rub.

"Would you mind?" I asked him. "Besides I have a feeling you'd like any excuse to stay."

"I don't need an excuse," Stafford said. "I'm not married."

I smirked. "Well," I said, "enjoy not being a woman who has to get married for her own survival."

Thomas furrowed his eyebrows at my comment. But Stafford merely doffed his hat and took off with Winston trotting alongside him.

"Bye, puppy!" I said.

"What do you mean, Lady Dreux," asked Thomas, concern on his face, "about 'having to get married for your survival'? Were you in danger before, or are you in danger now?"

I bit my lip. *How to explain my predicament about being a time-traveling single woman, without revealing that I'm a time-traveling single woman?*

"It is hard to explain. But I love to travel, and in order for me to travel, it became necessary for me to marry. Graham volunteered, more or less. He helps me with protection and my freedom, while I help him with my knowledge and abilities to..."

How to say this without being arrogant?

"—make people happy, perhaps? I have more smooth edges, whereas Graham can have a lot of sharp and rough angles."

"So," Thomas said, "yours is not a love match, but a matter of mutual convenience."

"I'm afraid so, yes."

"And are you happy with your arrangement?" he asked, as we started walking away from the party.

"Well, I'm very happy I'm here right now, with you! Seeing these incredible sights. Leeds Castle, Dover, Paris, and now Amboise. I mean, this is a fair old difference from my life spent reading books, immersed in my studies. And I've met two monarchs, one of the world's greatest ever painters, I'm at a royal ball..."

"But do you *miss* anything?"

"Come on, Thomas. Try not to bring my spirits down. Am I happy that we have to go back to check on Graham and leave this magical evening? No. Am I happy that I have to share a room with the man who snores, and is generally unpleasant? No. But, as they say, '*C'est la vie.*' Such is the lot of many women."

"Perhaps you'll be happier with Graham once you have children together," Thomas concluded. We began navigating our way back down the hill.

I couldn't help but snort out a laugh. "That is definitely not going to happen with him!"

His eyebrows knit together. "Are you... barren?" he whispered, looking discretely around. "Please forgive my indiscretion. It is none of my business, really."

I resisted the urge to snort. "No, I mean Graham and I will *never* have 'marital relations.' Never ever never."

"What does your husband think of this?" Thomas's eyes grew round.

"He's happy with it. He's not interested in me in that way. And *I* am not interested in him."

Thomas voice went even quieter. "Do I take it that you mean, and please pardon my extreme indelicacy, that you have never consummated your marriage?"

I nodded. It was an indelicate question, *yes*, but I wanted to be straight with him, and perhaps make him feel less guilty about our kiss in Dover. "We have, neither of us, attraction for the other, or desire to have a family with each other. I hope that you do not think terribly of me. I *do* believe in romantic love, but I had a chance for an adventure, and I took it. And so, I remain stuck with Graham."

He looked up at the sky, the moon full and shining its magical light down on us. "It is too bad that I was not there when you were called to adventure, Lady Dreux. I should very much have liked to have been a true husband to you. Not in name only."

Heat poured through every inch of my body when I realized what he was saying. "Oh wow—I would...*you* would have been the most—" my throat caught—"wonderful husband, truly. And one that I would have desired, not just to be my protector, but to be a companion, to love. I'm quite sure I could never ever tire of you, Thomas."

We were nearing the inn, with no one else around. He paused. "Please," he said. "Please, just for one night, for just one hour, can we pretend that it is you and I who are married? You were called to adventure once, yes, and took it? Why not be called to love?" He breathed these last few words into my ear.

Goosebumps went up and down every inch of me. My breath came in short gasps, and I could hear the pounding of my heart in my ears and beating up against my cinched in dress.

I knew I would never find a man like him again, so good, so decent, so interesting, so very handsome. It was torture.

My fingers were now in his hair, pulling him closer to my face. "I need to think this through," I said.

"You need to stop thinking and start doing," he said, putting his lips on my neck and nibbling my throat, and down, to where Anne had laced me so tightly no pair of lips could venture past a certain...

Unless you loosen the laces.

It was done, and now my brain was signed up for the next round of addiction, my heart had gone off into a complete flutter, and the rest of my body could have fueled the next space launch.

"I don't want you to stop, but let's not do *that* here," I said.

He moved his hands away from the back of my dress, and the front of my dress, and led me inside the inn. We quietly and cautiously made our way up the wildly squeaking staircase, loud enough to wake the dead, and tip-toed our way down the hall, trying not to giggle like teenagers at the ridiculousness of our situation, the sheer danger of our undertaking.

Hopefully Graham and Anne were exhausted from dealing with Graham's fever and aches and pains and were sound asleep. Stafford likely wouldn't be back for hours, and fortunately, the rest of the men in our party couldn't get rooms at the inn and were in a less "swanky" place.

Thomas retrieved the key tucked inside his jacket and creaked the door open. Moonlight streamed in from the window opening, the shutters slightly ajar. I almost hoped there was something within that would make me turn on my heels and walk out the door. Maybe a messy room, or a pile of trash with mice nibbling at it. Or rats! Something to cool the heat and be a wake-up call, a red flag, a warning. Instead, I found the opposite.

On the center of his still-made bed, lay a carved toy—a mini knight, complete with armor, helmet, sheathed sword, and boots.

I was suddenly shy in his room, not sure I was ready to take this step, and delayed. "Whatever is this?"

"That," Thomas said, "is Sir Gawain. My favorite knight from the round table."

"May I?" I reached for it, then withdrew my hand. It didn't seem right to touch it without his permission. Even if it was only a toy, it was his, and obviously held some special significance to him. Otherwise, why would he travel with it, remove it from his baggage, and set it on the bed?

"Of course," he said, picked it up carefully as though it was a great treasure, and turned it over to me. "My father carved it for me when I was just a small boy. It may seem silly, but I like to carry it with me on my travels, for good luck. I like to think my father carved him to keep me safe."

"What a special piece. I love that you love it. It appears to be working. Except for this strange woman you have in your room. I fear I am not keeping you safe at all."

Thomas held up Sir Gawain to look me up and down, and then held him up to his ear. It was really quite endearing seeing him act like a little boy, although I hoped it didn't stretch any farther than this…

"He says, 'She is lovely.' And so you are." He put the toy back down, this time on the nightstand, face down.

Once it was clear that we had consent from both parties, we managed to leave the 16th century code of behavior at the door. He pressed himself against me, and my hands naturally went around his waist, up and down his back, feeling the corded muscles underneath my fingers.

"Gabby," he said, "I have wanted to be with you, alone, ever since I saw you being so kind to that man at Wodeley Castle."

"William? Well, he was in a difficult position, I had to—"

"No, you didn't *have* to; not many in your position would. But you did. And that means your pretty face matches your beautiful heart."

The heat rose even higher in my face.

Although it looks romantic in films to go up on your tippy toes to kiss someone taller, I am here to attest that the strain on your toes does you absolutely no good in the long run, and eventually, either he has to arch himself downward risking a back strain, or you are like a ballerina and your calf muscles go out.

The glorious reality is that when kissing another at the same height, we match, and meld. I pulled him closer to me, and he pressed against me. There was no dimming of the lights because there were no lamps lit. Normally shy, knowing this might be our one and only time together, I asked, "Will you help me undress?"

I wanted us to be slow, deliberate, not rush. And the best way to slow down was to go through the laborious process of unlacing and untying everything on me. And him.

"I've been wanting to know what you looked like, underneath those clothes," he said, kissing the base of my neck, and then twirling me around so that he could have at the laces on my back. "I've had many sleepless nights imagining you." With each tug on my laces, I could breathe more, but I also became more breathless, as one of his hands did the unlacing, and another hand wandered, up and down my thigh, my belly, my...

"Ohhh," I said, leaning into him. "Yes."

"This one's done," he said, pulling away my outer dress. When he removed my sleeves, he ran kisses up the bare flesh of my arms, and when he pulled off my stomacher and farthingale, leaving me only in my kirtle and stockings, he pulled the material tight against my flesh, to see my true shape, all my curves straining against the thin fabric. "There you are. Now, these stockings no longer belong here, do they?"

He sank down to his knees. I am telling you now—there is no more glorious sight than a man down on his knees to assist you in any way that you need. Thomas's talented fingers slid up my legs and caressed the backs of my thighs as he reached for my garters, his breath puffing hot against my stomach... and with a simple movement, my stockings were released, and he pulled the one, and then the other off, running his hands up and down my bare legs.

I pulled my shift off slowly as he watched.

"You are magnificent," he whispered, voice ragged.

"Now it's your turn," I said.

When Thomas was stark naked, including the untying of his own stockings, I stepped back to have a look. "Stand there, in the moonlight," I said. "I want to remember this. Turn." The light came in from the curtain behind him, illuminating the outlines of his body, his muscled arms and shoulders, his strong chest and back, his flat stomach. A medieval lifestyle worked so very well for him. And for me, I thought, as heat spread throughout my body in anticipation.

His desire for me was clear. With the moon still casting its magical glow, bathing our limbs in the soft, silvery white, we both gave in, crashing together with pent-up tension, our tongues and limbs entangling, gently fell together onto the bed.

MUCH LATER, WHEN the moon was descending in the sky, I gave him one last kiss before I snuck out of Thomas's bedroom. When I opened the door of my room it was a painful snap back to reality. Anne was curled up on the floor on a blanket, and Graham was buried on the bed, underneath a pile of covers. I put a hand on his head; his fever had broken. He had either built up a super amount of immunity from his years spent as 007, was super lucky, or Anne was the best nurse ever. Or maybe it was a combination thereof.

I honestly had no desire to crawl into bed with another man, especially one who had been ill. Instead, I opened the window to stare at the moon; eventually I curled up on the floor with my cloak and a pillow. Anne inched herself closer to me, not quite snuggling, but hopefully getting comfort—if not warmth—from my presence.

I could not sleep, reliving every second of my evening with Thomas. I did not want to forget a thing and I promised myself I never would.

CHAPTER NINETEEN

NOT LONG AFTER sunrise, Anne was brushing my hair when there was a knock at the door.

"Come in!" I sat up straighter, hoping it was Thomas.

Would the cold light of day, and the dark circles likely under my eyes, dampen his enthusiasm for me?

To my disappointment it was Stafford, still dressed in last night's clothing. He was breathing fast, and there was the sheen of sweat on his forehead.

"What's happened to you?" I asked.

"Ummm, nothing. Just—have you gotten any inquiries for you, for me? Graham? Thomas?"

"No," I narrowed my eyes. "From whom would we have inquiries?"

He shrugged. He couldn't even look at me; instead, his gaze darted about the room. "Nothing, no reason."

Sneaky man. I wasn't giving up that easy. "Why are you still dressed in your finery from last night? And why so sweaty—have you been running?"

"My dear Gabriella, didn't we have a discussion about my policy on meeting beautiful ladies and then leaving them?" He winked. "Now I shall change, wash, and we'll be off to the Maestro's house."

Ah. Yes, *that* sounded like him. He excused himself and left.

I heard a grumble from across the room. Graham, still in his sick bed but looking healthier, said, "I don't trust that man. What happened last night?"

I explained how we'd had a good meeting with the king, the queen, Da Vinci, and that the last we saw of Stafford, he was taking Winston away to give him to somebody from Da Vinci's house. "Why—what do you suspect him of?" I asked.

"He could be just dallying around with some gal, but you know him and collecting artifacts. Seems to me the biggest prize of all would be a da Vinci, if I had his mind for treasure-hunting and stealing. It's just begging to be pilfered. He's already staked the place out, knows the entries and exit points. And he arrived here looking all guilty."

He was right. I gasped. "You don't think he—"

Graham held up a hand for me to wait and raised himself to standing. He wobbled a bit, then seemed to regain his steadiness. "I should be all right to go. But before we head to da Vinci's house I want to question that man."

And there was my answer. Anne finished up with me and started helping Graham. I went to find Thomas, who was already downstairs, trying to rustle up some breakfast.

There's not a lot that Tudor era clothing does for a man's body, except to accentuate his shoulders and his legs; however, I could get past the poufy shorts and the slightly sagging tights when I knew what I'd see when he turned around.

Those eyes.

"Hi," I said, more of a squeak, and less of a seductress than I wanted.

His face broke into a smile. "Lady Dreux," he said. The way he pronounced my name sounded like a love song. *Please put that on repeat.* "I don't know what to say to you, now that..." he paused, looking for the right words to speak in public. "Now that I've seen you in a different light."

I was desperate to hurl myself into his arms again. Damn these stupid restraints holding us back, this ridiculous tale of me being married, these absurd conventions! The 16th century, as wonderful as the manners might be, definitely had serious drawbacks for love, for women, for, well… everything.

I took a calming breath in. "I, too, have the same nerves. I honestly do not know what to do with myself anymore. I can't…" I was about to say, "keep up with this facade," when Stafford rushed down the stairs, cheeks flushed, traveling bags in hand.

"You two ready? Where are Graham? And Anne?"

"Isn't it premature to be packing up already?" I asked. "We still have business at da Vinci's."

"I thought we could leave from there," he said. "Thomas, are your lads ready to go? We'll have some precious cargo—we can't let anyone get close to our things."

"Of course," Thomas said. "They know the plans." He looked almost as suspiciously at Stafford as Graham had. I couldn't blame him.

"I'll go wait outside, then." Stafford strode out the door, one bag over his shoulder, the other tucked under his arm.

"He's usually the last one ready to go," Thomas said, eyes narrowing on the door where Stafford had just exited. "Perhaps the crows got him up early."

"I don't think he ever went to sleep." I explained about how Stafford had burst in earlier still in his fancy clothes.

"Hmmm. Can we trust this man? What do you really know about him?" he asked.

"I don't honestly know him that well. But from what I've been told, his reputation is mixed. He's both brilliant, and a bit of a cad. Graham is as suspicious as you with his behavior."

A server brought out bread, cheese, and *oh, thank God*, some fried ham. Yum. I needed some sustenance after last night's, er, activities. The rest of our party joined us (minus Stafford, of course; perhaps he hid in the shadows, or the barn, or *someplace*?). Soon we were all on our way, including Hugh, Edward, and Robert, this time riding along to accompany us for security purposes. We needed to protect this painting at all costs.

Graham, Thomas, Stafford, and I knocked at the front door to Le Cloux. Stafford stood in back, pacing. Minutes passed, us standing there awkwardly, shuffling our feet, waiting for the door to open. "Do you think everything is all right?" I asked the group. I got shrugs in response.

Finally, the maid pulled the door open, out of breath. "Yes?"

"I am so sorry to bother you, but we have an appointment with Maestro da Vinci?" Graham asked.

"I am afraid he has taken to his bed, my lord. We had a robbery last night."

"A robbery—oh no!" I said.

I turned to Stafford, my fears growing.

The maid ushered us into the foyer to wait. "I'll go fetch Melzi."

"Did you do something Stafford," I asked, hissing in his ear.

Graham seized him by the back of his coat. "Did you jeopardize us all? This mission?"

"Of course not," Stafford said, shrugging us off. "We're all here for the same thing."

Melzi came running in shortly after, glaring at the lot of us. Then he pointed an ink-stained finger at each one of us as he declared, "*You* have done the Maestro a most evil deed! How dare you!"

"What?" Thomas said, shocked. "I've heard there was a robbery, but we have nothing to do with it. We came here to buy art, not steal it. We are prepared to pay handsomely." He indicated his bag of money.

"The maestro would not dream of selling any art to you now. Get out!" He pointed to the door.

Little Winston came out, barking at us. "Winston," I leaned down to pet his sweet head, but he growled and scurried out of my reach; it was like he was already turned against us.

Melzi picked up the dog and nudged me. "Please leave!" he said, tears in his eyes, his voice trembling.

Thomas spoke up. "I don't know what you are accusing us of, but I swear that neither I, nor Lady Dreux, nor—" he looked over at Graham, quickly assessing him—"Lord Dreux, nor my men, have had anything to do with any ill-doings at your chateau. We have not been anywhere near this fine house, nor would we dream of stealing from the master."

"I've sent word to the king about what has happened. His guards are on their way."

Moments later, we were all on the other side of the door, locked out.

Awaiting the king's guard.

"I don't know whether to run or to burst back in those doors," I said, looking wildly around, first at Thomas, who looked horrified and white as a sheet, and then at Graham, who was clenching and unclenching his fists, as if ready to rough up the opposition.

Then I turned my eyes onto our number one candidate for having done something so stupid and totally reckless. "Well, my dears, I, for one, am running," said Stafford, turning back to where we'd tied up our horses. "It's been lovely." Anne was sitting innocently under a tree nearby, waiting for us, completely unaware we were all to be arrested and thrown into the Bastille. Or whatever awful prison they had in Amboise. *Dear God.*

My mother's voice sounded in my head. "Churchill said, 'If you meet danger promptly and without flinching, you will reduce the danger by half. Never run away from anything. Never!' Hold your head up to a fight, Gabby."

"You shouldn't run if you're innocent!" I yelled over to Stafford. "We need to tackle this head on. Find out what happened."

He ignored me. "See you back at Wodesley."

The run, the late night, the red face, the bursting into my room...it was obvious, and Graham had been right. He had to have been casing the joint yesterday. To Stafford, this was like robbing a bank, only better. And easier. The temptation had been too much for him. He'd completely lost his moral compass. It wasn't enough that we were buying something from da Vinci; he wanted his own piece too.

Without a thought, I took off after him. "Stop, thief!" I yelled.

Anne shot up and went into a crouching position to try to grab at Stafford, but he ran right around her, grabbed his horse's reins, and swung himself up. I noticed that his two bags were already secured to the back of his saddle. He took off at a gallop. *Crap.*

I had to get to those bags. Whatever he'd stolen were in there.

"Anne, get my horse!" I yelled, skirts flying, sprinting, all 5' 10" of me—thank heavens for long legs—and she held my horse as I mounted easily, thankful for all my years of riding making me quick. Even so, Stafford had the lead on me. He may have been just as much of an expert on horseback as I, but to lighten the load on my horse, we'd already moved my bags to Anne's horse since she was so tiny. A cloud of dust was in front of Stafford—the horse guards!—and he shot right past them.

"Thief! Thief!" I yelled to them, pointing at Stafford, and shot past them as well.

Half of them turned and followed me.

We'd reached the cobblestone streets of the city and had to slow, or else our horses would break a leg on the uneven ground. "Stafford—stop!" And I may have let out some choice swears, as anyone would do should they think their traveling companion had stolen priceless artwork and just left them to face a crime they did not commit.

After breakfast, I'd put a hard roll that I'd shoved in my pocket as a snack for later; Stafford was just ahead of me, but maybe if I could unseat him somehow with a well-timed hit, I could take him down. While I have the coordination that made me the last to be picked on every team at school, I needed to be endowed with the aim of David versus Goliath, or the accuracy of William Tell shooting an apple off his son's head. *Just this once, God, just this once!* I prayed. I made a decision of where to strike, and threw the bread roll at the horse's hooves. It stumbled, not falling, thank God—the horse was innocent after all—but when it stumbled it was just enough to unseat Stafford. I jumped off my horse, dripping with sweat, taking giant gulps of air. First, I retrieved Stafford's horse. Whatever he'd done/stolen, it was inside those bags. And then I ran to get him—how would I restrain him? I wondered. But by the time I got to him, he was gone.

I put my hands on my knees to catch my breath. *Where is my back-up?*

Thunderous hoof-steps came up behind me. I turned around to see the guards dismounting and coming straight for me.

"I don't know where he's gone. I got his horse first, and—"

My clammy hands were shoved behind my back. "Ouch!" I said. "Unhand me! I am not the thief! Look! I've got two horses!" I gestured to my horse, standing nearby.

"We were told to catch anyone who tried to run away. You were running," one of the guards said.

I used my most bossy and authoritative lecturer's voice. "But I'm not running now. Obviously. I'm just holding the horses. Well, his. But that one is mine. And he's running, still!" I swung around, wondering which way to point them. "Why don't you go after *him*?"

Next thing I knew, he commanded, *"Marchez!"* and pushed me forward between two of the soldiers, up toward the castle.

Humiliation and fear coursed through me. I had just triumphed in chasing down Stafford, and—I hoped—retrieved whatever it was that he'd stolen by capturing his bags, and now this? Hands tied together behind my back, burly and smelly men on either side of me, smirking, headed to what? The literal chopping block? Would it be my hands, my head? Both? There was no tolerance for stealing in these times.

How stupid it was for Stafford to risk it. Hadn't he seen Jean Valjean go to prison for years over stealing a loaf of bread in *Les Misérables*? I knew now that my jokes had been a foreshadowing; it wasn't funny anymore.

When I'd seen the show with my mum on the West End, and the character of Fantine had sung a song that made me cry in embarrassingly loud sobs, Mum had glared at me, handed me tissues, and hissed, "Chin up, everyone's looking." The tune came back to me as if I was back in the theater, honking and gasping, and then the lyrics filled my head. *I dreamed that love would never die...*

Once again, tears started to flow down my face and sobs wracked my frame. This time my hysterical crying made sense. I was being escorted into the dungeon. And my love was gone.

I hoped he was—I hoped my beautiful Thomas wasn't suffering the same fate as I. Had he run as well? Had he come after me as I raced after that piece of human refuse, John Stafford? I had no way to find out, and no one to ask. Instead, I was pressed into a dark, damp cell that stank of real refuse and God only knew what else. As the door slammed behind me, it boomed with an echo that resounded through the stone corridors.

I sank to the floor and immediately wished I hadn't. I don't know what was underneath me on the floor of my cell, but it smelled to high heaven, and let's just say it squished as I moved.

If Anne could see me now, sitting in a pile of filth, in the lovely—rented!—dress she had only just aired and spot-cleaned as best she could, the kirtle fresh that morning, my hose washed and dried...well. She would have been most disappointed.

I hoped and prayed she was all right. Who was taking care of her? How would she get home?

How was *I* going to get home, for that matter? *Is this how it's all going to end for me?* I hoped Ellie and Jane would come up with a really good story for my mum when I disappeared? Perhaps they'd concoct some sort of last words email from me that would give her comfort.

After I'd cried my eyes out, I sat in the darkness. With nothing to do—nothing to read!—I started playing my memories in my mind's eye. It wasn't long before I remembered how I'd argued with Graham about how I was a glass half-full kind of girl.

Well then. That was the answer—my very essence, right? I wasn't going to dwell on the negative (as hard as it would be not to be negative, given the circumstances), I was going to focus on the good. I began by making a list of things I was grateful for, all the thrilling things I'd done in my lifetime, the sights I'd seen, the friends I made, the horses I'd ridden, the doggies I'd loved, the food I'd eaten. And meeting Thomas. And especially, spending the last night with Thomas. At least I'd had that.

I closed my eyes. Yes, I could die happy. My life had been short, but it'd been 99.95% good. I refused to think about my torture or manner of death, but if I kept a loop of happy thoughts in my head, I knew I could endure it.

The sound of iron doors screeching open and booming closed shattered the silence. My fellow inmates cried out, sounding terrified, angry, and insane...then the sound of shuffling footsteps echoed steadily down the hall.

"Lady Dreux?" a soft, scratchy voice called.

Was it? *No.* It couldn't be! But then there he was, in the dim light. Leonardo da Vinci.

"Maestro, what are you doing here!?" I pulled myself up to a stand using the bars as an assist. My legs had gone numb. "Here! In here!"

And there he was, with his flowing robe, crazy floppy hat, and his long silver beard and hair. He stood on the other side of the locked door, studying me with those bright, sharp eyes of his. "I've come to see you. To see whether I could figure out for myself what has happened. I'm sorry you've been locked up without me first determining your guilt or your innocence."

I reached through the bars, and he put his hand on mine. "No, it is I who am sorry, terribly sorry that Stafford stole from you. Or at least, that's my assumption—that he stole from you. I did not have time to look in his bags before the guards hauled me here."

"What has been stolen has been retrieved, thankfully. A notebook of mine, full of my writing, my notes, my studies. I want Melzi to organize them after I'm gone. Without that one, so much of my work on earth would have been lost. Now, please tell me where you went last night after I saw you."

I recounted what I told Graham—that Stafford had taken Winston in search of one of da Vinci's household, and that Thomas and I had left the party to go back to the inn.

"Did anyone see you go back in?"

"It was late."

"Can your husband testify that you came back into your room at a certain time? I have heard he was ill, and your maid stayed with him."

I blushed. I was already sunk so low, what harm was there in telling the truth? "Thomas and I spent hours together alone in his room. Only he and I can vouch for each other. I know that might sound shocking to you, but Lord Dreux and I aren't really—"

He held up a hand. "*Arrete*. Stop. He has told me the same thing. In front of Lord Dreux, which I thought quite bold, as he could be whipped for taking another man's wife. And you could be whipped, your hair shaved off, and you could be paraded through the city, publicly shamed, and then sent to a convent to live out the rest of your days in the service of the Lord."

I had not thought of that. Both Thomas and I had taken a foolhardy risk in being caught. We'd been too frenzied in our "seize the day" mentality.

Hair would grow back. Escaping from a nunnery, however, was another issue. But I knew I could handle those nuns. After all, Harry had taught me self-defense; even if they whipped out the rosary beads, I was sure I could take them down.

What I'd do then, I wasn't sure. But I'd be ready. Maybe— hopefully—I'd figure out a way to make my way back to the labyrinth and be lucky enough to get back. Somehow.

"We only came to Amboise to meet you," I said, "to see your artwork. To meet you was a huge honor, and hear you speak about your creative process… It has all been like a dream. And now it's turned to a nightmare because of that evil man who accompanied us." I paused, trying to figure out the best way to articulate my thoughts. "I never quite trusted him, but I had no idea that he would ever do such a thing."

Da Vinci patted my hand. "In my many years on Earth, I have learned that we cannot predict the cruel intentions of another man, especially when they have such nice manners and a way with words. But as an artist, I believe I can measure out what facial expressions make up kindness, respect, even love. You and Thomas have the elements in your face—" he reached through the bars to hold my face in his palm—"that belie a certain kind of nobleness to your deeds. I know you would never wish me harm, nor my work. And by revealing yourselves so honestly to me, both at possible harm to yourselves, I know your words must be true."

"Oh—thank you for believing me." My voice broke, my throat suddenly so tight, as if the tears were going to burst out again. "Does that mean they're not going to chop off my hand?"

"Oh," he laughed, "most definitely not."

"Wait—what do you mean? Yes, they are going to chop off my hand, or yes, they are *not* going to chop off my hand?"

"Oh, aha! I see what happened. I apologize. My French is not as good as it should be." He stopped to laugh and give his head a little shake. "You keep your hands, my dear. No punishment, but what Lord Dreux might do with you, I cannot say." He leaned in a little closer. "But before I call the guard, I would like to know one more thing: what is the future like?"

It took me a few moments to gain control of my thoughts and my tongue. "What?" I asked, clamping my hand over my wide-open mouth. "*What?*"

He waggled a finger at me. "You must tell me the whole truth."

"I'm not sure what you're talking about. The future? That… that sounds crazy!"

"No, it is not crazy. I see everything. And I see your teeth. I saw your teeth click in, and out. At our midday meal. Such wonders we do not have.'

My snap-on veneers—he'd seen me unsnap them. *Oh no.* This was a disaster. What kind of repercussions would this have?

I tried to remain calm. "Your powers of observation are re-markable. I thought you could not see me when we were eating."

"Even so, I need to get you out of here," he said. "It smells bad, and I think a rat just ran over my foot." He lifted his shoe and pointed his toes to give it a little shake.

It took about an hour or so for the guards to let me out. I'm afraid I practically ran out, dragging poor Leonardo behind me, but he'd chuckled and was a good sport about it all, seeming to understand my desire to put as much distance between the dungeons and ourselves as possible.

Once outside, I slowed to a mincing, elderly-man pace of a walk and gave the Maestro a little lesson on modern dentistry. He listened intently, asking many questions about materials and design, but I didn't much know about compounds and plastic or resin or whatever they had made this vanity saver out of. Eventually, I started to fill him in on what my modern life was like.

"But how," I asked, stopping in the middle of the well-worn path, "did you make the leap from looking at my playing with my teeth to knowing that I was from the future? Wouldn't you just assume that I came from a place that just had better inventions?"

"I have always been open to possibilities both big and small in explanations to questions that I have. Nature is the source of all true knowledge and makes her own laws." He held his arms out wide. "Plus, Thomas told me about your writing instrument. Not to mention you are cut from a different cloth than other women, although I cannot explain why. And if I had asked the question about the future and guessed wrong, you would just think I was an old man who had gotten confused. Right?"

"True!" I said. We sat down on the path, not wanting to be interrupted, and he also need a bit of a rest. I wanted to tell him everything, but we had to get back and let everyone know I was okay. So, I told him that all his inventions would come to life in the future—the plane, the helicopter, the robot, refrigerators, submarines. I told him about our special labyrinth, and our mission to help save his painting. His paintings would become world famous, as would his manuscripts like the one Stafford had stolen, every single scrap of paper on which he wrote would be treasured.

And then I told him that *The Three Sunnes* had never been found or seen, which is why we'd come to buy it and to save it, to show it to those in the future and put it in a museum for all to see.

"Are you ready to see it?" he asked.

"I cannot wait!" I said, "And thank you for believing in us. I would be devastated if you were to think ill of us." I paused my steps and my thoughts before admitting (God forbid I did the fangirl thing again), "In all my studies of art and history, you have always been the person I've most admired."

He patted my cheek. "It has all ended well. Stafford will be found soon, I hope, and punished for his crimes, and you all shall return to England—to your time!—with what you have sought."

We continued walking, into the foyer of the chateau, his arm passed through mine. "Ah, now here is Melzi."

"Lady Dreux!" he looked at me in horror, and visibly recoiled, likely at how I smelled. "Would you like to change? And…bathe?"

"Most definitely, but I don't know where my clothes are. Do you know where—"

"Lady Dreux!" Anne called out as she rushed in from the dining room. I could tell she wanted to hug me but held back. (Either from my stink or my stature, I'm not sure.) Graham and Thomas emerged a moment later. They too, restrained themselves from going near me but the tears in their eyes showed me how relieved they were. "Thank God, thank you, Maestro da Vinci," Thomas said.

"I'm so sorry to have worried you all. Anne, is it possible you could get some warm water so I can get cleaned up, and can you help me find some clean clothes? I fear we have to burn these. Gentleman, I shall return as quickly as I can. Maestro da Vinci here is going to have *The Three Sunnes* for us to see at last."

I knew I would not feel clean again until I had a two-hour long, scalding hot shower, had my hair scanned for lice, and for who knows what else might have gotten onto me in the time I sat in that dungeon. But I made do with what Anne could muster up for me to wash with, and I changed, eager to see the painting.

"Lay it out on the desk for them to see," da Vinci instructed Melzi when I finally returned in fresh clothing, with wet hair, and no foul odor.

What we saw—well, it wasn't a full painting. "It is not finished, as you can see. I am learning to part with things that I will never finish, I fear, at my age. There are three other works I wish to devote my time to, so since your arrival here on behalf of your king, I think this is the perfect time to part with it—aided by Lady Dreux's persuasive reasoning today."

The work was unlike anything I had seen by him before. There was the sky with the three suns, the cold of the February landscape in the background, majestic and mighty like the one in *The Annunciation*. There was the gathering of men, with Edward of York in the foreground, his soldiers before him, some dazzled by the appearance of the parhelion, some alarmed, showing the true range of human emotion when confronted with something that they didn't have a rational explanation for. For them, it was a supernatural event and it caused history to change when Edward won the battle.

"It is more than I ever hoped for," I said. "This shows us— mankind—in our true state. In one, we are encouraged, amazed, and astounded. In the other, we are curious, fearful, worshipful. But either way, we are smaller than the events that surround us and we'll never know—in our lifetimes—how what we've seen will affect us." Da Vinci nodded, giving me a wink. "All the miracles, the beauty, the heartbreak, the betrayals," I said, pointing to the menacing forces of the enemy not far behind. "As clever as we are, as much as we try to learn, and study, and read, and meet great wise people like yourself, Maestro, we just cannot know."

He squeezed my hand. "I will never stop trying until I draw my last breath. But there is comfort knowing that other people are seeking answers too, and in the company of loved ones. And my notebook, which you have returned to me, contains so many of my thoughts. I've put Melzi in charge of organizing and publishing them for all to read."

I whispered into his ear, "But we must keep our discussion a secret, yes? People cannot know—it would be too much for them."

The great man winked at me, his eyes twinkling. "It's our secret."

Just then, there was a scuffle and a shout, and a man in official-looking dress strode into the room. He looked like a representative from the palace, sent to collect the Maestro. "Everyone! Out!" he declared.

I meekly gave da Vinci a little wave as we were being scooted away. "Grazie Maestro! A thousand thanks!"

Before we left, I took Melzi, aside, as I didn't have time with Da Vinci. "I know you have a great task before you in organizing your father's notebooks. They deserve every care in the world and must be treated as the treasures they are. Please do your best to make sure they are preserved for the future. And again, we are so sorry for all the trouble Stafford caused."

"Of course, my lady," Melzi said, before going to be with his father.

As we left, I hoped that my entreaty might help make a difference, that maybe when we returned back to our time, there would be many more notebooks preserved. But I'm not sure what kind of difference one rushed twenty-second conversation by an Englishwoman would make on this young man, who already had so many responsibilities.

Winston came running out of the door, looking confused. He

rubbed up against my leg, and Anne's as well. It seemed all was forgiven, but his loyalty was torn.

"Winston!" called Melzi, and he turned and ran back inside to his new big brother.

I was going to miss our sweet, fluffy boy. But he was never truly ours to begin with.

CHAPTER TWENTY

NOW IT WAS time for hugs. Anne had given me one after she threw out my dungeon clothes. Jane would owe quite a few quid on that loss. Then from Graham, who said, "Girlie, you about gave me a heart attack. But you saved us all."

And finally, from Thomas. When his arms came around me, I wanted to collapse into him, seek refuge in the folds of his clothes and against the heat of his body, let his woodsy scent envelope me and to just rest awhile, processing my hurt and shock in the safety of his arms "I was so worried—it should have been me that went after him," he murmured into my hair as he stroked my back.

"No," I said, "I'm the better equestrian." I gave him an affectionate shove, then settled my face into the crook of his neck for a brief second. We still had to keep up with our pretenses.

Once we were safely out of town, Graham and I planned a brief meeting with Thomas. "It's the easiest way to at least try this now," Graham said. I nodded, afraid of either scenario working out. We took Thomas aside while the others rested the horses.

"Graham and I were thinking," I said, "that maybe we should just be the ones to take the painting back to Henry. Maybe you and your boys should go on ahead to Italy and use your letter from da Vinci to scout out more art for the king."

"Yes," said Graham. "It's such a long way back to England when there are so many other great artists you could buy more work from in Italy. We could let the king know that you've continued on. We could take a note for him from you, informing him of this plan. It would be our great honor to hand the painting to the king. What say you?"

Thomas looked first at me, and then at Graham, and then back at me again, his mouth slightly ajar, as though he couldn't believe what we were asking. But didn't get to his rank in Henry's court by making poor decisions. "No," he said. "This is my commission. I must see it true to the end. Thank you for this..." he cleared his throat in what sounded like an *ahem*, "offer."

And he gave me a slight look of disgust before he walked away, which hit like painful daggers. Graham and I stood there like the worst, most incompetent swindlers who'd ever lived.

"Well, onto Plan B," Graham murmured.

"Are you sure you do this sort of thing for a living?" I asked Graham.

"Oh, no. I never negotiate," a wry smile on his face. "I take before they even know what him 'em. Perhaps this is why we didn't do so well."

I shook my head. I really hadn't wanted to separate from Thomas that very day, but I also would rather he looked upon me fondly and we parted in good graces, rather than he saw me for the thief I was about to become.

⟫⟩⟨⟪

OUR PROGRESS BACK to Calais was already half a day behind. We had our prized painting, and we had left da Vinci happy, knowing that his son would be taken care of with the extra money, and that his painting would be saved. And all the information I'd given him on the promises of the future and what he meant to the world, I hoped, made up for the stupidity of Stafford's actions.

I didn't care one whit about what had happened to Stafford, but it was hard—seriously hard—to not just say "see ya later" to everyone in our party and have my way with Thomas. At the very least, I wanted a kiss. And if fact, I could think of nothing else. When I closed my eye, I could only relive the night we had in his room. With every glimpse of his body, his face... I had so many memories and I wanted to make new ones too.

You won't be surprised, given my obsession with his scent, that I stole a scarf that Thomas usually kept knotted around his neck. One day, when we stopped to water the horses, he took it off to cool himself and laid it down; when he turned his back, I took the opportunity to swipe it. He looked everywhere for it, poor man, looking most perplexed, until we signaled that it was time to go. His angst reminded me of what I must look like when I lose my phone in my flat; I turn over every couch cushion, pillow, look under furniture, and generally panic until somebody rings me so I can find it again. Thomas had no such luck because I'd secreted his scarf away in my pack.

That night, back-to-back with Graham in our room and Anne on the floor, I retrieved it from my hiding place, pressed it to my face, and inhaled deeply. Heavens above, it smelled exactly like him. In an instant I was transported back to his room in Amboise. It was the only reminder I would have of him once we returned to our own time. I clutched it until I fell asleep.

ON THE SHIP back to England, with Graham was up on deck and Anne below helping the kitchen staff, I was able to sneak down to the galley at exactly the right time to catch Thomas as he was going up the steep, almost ladder-like stairs, and I was going down. This time we did not have a collision: he stepped to the side, and I slid my body past his, pretending to lean on him for support, but really, that was an excuse. I ran my hand down his body to feel the outline of his shoulders, the narrowing of his waist, the curve of his bottom. He let out a subtle moan.

"Had to do it," I said. "Because I don't think I'll get another chance."

"You're torturing me," he said.

I pulled a small strip of fabric out of my pocket. "I have something of yours to remember you by," I whispered. "And here is something of mine," I slipped the token—one of my garters—into his hand. I'd made sure it smelled of the perfume I'd brought with me.

"A token," he said, closing his eyes with a mixture of pleasure and pain on his face. He tied it around his arm. "I shall always wear it in honor of you."

➤➤➤◄◄◄

ONCE OFF THE ship back in England, the clip clop of the hooves of our horses seemed to echo out messages to me, simultaneously saying, "We did it! We did it!" and, "Thomas is gone, Thomas is gone." Of course, he wasn't gone yet; instead, he was riding gamely beside me or in front of me, but all I could think of was that in less than 72 hours, *I* would be gone—and he would be a ghost. Buried under centuries of earth.

He'd live out a life, hopefully a full and happy one if he didn't get in serious trouble with the king for the disappearance of his painting. But I felt optimistic that, with his quick wits and friendship with Henry, they would get past it. In my mind, Thomas would marry and have kids. I envisioned that I'd spend a lifetime of research looking for what happened to him, any trace of him, who were his children, and was he happy?

I had visions of me in church graveyards, hunting amongst the long-faded stones for his plot, weeping over his grave, tracing my fingers over his name on a gravestone. And I'd be looking for any art he may have left behind, any record of him. Any indication that he might be thinking of me.

The hooves continued to gallop, canter, trot, and walk out their messages to me, da Vinci's painting safely rolled in the leather bag, protected. Graham and I were making our final plans to escape back to Wodesley with that bag in hand, leaving Thomas and the guards none the wiser until it was too late for them to stop us.

But then, my conscience spoke up. I had to tell him the truth. I didn't think he would understand, comprehend the sheer preposterousness of what I was going to tell him, that it would probably take him hours, or days to even grasp onto the reality that I was about to tell him, and that it was not just that we were going to steal from him, but that we were from the future and preserving the art for the sake of history. For its protection.

In lieu of his.

CHAPTER TWENTY-ONE

W E HAD ONE last night in an inn. It was Anne's home village. She slid off her horse and went running to see her mother, who after many hugs and tears of relief, admired the fine new clothes that I'd given her, and the way her daughter had filled out when she finally had three proper meals a day. Anne shared some of the stories of her travels. I gave her my own hug goodbye, told her to rest, handed her a written reference as a most excellent lady's maid, and gave a huge tip for her troubles.

The reality of our party splitting up hit me. I sobbed when I was alone in the stables, hugging my horse's neck, taking comfort in its warm scent, and the way it snuffled into me. Soon, I wiped my eyes and nose, more calm. Horses never fail to soothe me.

"Why are you so sad, my lady?" Thomas stood near the doors of the barn, the fading light catching the top of his hair, lighting him up as though he had a halo around his head.

"This is our last night together."

He looked stricken, his mouth dropping open. "Why?" he asked. "I thought you and Lord Dreux were returning to Leeds with us?"

"No. We cannot, I'm afraid. We must go back."

He wrinkled his nose. "To France? We just came from there—why?"

"No. To Wodesley Castle, where we first met. That's where

we came from."

He shook his head. "But I thought you came from Rennes, and were in England visiting?"

"We *are* just visiting." I twisted my sleeves. "I must tell you the truth of what's happening. What Graham and I are doing... what *we* have been doing."

I continued, looking into his eyes, his heartbreaking eyes, already so sad, so upset with the world, now clouded with confusion and concern. I took a deep breath—I was really doing this. "This is going to sound...unbelievable. But it is true. I swear to you...We are not from this time."

He held up both palms, as if he wanted to shake my shoulders but restrained himself. "What does that mean? 'This time' being night? Dawn? You confuse me."

I shook my head. "We come from the future. 500 years in the future. Our mission was to fetch da Vinci's painting, and take it back with us, preserve it, as nobody has ever seen it in my time."

Thomas sat down on the floor then and there, looking flabbergasted.

"Stafford had found a way, through a labyrinth, the labyrinth at Wodesley, to travel through time. When we walk on the labyrinth, it sends us back, and then when we are done with our adventure, we walk the labyrinth again, and we return to our time."

His eyes widened in his whitened, shocked face. As though I were a ghost. Or insane. "A labyrinth does this? You are surely making a joke."

I shook my head. "I am not. Thomas, I was born in 1996. In my time, there are mechanical wagons, flying machines, moving pictures. People can talk to one another even though they may be on different sides of the earth."

He put his hand on his head. "No, no, I fear you have had some bad water, that you have gone mad. Shall I fetch Lord Dreux...Graham?" He got up and made toward the door.

"No!" I said. "Stop!" Graham would be furious if he knew I

was telling Thomas the truth and potentially blowing the "mission." I continued. "I have something that can prove this to you.

Ellie and Jane had made sure that there was absolutely nothing on me that would ever give away my status as a time-traveler to anyone except for the agreed upon veneers. And I'd slipped in that notebook and pencil, that had aroused Thomas's radar.

But they hadn't seen that I had sewn into my purse an iWatch minus the straps, wrapped in the cloth that lined the bag. I never parted with my purse, at any time, so Anne wouldn't have found it. I had turned it off to conserve batteries; now I pressed the button to power it up. On it, I had downloaded pictures, songs, videos. Enough to convince someone that I was really from the future if that case ever needed to be proved.

I had thought long and hard about what to include, and what a better way to introduce someone to the 21st century (okay, 20th) than Julie Andrews, and the most beloved movie of all time: *The Sound of Music*. I powered up the watch and it sprang to life, with the date, the time, the year: *2023*. I pushed the *movie* button and there was the opening scene of the alps, and then zooming, zooming in from on high, Maria singing *The Hills are Alive*.

Thomas peered at my little watch face, his elegant jaw agape, hand over his mouth to muffle his "whoa." When he'd finally collected himself, he said, "It can't be real. It is I who must be the one who is truly ill." He held his fingers to his head, checking for a fever.

"No, you aren't. Wait, here are pictures of me. Here are me and my friends outside of university, here is me riding a horse, here is me when I was a little girl, sitting on my mother's knee..."

"Are these paintings? They are so lifelike!"

"No, they are something called photos. I don't know how exactly they work, but it's like magic. This little gadget can hold hundreds of photos, and songs. Here," I said, "this one is my favorite." *September* by Earth, Wind, and Fire played. Surely there is no better song. At least, not for me. I started dancing to the music, wiggling my hips. He laughed out loud, which I tried not to take personally.

"I like this song! Do you have others?"

I did. Hall and Oates was next, with *Your Kiss*, then Prince's *1999*, for both the date and the funk, and then, *Happy* by Pharrel Williams.

While it was playing, he asked, "But if you are saving *The Three Sunnes* for your time, what about *my* time? The people will never see it. That doesn't seem fair."

His point literally hit me like a punch to the gut—I clutched at my stomach. "You're right—it doesn't." I gulped. "But, on the other hand, if we don't save it now, it will be lost to eternity. In my time, however, we can preserve the image through photos. It will be protected from fire, storms, theft...forever."

The song switched to Rachmaninoff's *Piano Concerto #2*, my favorite classical piece; the violins swelled, and the pianist banged out the dramatic notes.

It was at this moment that a man came into the barn; I jabbed the device off and shoved it into my pocket. He paused, moving his head to and fro, as if looking for something. "What was that noise?"

"I didn't hear anything," Thomas said.

"It was coming from you!" the man said, pointing to me.

"Good sir! I think you must be hearing things," I said, and frowned.

"You've got a funny accent," the man said. "And you make music play with your hand. You're a witch!"

How could I have been so careless? I'd been so good all this time, and at the end, I blew it. The man opened his mouth to yell, but then he stopped. Thomas had pulled a dagger on him. "I wouldn't do that if I were you." He turned to look at me. "Go now—go back to where you came from. I'll have Graham follow you."

"But..." It was if my heart was being torn from my chest. "I don't want to leave you!"

"You must." He tossed me the bag containing the rolled-up canvas of *The Three Sunnes*. "I trust you with this."

"No!" Tears filled my eyes. "You can't do this! You'll get in trouble!"

The man started inching his way toward the door, but Thomas turned to grab his arm. The man was short but wide, and not built for quick exits. "Not so fast, sir. Don't you dare speak against this fine lady. Upon my oath, I shall gullet you! Get down on your knees."

As the man got on his knees, Thomas pulled out a rope from a stall to bound him with. While he disabled the man, I led my horse from its stall, and readied it to ride with saddle and bridle. Then I mounted, ducking low to avoid banging my head on the raftered ceiling of the barn. "Thomas! I'm sorry!" I cried before pressing my heels into the horse's sides and galloping out of the barn and down the road.

I was off, on my own.

CHAPTER TWENTY-TWO

O H WITCHCRAFT. IN our time, to be a witch is trendy, sexy, marked by the use of crystals, paying attention to the cycles of the moon, burning sage to clear bad energy, driving Subarus, and... I don't really know what else. I had one friend who was a Wiccan, and apart from giving me a crystal to attract love after Albert left, we just mainly shared a love of the series *New Girl*.

But any time before the 1700s, somebody could yell "Witch!" at a woman, and that was it. Reputation damned forever, you were forced to be on trial, thrown in a river to see if you drowned (and then hurray you're not a witch, but unfortunately, you're *dead*), burned at the stake, or driven out of town to live an exiled life.

Yes, that man in the barn had every right to be scared of me. I had taken a very foolish risk in showing proof to Thomas. Graham—if he ever caught up with me—would be furious. And what did Thomas think of me, for just ditching him like that? But what choice did I have? I wasn't about to end our quest by being burned at the stake.

Still...I was taking an important painting by one of the greatest men of all time away from the people of its time. I'd always considered myself a morally straight shooter, but in the course of a day, I'd turned a corner, and I wasn't sure I liked at all what I'd done.

I galloped for what seemed like forever in what I remembered was the route from whence we'd come. Fortunately, I have an excellent sense of direction, as well as a good eye for landmarks. Yet I worried. Had I been so upset that I'd missed a turn, a house, a tree? Should I leave this road and go in the other direction? I went for what felt like miles before I saw something familiar: a mill on a river I knew we'd passed before.

I decided to go farther; by then it was dark, yet above was the waxing moon (what would my Wiccan friend say what that portends?) and I kept going until I found a thicket of trees where I could hide me and my horse, but still have a good view of the road and wait for Graham.

I had no food, no blankets. My belongings were at the inn, including my sketchbook. Would Graham come? Would both he and Thomas be caught as sympathizers to the accused witch woman? Would there be a search party of scared and angry people with pitchforks sent after me?

Eventually hunger, low blood sugar, and worry kicked in. I got dizzy and nauseated all at once. I ended up vomiting yet again on this trip, then had to lie down.

I'm not sure how much time had passed before I heard hooves on the hardened dirt, and I rose to peer through the trees. Not Graham; another random man. I hid again, hoping that my horse was not visible, as obviously he was harder to hide.

A few more men and horses passed. And then, unmistakably, I saw yellow tights! In the moonlight, they glowed. I shot up and waved to Graham, still cautious enough not to shout. He pulled his horse over, and after a brief hushed exchange, we decided that if he'd been followed, this was not safe, and we needed to hide farther off the road, and better yet, after a crossroad. We'd stay there for the night.

"Did you bring any food?"

He nodded, handing me a couple of hard rolls. I didn't care how hard they were, I gnawed at them anyway like a squirrel with acorns.

"You're an idiot you know," Graham said. "What a stunt to pull. Thomas told me everything. We hid the man away and left Anne with instructions to pretend to find him after we all left."

"And what about Thomas?" I asked. "How is he?"

"Very, very confused. Conflicted. But I acknowledged that what you told him was the truth."

Guilt. Heartache. An unbelievable sense of loss. I stood up, walked over to a tree, and vomited again.

The next day, we found our way back to Wodesley Castle. Empty. No more William, who—hopefully—was enjoying his new life surrounded by people at the court of Henry VIII.

Graham had not chastised me too much over what I'd done. "Hey, if I found somebody who I thought was the love of my life, I might have taken a chance like that too. But thank God you did it at the *end* of our trip."

I wondered why he was suddenly so understanding, why he hadn't yelled at me about "the mission" and safety first, and "not getting attached" and "focus," but I was just thankful. Maybe he knew better than to hit a witch when she was down.

We released our horses out into the wild. No more traveling for us in 1517.

"Tell me again what he said to you," I asked Graham, as we sat on the hillside, overlooking the overgrown labyrinth.

"It was mere minutes, Gabby. That's all the time we had for him to tell me what had happened and for me to make a plan."

"But I don't understand... if he had tied the guy up, why he couldn't just come with you?"

"He'd said something about needing to give us a head start, to make sure that nobody came into the barn to find the man before you had had time to get away. And then he said he would try to follow us."

"Here? He'll meet us here?" Hope rose in my chest and joy spread through me like the sun burning through clouds after a storm.

Typical of dour, grumpy Graham, he quashed my happiness

in an instant. "Yes. To say goodbye."

Also typical mission-minded Graham didn't want to wait too long for Thomas to show up. As much as I wanted to argue with him, I knew I belonged in 2023. If I stayed here, I'd be burned for witchcraft—if not for the iWatch, for my knowledge and forward-thinking ways. Not everyone was as smart as da Vinci and could figure out that I didn't belong there, but they could certainly come up with other reasons for my being different. Witch or feminist—in the 1500s, there was no distinction between the two and I knew it.

I searched through our bags that Graham had grabbed from the inn, and couldn't find my little notebook and pencil. Damn it! *Where had they gone?* I left Graham in charge of da Vinci's treasure and went to William's old apartment. I needed to search for something to write on and with. For a moment I was sure I'd gotten lucky when I'd found a scrap of parchment, and a quill, and some dried-up, old ink.

I added a bit of water to it and shook the bottle; as much as I tried, however, I couldn't get any ink that worked. It wouldn't mix and remained as a layer of darkened water with a mass like hardened glue at the bottom of the bottle.

Mud maybe? I could write with mud. But if I left a paper out in the labyrinth, and he came a day later, and it rained on the paper, and the mud ran, there would be nothing left of the note. Just a sad, wet scrap of dirty paper with no indication it was from me.

I broke down and had a rather desperate cry on William's old table. *This was not how I wanted to leave things. At all. What did Mummy always say? Leave things better than you found them?*

Had we left things better? First we had met William, and he'd gone on to better things. We did so with Leonardo, who now was reassured about his son being more settled financially, and his own future legacy. We did so with Anne, who had gotten out of the village, seen a bit of the world, and had some good nutrition and training and a nice new wardrobe, and hopefully she'd take that and get more employment.

But Thomas? I'm not so sure his life was better off. I'd ruined his quest for his king, taken his prize away from him in broad daylight. But on the other hand, I'd introduced him to some puzzling media from the future, had some good discussions about art and love and death, shared a really spectacular evening in Amboise. Maybe, *maybe* we could leave him our remaining coins, I thought, to repay King Henry. And then after that, he could go to Italy and France, to make a new life for himself.

I gave the ink one more try to see if anything remotely resembling a legible substance came out, but it was no use. I gave up.

It was like being crushed by the greatest sadness I could imagine. There was no hope at all.

And then, I heard Graham shout. "Gabby, he's here! He's here!"

I ran down that hill so fast, you can guess what happened. Head over heels. Eventually I came to a stop, but I didn't feel any pain—only joy. (Later, I'd discover quite a few bruises and scrapes.) I bounced up and ran again, this time on flat land, to Thomas and his horse, standing next to the labyrinth.

"You're here!" I threw myself at him. To his credit, he didn't fall down but managed to catch me and stay upright at the same time.

"I'm here." He pulled me close.

"I was so afraid I wouldn't get to see you again. I was trying to write you a note, but the ink was dried…"

He wiped a tear from my eye. "You can tell me now. What did you want to say?"

Graham moved near us, but only to take the reins of Thomas's horse; he led the animal away, giving us some privacy. "It's just…" I searched his face, trying to memorize each and all of his features that I adored. It didn't seem fair that I'd never see him again, this man that I loved, that I knew I was meant for… "It's just that… I'm sorry. I was thinking of what my mother always implores me to do—to make things better. And for you, I made things worse! I screwed everything up for you. We've taken your painting meant for the king and he'll be furious with you!"

Thomas looked me straight in the eyes. "No, you haven't made a mess of things. At all. You've changed my life completely. Before I met you, I was living under a dark cloud. I was angry. So terribly sad. You made my see things differently, opened my eyes up to possibilities I'd never seen before, even before you showed me your magical contraption. So—thank you."

So relieved that he did not hate me, I hugged him so hard I'm still surprised I didn't snap his spine. Yet now I had to say goodbye to him.

"I just have one favor," he said then, his voice soft.

I leaned back to look up at him, my hands cupping the sides of his face. "What? Anything!"

"Take me with you." His voice caught. "That is, if you would consent to be with me. I can't imagine living in this world without you, so if you please, my lady, my love—take me to yours?"

My mouth fell open and I fought to regain control of it. Finally, I managed to squeak, "Are you sure? It's so very different. It'd be a huge shock for you."

"I have a feeling you'd help me, though, yes?" He ran his hand over my hair, and I tilted my head to lean into his caress.

"Of course! I wouldn't dream of leaving you alone in a strange new world," I held his hands tightly. "I don't want to leave you—anywhere, anytime—again."

He smiled. "*That* sounds like an adventure I'd like to be a part of. But this one would be with somebody that I love."

I gave myself a fist pump. He loved me!

Thomas turned around. "Graham, is it okay if I steal your wife from you?"

"She was never mine to begin with, you know now. You want to try this labyrinth thing out?"

"I do, actually." He laughed.

"Let's go then." Graham turned and started into the labyrinth. Thomas and I looked at one another, stepped apart, but linked hands. And then, we walked into the labyrinth—into *our* future—together.

EPILOGUE

"**D**ARLING?" I CALLED from bed.

"Yes?"

"I think you're ready to go to Windsor. I want to—"

I stopped at the sight of him. Thomas had emerged from brushing his teeth in the bathroom, clad only in his boxer shorts, and a pair of cozy socks. I had to remember to breathe again. Modern underwear suited him. He smacked his lips, probably appreciating the minty freshness of toothpaste.

Jane was gracious enough to let us stay as long as we needed to get Thomas acclimated. We'd had a quiet week at Wodesley Castle, introducing Thomas one-by-one to such modern concepts and conveniences as electric lights, indoor plumbing, oven ranges, bicycles, and yes, a full showing of *The Sound of Music*. Which brought up a lot of questions about Nazis, World War Two, and Julie Andrews.

This beautiful, 16th century man leaned down to kiss me, this 21st century woman. "Umm," I said, after a while, forgetting what I had on my mind. A dizzying make-out session will do that to you. "As I was saying, I think maybe it'll be time to go to Windsor soon, and introduce you to my cousin, the new king. He's about as unlike your friend King Henry as can be imagined, but I think he is really going to be ecstatic about what we have to show him."

The painting had been carefully framed, preserved behind glass, and was temporarily hanging in our bedroom.

"First, though," I continued, "we must take you for your first ride in a car."

"Only if you'll be beside me, Gabby." He thoughtfully placed a pillow under my head, and kissed my forehead, then both cheeks, and nibbled on an ear.

"Aren't you are the sweet one," I said, murmuring into his hair. "I can't wait to see the look on your face, Thomas. You're going to love it."

The End

About the Author

Hope Carolle is a professional book editor by day, and a historical romance/time travel writer late by night. She was inspired to write the series based on her own experiences getting a Masters in Middle English Literature before 1525 at King's College London as an American studying abroad. Now living in Charlotte, North Carolina, she is a proud mother of two young women, a giant rescue dog named Charlie, and looks forward to living abroad and walking more labyrinths soon.

CPSIA information can be obtained
at www.ICGtesting.com
Printed in the USA
LVHW021941280423
745572LV00009B/521